Unforgettable
You

Cover design by Okay Creations
Book layout by Lori Colbeck

ISBN: 978-1-950348-62-6

Unforgettable You

MARCI BOLDEN

PINK SAND
PRESS

PROLOGUE

A shiver rolled through Carrie Gable when the vent high above her head began filtering cold air into the small office where she sat. The current was strong enough to stir strands of her dark hair across her face. Frustrated, she twisted her long hair into a haphazard bun at the nape of her neck and secured it with the elastic hairband she'd worn around her wrist. Glancing up at the outlet in the ceiling, she ground her teeth to prevent herself from complaining about the already frigid temperature.

When she and her mother-in-law had come to the clinic to get Doreen's test results, they'd been led to the doctor's office rather than an exam room. In the time they'd been waiting, Carrie had read over each certificate and degree hanging on the wall, memorized the faces of Dr. Schultz's wife and children, and had replayed over and over every moment that had led her and Doreen to this point.

Six months after burying her husband, Doreen's son, Carrie had noticed Doreen's mind slipping. At first, she chalked it up to the stress of losing Mike. He'd walked into a convenience store one afternoon and never walked out. A point-blank gunshot to the head from a junkie robbing the store had taken Mike's life far too soon. Carrie had become a widow, and Doreen had lost her only child.

Though Carrie and Mama had always been close, the bond between them had grown even stronger after their mutual loss, so Carrie noticed right away when Doreen started losing words, forgetting things she shouldn't, and seemed to get lost in her own world more and more often. When the symptoms didn't start to clear as life moved on, Carrie became worried and convinced Doreen to see a doctor.

Now they sat in a freezing cold room waiting to find out if the latest rounds of tests, scans, and exams had finally given them insight into what was causing the confusion.

Doreen twisted her hands together. She did that whenever she was upset. Despite trying to maintain a confident exterior, her entangled fingers with their white knuckles indicated the anxiety raging inside her.

Carrie wrapped one of her hands around both of Doreen's to try to soothe her. "It's okay, Mama. Everything is going to be okay."

Doreen glanced up at the offending vent too. "Is this a doctor's office or a meat freezer?"

Thankful for her mother-in-law's signature spunk, Carrie smiled. "A little of both, really."

Doreen snickered and pulled one of her hands free to tug her light blue cardigan closed. "How long have we been sitting here?"

Carrie checked her watch and did her best not to sound too disgruntled when she answered, "Almost half an hour."

"Well, then the diagnosis can't be too bad, can it? Dr. Schultz clearly isn't in a hurry to give it to us."

Faking a smile, Carrie said, "It's going to be okay."

Tears created a shiny layer over Doreen's dull gray eyes. Those eyes used to be so sharp. She'd never missed a thing. Twelve years ago, when Carrie had just turned eighteen and had gotten her first job at Gable Inn, Doreen's eyes would sparkle whenever Carrie and Mike were in the same room. Mama had figured out the two were in love long before they'd even started dating.

Mama blinked several times and tugged out the tissue she had tucked up the sleeve of her sweater. After wiping her nose, she clutched the wrinkled paper in one hand while she gripped Carrie's hand with the other. "I want you to promise me something."

Carrie's heart ached at the vulnerability and fear reflecting in Mama's trembling voice. "What?"

"Don't put me in one of those homes. I don't ever want to go into one of those places."

The words cut through Carrie's heart like a serrated knife. She tightened her hold on Doreen's hand. "I won't. I promise."

"Hire someone if you have to. But don't send me away."

Shaking her head, Carrie said, "I won't. I'll take care of you."

Doreen's lip quivered, breaking Carrie's heart further. Carrie was thankful when the door to the small doctor's office opened. The neurologist they'd been working with offered a sorrowful smile as he entered, and what was left of Carrie's broken heart completely shattered.

She'd seen sympathetic looks on doctors' faces before. Those looks never preceded good news.

Mama lowered her face and sniffled, brushing her nose with her tissue once again. Carrie tightened her hold on the cold hand in hers, bracing herself for whatever diagnosis the team of doctors had finally settled on.

CHAPTER 1

TWO YEARS LATER

Carrie struggled to tuck a royal blue fitted sheet around the corner of a queen-size mattress. This was the seventh bed she'd made in the last hour. Since she and Doreen had stopped having overnight guests at the inn a little over a year prior, Carrie was completely out of practice. She hadn't had to work at this pace in some time and was cursing herself for not planning her morning better. The old Colonial mansion turned bed-and-breakfast had nine guest rooms, and each one had been booked for the foreseeable future.

She was already exhausted, but there were several more beds that needed fresh sheets before the boarders were due to arrive at Gable Inn.

Even though the company who had booked the rooms had paid a deposit, Carrie couldn't afford to hire help. She'd used that money to catch up on bills. Rather than hire someone, she had recruited her best friend, Natalie, to help her get the inn ready. Though, as she watched Natalie collapse into a chair and let out a miserable moan, Carrie couldn't really remember why she'd thought that was a good idea. Carrie adored her, but Natalie would never be known for keeping her thoughts to herself.

"Remind me again why you're doing this?" Natalie swatted at a wayward chunk of black hair that fell back into her eyes as soon as she dropped her hand.

"Because," Carrie grunted, "I love to torture myself."

"Besides that?"

Carrie stood upright and rested her hands on her slender hips. For a moment, she debated asking Natalie to do something in another room. Instead, she threw a pillow at her smartass friend and instructed her to put on the top sheet and comforter.

"They offered *a lot* of money to stay here, Nat."

"Some guy named Confucius once said that money can't buy happiness."

Carrie pulled a rag out of the bucket of cleaning supplies. "This place is expensive to maintain. I can't keep going without some kind of income. They'll only be here for a few months."

"A few months," Natalie said with a muted tone, "of being their bitch."

Natalie's image blurred as Carrie sprayed a hanging mirror with bright blue cleaner and wiped dust and smudges from the reflective glass. Once the mirror was clean, Carrie frowned at her reflection. "I'm not going to be anyone's bitch."

A laugh bounced off the light blue walls. "You're going to have a house filled with Hollywood's snobbiest," Natalie reminded her. "Who do you think is going to fetch their mineral water?"

The dread in Carrie's gut grew. She'd been regretting this decision since before she'd made it, but one look at Doreen's bank account was all Carrie needed to know they really didn't have a choice. Either Carrie would have to tell Doreen the time had come to sell the historic property that had been in the family for generations, or they took in a group of over-rated actors who were filming a period piece in town.

The actors would be at the inn three months, four tops, the location manager had promised. When Carrie looked at the offer from a business standpoint, the deal had been too good to pass up. However, on a personal level, she'd stopped opening the doors to overnight guests because the amount of work was more than she could handle with Doreen's mental clarity declining. Other than weddings, parties, and other short-term events, Carrie had rejected most opportunities to rent rooms at the inn.

Having her home invaded for *any* length of time, let alone months, didn't appeal to her at all. But she could open the inn, or she could sell the inn. Both options would have been unpleasant, but only one was temporary.

"Do you think Doreen can handle this?" Natalie asked.

Carrie finished wiping dust off a dresser. "She'll be fine. She'll have to be. The contract was signed weeks ago, and the deposit has been made. There's no turning back."

Carrie had been trying to reassure herself that she'd made the right decision ever since she sent the paperwork back to the production company. For the most part Doreen was clear-minded, but there were times when the early onset Alzheimer's made things challenging. Even though Doreen had been symptomatic for the better part of three years, every episode shook Carrie to the core. Carrie hadn't adjusted to the disease yet, but she didn't think anyone ever did. Watching Doreen fade little by little was heartbreaking, exhausting, and frustrating all at once.

Focusing on the antique cherry vanity, Carrie swiped away nonexistent dust. "I think she'll enjoy having a few new faces to look at. Don't you?"

Natalie stopped adjusting the bedspread. "I think you're adding more to your plate than you can handle. She's getting worse. You know she's getting worse." Natalie softened her tone. "She made it all the way across town last week before you knew she was gone."

"I know," Carrie said, trying to keep her voice from cracking.

"Anything could have happened to her."

Carrie didn't need to be reminded. The fear of realizing her mother-in-law had made her way off the property unnoticed had taken at least ten years off Carrie's life. She'd been in tears for the better part of an hour, terrified of what had happened to Doreen, until a store owner called the inn to report that she'd been wandering their aisles. "I *know*."

Natalie rounded the bed and eyed Carrie with a sympathetic look that was far too maternal for Carrie's liking. "I'm not saying it was your fault. It's not like you can tether her to your side. But if you can't keep up with her when it's just the two of you, how are you going to keep up with her and a houseful of guests?"

"With the help of my very dear friend."

Natalie frowned with obvious disapproval. Carrie shook her head, silently warning off the impending lecture. She'd been hearing the same song over and over since she'd told Natalie of her plans. Carrie understood Natalie's concerns. She shared them. She agreed she was already spread too thin, and taking on guests would be more than she could handle. She *absolutely* agreed. But she didn't have the heart to sell Mama's home without trying everything she could to save it. This wasn't only Mama's home. It was Carrie's too. She'd spent so much of her life here; she couldn't give it up without a fight. Natalie didn't have the same sentimental ties that Carrie did. She didn't have the same memories. She couldn't possibly understand how much leaving this place would hurt Carrie *and* Doreen.

Turning at a round of cheerful knocks on the bedroom door, Carrie smiled at Doreen. Even from across the room, Carrie noticed a happy glimmer in her eyes and a flush to her cheeks. "I've stripped all the beds, girls," Mama announced. "Let's get to cleaning."

Carrie's face fell. *No.* They'd just made all the beds. "You did what?"

"Come on," Doreen said with a wave. "We don't have all day. Our guests will be arriving any moment."

Stepping into the hall, Carrie and Natalie looked at the linens piled in front of every door all the way down the long hallway.

"Oh, shit," Carrie moaned, realizing they had to start all over.

———

AT THE SOUND of gravel crunching under tires, Carrie pulled back a sheer curtain and confirmed several black SUVs were coming up the long driveway toward the inn. "Well, there's no backing out now," she muttered. Letting the curtain fall back into place, she turned toward the den, where Doreen was moving a vase of white roses, trying to find the perfect position. "Mama, the guests are here."

The older woman flashed a brilliant smile as her quest was forgotten. "*Wonderful.* I love this part."

"Yeah," Carrie whispered, wishing she felt the same. Instead, she felt overwhelmed at what she knew was going to be a few chaotic and likely exhausting months. She returned her focus out the window as car doors began to shut. Each slam increased her sense of dread until she found it difficult to breathe.

Doreen started humming a happy tune and ran her hands over her slacks as if to smooth out any wrinkles. "Do you know how many presidents have slept in this house?"

Carrie glanced at her. She did know. She'd known for years. Part of the selling point of the out-of-the-way inn was the long history of politicians and celebrities who had found refuge there. While Gable Inn couldn't boast that George Washington had slept there, they did have plaques on the Presidential Suite with a list of who had.

"No fewer than six." Doreen grinned. "Of course, they weren't president when they were here, but this was one of the stops on the way."

Her voice faded from Carrie's ears as she continued on with the speech she'd given to visitors for years. "Here we go," Carrie said to Natalie.

"Here *you* go."

Carrie glanced down at her jeans and blouse to make sure she was presentable before patting her hand over her French braid to make sure her long hair was out of the way. Finally, without any other reason to procrastinate, she opened the front door and let Doreen go first—she had been through this a hundred times, after all. With a forced welcoming smile on her face, Carrie stepped onto the porch as people continued climbing from cars and looking up at the old white house with its two-story pillars and tall windows.

Carrie recognized several of them from movies and

magazine covers. She thought she should be more impressed that they were there, planning to stay in the house where she'd spent so much of her life. Everyone in town was talking about the movie, even though the small Iowa town wasn't unfamiliar with celebrities—plenty passed through during election season to support their favored candidate before the all-important Iowa caucuses. This, however, was the first time a big-budget movie was filming in the area. Speculation on who, what, when, and where was all anyone could talk about. Even though the nondisclosure Carrie had been forced to sign forbade her from telling anyone the actors would be staying at the inn, there weren't many places in the area where the actors could have privacy. The powers of deduction had nearly everyone in town green with envy that the actors were staying at the country inn. Carrie had fielded more calls about the actors and done more dancing around the truth in the last weeks than she'd been comfortable with.

Stepping down from the porch, Carrie smiled at the man approaching her. Unfortunately, her assessment of him after doing some search engine stalking had been on point. The man came across as fake and sleazy in person as he had in his online persona. Even so, she kept the big smile on her face as if she were so happy to meet him in person. "Donnie?"

"Carrie," he said with a forced cooing tone. He embraced her as if they were old friends. "Darling, this is exactly what we were looking for. Fantastic," he commented, eyeing the house.

"I'm so glad." She tried to come across as enthusiastic, but it sounded as false to her ears as his greeting had.

Draping his arm over her shoulder, not hesitating to violate her personal space, he huddled close to her. "You did what we talked about? A south-facing room with heavy drapes for Ms. Ramirez?"

Carrie had begun forming a strong dislike for Donnie when he'd started sending her detailed lists of requests. As someone who had worked in hospitality most of her life, Carrie understood the need to make her customers happy. However, Donnie's long list of demands had gone beyond the normal expectations, sometimes bordering on preposterous. Hearing him run down the list as if she were incompetent cemented her dislike. "Yes."

"Absolutely no baked goods on the menu. Remember?"

"I remember."

"No down for Mr. Walker. He's allergic."

"I've taken care of it," Carrie assured him.

"Some of the other actors will push their way around a little, but Ramirez and Walker are the ones you *must* concern yourself with. We want them happy."

"Of course."

"Just do your best to stay out of their way, and everything will go smoothly." Finally putting some space between them, he grinned down at her, and she had the eerie feeling he would eat her alive if the opportunity arose. "You're a doll, Carrie. I knew you would be. Let me introduce you."

She smiled her way through shaking hands with some of the cast members who would be staying in her house. In turn, she introduced Doreen and Natalie. Carrie had been told in advance that Juliet Ramirez and William Walker were to be checked in first, but the two stars had yet to emerge from the limousine. Her anxiety began to rise as she wondered what she should do with the small gathering of guests while she waited for the VIPs to emerge.

Normally, guests would walk into the foyer, where they

were greeted and given a tour after they signed in. This was different, and Carrie suddenly felt unprepared. Mama saved the day by taking Grant, an actor who had a supporting role in the film, by the arm and starting a tour for the group. Seeing how easygoing Grant and the others were calmed Carrie's nerves and gave her hope that the next few months wouldn't be as stressful as she had imagined. The group was nearly to the side of the house when the driver of the sleek black car stepped out. Her moment of relief faded.

Carrie expected she should feel some kind of excitement since she was about to meet two of Hollywood's most popular actors, but all she felt was trepidation as her fate unfolded before her. As if taking care of Mama and this house weren't enough, now she was committed to a houseful of people, two of whom she was instructed to kiss up to yet stay away from at the same time. Carrie's head throbbed as she hoped the house of cards didn't come tumbling down.

The first to step out of the car, with the assistance of the driver, was Juliet Ramirez. Her near-black hair fell around her face in long waves full of body and auburn highlights that caught the light. She pulled dark glasses from her face as she looked up at the house, and Carrie almost expected the birds to sing louder and the sun to shine brighter. The woman's features seemed unnaturally perfect, and her stiff posture seemed mechanical.

For a moment, Carrie likened the actress to a mannequin in a store but forced the judgment away and held her hand out. "Welcome, Ms. Ramirez. I'm Carrie Gable. It's very nice to meet you."

"This is lovely, Donnie," Juliet said, turning away as if Carrie weren't standing there. "I think I'll like it here."

Donnie's smile grew. "That's wonderful, darling."

Juliet finally looked over her shoulder at Carrie. "Have someone get my bags. I'd like to see my room."

Carrie quickly realized she would be the one getting Juliet's bags. She hadn't hired anyone else to play bellhop. "Right," she whispered as two large suitcases were pulled from the back of the SUV. "Natalie?" She smiled at her friend. "Would you please show Ms. Ramirez to her room?"

Natalie stared wide-eyed at her. She, too, already had an immense dislike for the woman. Natalie kept up on Hollywood gossip and had warned Carrie against renting to the actress. Apparently Ms. Ramirez had a not-so-nice reputation, despite her angelic face. "Sure," Natalie said with fake cheer. "I'd *love* to."

"One moment, Carrie," Donnie said before she could head for the luggage. "This is William Walker."

Carrie turned and realized for the first time that there was a man standing next to the open SUV door. Carrie had to admit her heart did a little flip as he stopped taking in the architecture of the house to smile at her. His teeth were straight and blindingly white, but it was the deep dimples in his cheeks and perfectly aligned nose that gave him the signature good looks that kept the world enthralled. Seeing them in person, Carrie had a new appreciation for them. He wasn't as tall as she'd anticipated him to be. He was only an inch or so taller than her. For some reason, she'd expected him to be unnaturally tall and built, but he was no more a Superman than any other man she'd ever met before. William Walker was, to put it the kindest way Carrie could think, average. Good-looking, but not the Greek god she'd been expecting.

"Will," he clarified. "Only critics and producers call me William."

He held out his hand, and she slid her palm against his,

instantly taking notice of how smooth and warm his skin was against hers. She'd seen his gray eyes on the television many times, but having him look directly at her did make her heart skip a beat, despite her determination that he was only human. The heat of a blush touched her cheeks when he held her gaze for a long moment, making her wonder if she looked as starstruck as she suddenly felt.

"Carrie Gable," she managed to say around the lump in her throat.

"Carrie. This is your home?"

She looked up at the house as she pulled her hand from his. "I live here, yes."

"It's fabulous."

"Thanks. Feel free to have a look around."

"I will," he said in a tone that implied genuine interest. He stepped to her side as she headed for the luggage. "Let me help."

"Mike can help with that," Doreen said, walking back to the vehicles. "Carrie, let Mike do that."

Carrie glanced up at Doreen. She had given up trying to explain Mike had died years ago. Instead, she offered up what had become her usual excuse for his absence. "He's at the store, Mama."

"Oh." Mama frowned and headed for the luggage. "Well, let me help."

Carrie lifted a suitcase, testing the weight before gesturing toward her mother-in-law. "Will, this is Doreen."

"Everybody calls me Mama." The petite woman held out a hand to him. "I expect you to as well."

Will smiled as they shook hands. "Yes, ma'am."

Will and Carrie grabbed two suitcases each and headed toward the house while Mama stopped to tell someone how many presidents had slept at the inn. There was going to be a lot of that going on.

Will stepped into the foyer and paused to scan the dark wood flooring that perfectly complemented the cream-colored walls and crisp white crown molding. The light shining through the decorative windows cast mesmerizing prisms of color about the room. Carrie was used to the display now, but as she watched him, she was reminded how amazing the spectacle could be.

"This is incredible," he said as he turned in a circle, taking in the room from the high ceilings lined with dark wood support beams to the natural wood flooring that had been polished to an unnatural shine.

Once he stopped spinning, Carrie gestured to the den, silently encouraging him to move along. As he'd done in the foyer, he scanned the room, focusing on the massive built-in bookshelves that matched the dark wood of the support beams. The shelves were lined with old books and family photos, creating a cozy feel to the large room.

"There's a TV and a fireplace in there," she said. "Though it's still summer, it can get chilly in the evening, so feel free to build a fire whenever you like. All of the inn's rooms have TVs as well, if you prefer solitude. The dining room is there." She pointed ahead. "We'll be serving breakfast and dinner in here. Lunch is on you. There are plenty of restaurants in town. Most deliver."

He looked through the framed doorway. "Is that table hand-carved?"

He walked into the room and ran his hand over the intricate design that outlined the tabletop. The carved oak table and chairs took up the majority of the room, leaving little space for the buffet that sat against the far wall. As in the foyer, the windows were decorative, splitting the light that shone through them and sending it in a thousand different directions. Carrie figured he was used to far more modern surroundings. However, the way he was examining the table made her wonder if he preferred antiques.

"Yes," she said. "Most of the furniture here was made long, long ago. Mama is determined to maintain the original charm of the place."

"Good for her," Will said. Still bent over the table, he looked up and smiled like a kid at an arcade. "My grandfather used to make furniture. I helped him sometimes. When I was younger," he added as he stood upright. His lips fell, and for a moment, he seemed sad before he caught himself and plastered the smile back to his face. "It's beautiful."

"Thanks," she said and moved him along to finish the tour. As she went, she pointed out the bathroom and a sitting room with large windows that looked out over the acreage that surrounded the house. When Doreen's ancestors had bought the land, they'd had well over a thousand acres of farmland. Over the years, that had been sold off piece by piece until only the five acres around the house remained, but that was more than enough for Carrie now that she was in charge of maintaining the property.

She pushed a swinging door open for him to step into the next room—her favorite room. The white walls were lined with dark wood cabinetry, and a marble-topped island sat in the center. Several stools lined the island, but the area was used more for rolling out dough and preparing meals than for sitting. "The kitchen is mostly off-limits to guests. However, through here"—she opened the back door and gestured—"is the patio. There's a built-in fire pit. We have a never-ending supply of firewood, so feel free to use it whenever you'd like.

Make sure to put the top on before leaving it unattended. We don't want to burn the house down."

When he looked at her, she put a smile on her face, but she suspected he could tell she wasn't feeling nearly as welcoming as she was trying to be. She loved sitting by the fire after getting Doreen settled for the night, and having that routine interrupted was one of the bigger disappointments she felt at having made this decision.

"How long have you lived here?" Will asked.

"This is Doreen's family home. Her great-great-something-grandfather built it. She'll happily tell you about it sometime. Or all the time," she amended, thinking of how many times she'd heard the story.

"So your entire life?"

"A lot of it." Carrie intentionally kept her answer vague as she headed back inside. "Shall I show you to your room?"

"Lead the way," he said around his famous smile. Stopping in the foyer, he picked up his suitcases and stared up the long stretch of stairs. "Wow. That's some staircase."

Carrie followed his gaze up the red runner to the second-floor landing made out of the same dark wood that was found throughout the lobby, den, and kitchen. "Try not to fall down it. I'd hate to have to call all the king's horses."

Will laughed as he started up the stairs, hauling his bags with him. He followed her down the hall until she stepped inside the middle room on the left side. As he had throughout the tour, he paused and took in the light blue walls, dark wood accents, and the large windows overlooking the fields. "This is me?" he asked as he eased his suitcase onto the big, round, vintage rug that covered much of the bedroom floor.

"This is you. Grant is across the hall, Donnie is the last

door on the right, Juliet is the first room on this side, and Mama is on the far side of you."

"So you're the first room on the right?"

Carrie stared at him, wondering if he intended to knock on her door at three in the morning to request his tea.

He must have read her mind—or at least her furrowed brow. "I promise not to stalk you. I was just curious."

She smiled with embarrassment and let her defensive posture ease. "Yes, first door on the right. Everyone else is on the third floor."

"Good to know."

Moving past her, Will set his suitcases down and examined the fireplace. "Does this work?"

She pointed to a switch on the wall. "It's gas. All you have to do is turn it on. The bathroom is through there."

"And a sitting area." He looked to several dark blue high back parlor chairs grouped by a large window.

"So, that's it. Let me know if you need anything."

"Carrie," he called before she could leave. When she stopped and lifted her brows curiously, he gave her a warm smile. "You have a beautiful home."

"Thanks." She backed out of the room, closing the door behind her. Turning, she nearly bumped into Juliet Ramirez standing with her hands on her hips and narrowed eyes. "Ms. Ramirez."

"The sheets on my bed are *not* what I requested."

Carrie searched her mind, delving into the very depths, but nothing came to her. "I don't recall a request for sheets."

"What is the thread count?"

She nearly laughed but managed to contain it because the woman before her was clearly serious. "I don't have any idea."

"Well, it's not high enough. They feel like sandpaper."

Donnie came out of his room, appearing as if panic were about to overtake him. "Is there a problem?"

"My sheets are cheap," Juliet told him.

Donnie put a reassuring hand on Juliet's shoulder. "Well, Carrie will take care of that. Won't you, Carrie?"

Carrie forced a false bright smile. "Of course."

"Now," Juliet demanded. "I will not sleep on those sheets."

"No, of course not." Carrie grabbed the suitcases she'd left by the door and stepped around Juliet and into her room to strip the bed of perfectly soft sheets.

CHAPTER 2

W ill hesitated when he found Carrie in the dining room the next morning. He had sensed through the check-in process and dinner the night before that she wasn't thrilled to have the actors as her guests. He didn't think anyone else had noticed, but he had found himself fascinated by the thinly veiled resentment. Where most people fell over themselves to suck up to movie stars, Carrie had only taken the necessary steps and, if he'd read her correctly, had done so begrudgingly.

While his peers were busy gossiping about the industry, Will had watched Carrie move about the room with a subdued poise that matched that of any actress he'd worked with over the years. Her slender frame, gentle voice, and soft smiles betrayed the strength he'd seen in her dark eyes every time she glanced at him. She had a quiet confidence that was likely missed by most. He was intrigued by her muted behavior.

When their hostess turned and noticed him standing in the dining room, she gave him one of the smiles he'd seen all throughout dinner—kind and professional—but the smile didn't reach her eyes. "Good morning, Will. I hope you slept well."

"Like a baby. That room is wonderful and..." His words drifted off as he sniffed the air. "Do I smell sausage?"

"You do," she confirmed. "That's what I had for breakfast. Your menu consists of fresh-cut fruit, yogurt, and granola."

His face sank and his stomach protested. "No. No, no, no. This is Iowa," he stated with a firm tone. "I'm not eating granola while in Iowa. I want farm-fresh sausage and eggs over easy."

She laughed, she *actually* laughed, and her eyes lit in a way he hadn't seen in his short stay. "I thought someone might. I made extra sausage, and I'm happy to fry you a couple eggs."

Will's mouth started to water as he flashed back to break-fasts during his childhood. His mom always made a big meal on Sunday mornings with more food than their family could eat. Leftovers were dropped off at his grandparents' homes by noon. The routine was the same every weekend—they'd eat, then head to his father's parents to check in and leave the meal. Then they crossed the small town where he'd grown up to visit his mother's parents. His maternal grandfather had been Will's favorite person in the world.

"Did you happen to make homemade sausage gravy?" Will asked hopefully. "Biscuits?"

Carrie's laugh returned. "Sadly, I did not. I'm happy to add biscuits and gravy to the breakfast menu *tomorrow* if you'd like."

"I'd like that," he said. "I'd like that very much."

"Okay. For today, I have sausage and eggs over easy, coming right up."

"Thank you. In the meantime, I think I'll have some of that delicious-looking fresh fruit," he said and began loading up a plate as she disappeared. He was settling into his spot at the table when Mama came into the room, a pitcher of orange juice in her hand. "Good morning," he said with a cheerful tone.

She stopped and looked at him for a moment, and then a bright smile spread across her painted lips. That was one thing Will had noticed straightaway when he'd arrived the previous day. Carrie was casual in her jeans and barely there makeup, while Doreen wore slacks and blouses and vibrant red lipstick. Carrie's long brown hair was swept back in a braid, but Mama had a fashionable silver bob. They seemed to be complete opposites. Where Carrie was more down-home comfort, Mama added just enough splash to be noticed. Carrie seemed to want to blend into the background, but Mama wanted to be seen.

"Did you sleep well?" Mama asked.

"I did."

"That's nice. Would you like some orange juice? It's fresh-squeezed."

"That sounds great. Thanks."

"You're very welcome." She filled a glass and sat down across from him. "Is today the first day of your film?"

Will shook his head as he finished a bite of pineapple. "We shot some scenes in LA before heading here. Those were the indoor shots that needed to be done at the studio. Most of the scenes here will be filmed outside. We don't have scenery like this in California."

"Iowa is beautiful. I couldn't imagine living anywhere else. I grew up right here in this house. I'd never want to leave."

She gave him a wide smile that made him feel at ease, like he was family instead of a guest and certainly not an actor she needed to put on airs with. Despite her salt-and-pepper chin-length bob and fresh makeup, she came across so grand-motherly, he half expected her to pull an oven-fresh cookie from her apron pocket and serve it up with a glass of warm milk.

"It's not what I imagined," he admitted.

"Did you expect toothless farmers and endless corn fields?"

His image of the consummate grandmother faded as her warm smile turned a bit mischievous. "I wouldn't go *that* far," he said with a wink.

She laughed—a sound that was surprisingly strong coming from her small body—and it made Will smile even more.

"Mama," Carrie said, carrying a platter in one hand and a plate in the other, "did you cut up all this fruit?"

"I was up with the sun this morning. I knew you'd have your hands full, so I put myself to good use."

"Thank you." She eased the fruit down on the buffet and then put a plate in front of Will. "Between the two of us, we may have made too much, though."

"Mike and the boys will finish up what they don't, I expect." Mama's eyes glazed over as if she were deep in thought. It lasted only a moment before she snapped back. "I should make more juice. One of those girls is bound to be on an all-liquid diet."

Doreen left, and Will focused on Carrie, who was wiping her hands down her apron. "This smells amazing," he said, and his stomach grumbled in agreement. He cut into an egg and watched the yolk ooze out. "Who is this elusive Mike person Mama keeps talking about?"

Carrie paused in her movements for a moment before she finished straightening a place setting on the table. "Her son. My husband."

The distant sadness in Carrie's voice was unexpected, not

the usual tone someone took when referring to a spouse. "Oh?"

"He died. Three years ago. She has early onset Alzheimer's, so...she forgets."

"Oh, geez." He cringed. "I'm sorry."

Carrie glanced up long enough to meet his gaze.

As he looked into her eyes, he again saw the underlying strength he'd noticed the day before. She was going through something bigger than anyone would have ever guessed by the soft grace she presented to the world.

"She's okay most days," Carrie said. "We have some excitement once in a while, but we do all right."

"Excitement?"

She returned her focus to prepping the table. "Last week she decided to go visit a friend. Only, she left at four in the morning, and her friend doesn't live in the house Mama walked to. The couple who does live there were nice enough to sit her down with a cup of tea and call the police. I didn't even know she was gone. It was more frightening than exciting, really."

"That's tough," he said. "I'm sorry."

She shrugged casually. "We do okay."

"So, it's only you here to take care of her?"

"Mike was her only child, and her sister passed away years ago. She doesn't have any family other than me. Besides, she doesn't need around-the-clock care. Other than occasional bouts of confusion, she can still take care of herself. For now."

"That's good."

"Yeah, it is good."

He looked at the doorway when several of the other actors came in and walked around her without so much as a "hello." He was immediately irritated to see how demanding yet dismissive they were of their hostess. That was the way with most rising stars, though. What better way to make oneself feel important than by making someone else feel less so?

Will hated to admit he used to be the same way. When he'd had his first brushes with success, his head had filled with all kinds of egotistical thoughts. If he were honest with himself, those thoughts had only recently started to fade. Reality had taken a bit longer to catch up to him than it did to some others, but the truth couldn't be denied forever. As much as Will and the others fancied themselves above it all, they weren't better than anyone. On some levels, they were worse than most.

He watched, eating his unhealthy breakfast, while Carrie catered to every whim with the same ease and calm that had lured him in the night before. When she ran out of juice, she announced she'd be right back and disappeared.

Juliet sauntered into the room then abruptly stopped. "What is that smell?" She scrunched her nose and put her hand to her chest. "Is that...*meat*?"

"It's sausage," Will said, "and it is spectacular."

"You ate that?" She widened her eyes at him. While some might have been taken in by her innocent deer-in-the-headlights looks, Will had to wonder if she ever stopped putting on a show for those around her. "Do you have any idea what that will do to you?" Juliet demanded.

"Fill me up until lunch, I expect." He stuffed the last of his breakfast into his mouth as he stood. "Excuse me, I need more juice."

As Will neared the kitchen, he overheard Mama say, "The troupe seems happy."

He slowed his stride at the sound of Carrie's flat response. "They seem to like the house."

"My great-great-grandfather built this house right after—"

"Mama," Carrie said with a hint of impatience. "Would you slice more oranges?"

"I can do that." Mama walked to the island and took a few oranges from a bowl as Will stood in the doorway unnoticed. "I like cooking with you," Mama said.

Carrie rinsed a dish in the sink and grabbed a towel. "I like cooking with you too. We make a good team."

"Mike always tells me how much he likes your food," Mama said.

"That's nice."

Will couldn't see Carrie's face, but he heard her voice. She said the words, but there was a sad undertone. He couldn't imagine how difficult it must have been for her to constantly be reminded that her husband was gone.

"This isn't going to be too much work for you, is it?" Mama grabbed a few more oranges. "All these people needing your attention."

"I can handle it. Why? Do I look overwhelmed already?"

Doreen laughed. "You looked overwhelmed when you woke up this morning, dear."

"Well, I can handle it. I'm Superwoman, you know."

"You try, that's for sure. I don't want to see you working too hard. You always work too hard."

Carrie snagged an orange half from the pile Mama had cut and put it in the hand juicer. "Don't worry. I won't work too hard." She pushed the handle down, and the juice ran into the bowl beneath.

The scene was so common, so *normal*, Will could have stood and watched them working together all day. There was a kind of harmony in the room that seemed to be an extension of the two women. Something there drew Will in and made him want to sit at the island and partake in their joint effort to make juice. Carrie had squeezed three orange halves before she glanced up and noticed him in the doorway.

She plastered a forced smile to her lips as soon as she noticed him. "Did you get enough to eat?"

"More than enough." He patted his flat stomach. "It was wonderful."

"Thanks."

"I've got this," Mama said, practically pushing Carrie away from the juicer.

As Carrie stepped around the counter and closed the gap between her and Will, he offered her a much kinder and genuine smile than she'd offered him. "I'm sorry about them."

Carrie creased her brow. "Sorry about what?"

"The superstars out there." He nodded toward the dining room. "They're jerks."

She didn't dispute his assessment. "Well, it happens."

"Yeah, unfortunately it does. Doesn't make their behavior okay, though."

"I'll take this out," Mama said, bypassing them with a glass of orange juice.

Carrie started to stop her but clamped her lips shut. "Hopefully only one person is thirsty," she said lightly. Once they were alone, Carrie returned her dark eyes to Will. "It isn't out of line for them to treat me like what I am: their chef and their maid. That's my job."

"They can be respectful about it."

She shrugged slightly. "Some are more respectful than others. That's par for the course. I appreciate you being concerned, but I don't take their treatment personally, Will."

He glanced around the kitchen. "Okay, but if anyone takes that too far, let me know."

A slow grin curved her lips, and he realized, belatedly, that he'd sounded like some kind of wannabe hero, a tough guy coming to the rescue of a damsel in distress.

"You'll be the first to know," she said in a way that wasn't quite patronizing but close enough he was slightly embarrassed by his bravado.

He had no idea why he felt the need to come to her defense. He'd never been one to go out of his way for others. Then again, he supposed he did know. The last few years had changed him in a lot of ways he was still trying to sort out. Being part of this film made his skin crawl. Not because it was a bad movie, but because he felt like he'd sold himself out to be part of it.

"They're about done," Mama announced, walking back into the kitchen. She stopped, looking at Carrie and Will standing next to each other as if she was confused, and then eased the dishes in her hand onto the counter. "They did ask for more juice. I must have forgotten. Other than that, our first breakfast was a complete success!"

"It was delicious," Will said to Doreen.

Giving him a slight bow, she said, "Thank you very much, sire."

"We'll be heading out soon." He focused on Carrie one more time. "I should get ready. Have a good day, Carrie."

"You too, Will."

He winked at Doreen. "Try not to get into any trouble today, Mama."

She laughed as she grabbed a few oranges from a big bowl. "Oh, that's nearly impossible."

———

CARRIE CLICKED open the container that held Mama's evening medications and dumped them into Mama's palm.

"I so love having actors in the house," Mama said, ignoring the pills. "They appreciate my theatrics."

Carrie smiled. "They certainly do."

"You know, I was going to run off to Hollywood when I was younger."

"Until you met the love of your life," Carrie said as Mama popped her pills into her mouth.

"Oh, he was so handsome," she recalled after swallowing the medication. Handing Carrie the glass of water she'd used, she heaved a dreamy sigh. "I had such a weakness for bad boys."

Carrie chuckled, thinking of all the rules Mike used to convince her to break. Sneaking off to make out in the field when she was supposed to be washing dishes or slipping into a room while she was making the bed and pulling her into the closet for a few breathless kisses. Despite having a heart of gold, Mike had been a rebel all his life, and she suspected he never would have changed. If he were alive today, Carrie imagined he'd still be dragging her into the pantry while she had flour on her hands and dough under her nails.

Damn, she missed that.

"Me too, Mama," Carrie said as she pushed thoughts of her late husband from her mind.

"He takes after his father, you know?"

"Hmm?"

Mama grinned in a knowing way. "That blush on your cheeks, missy. I know what you're thinking. Mike's father was just as bad."

Carrie gasped and tried to stop a giggle from slipping out. "Go get changed. It's getting late."

Mama disappeared into her bathroom, and Carrie sat on the edge of Doreen's bed, lifting the old photo of Doreen and her husband. He'd died in a farming accident when Mike was a boy. As far as Carrie knew, Doreen had never even considered allowing another man into her heart. Carrie loved Mike, she missed him every single day, but she hoped someday she'd be able to move on. She didn't know when someday might be, though.

She supposed that didn't really matter. With Doreen's memory loss and steadily declining health, Carrie didn't have time to even consider dating. She didn't have the energy to give to anyone else. As Natalie loved to remind her, she was already spread too thin.

"And then he said," Doreen said as she came into the room.

Apparently she'd been talking but Carrie hadn't heard her. She didn't need to. Within a moment, she recognized the story about how Mama was won over by a farmhand.

Mama rested her head on the pillow. Taking Carrie's hand, she smiled up. "I would be lost without you."

Leaning down, Carrie kissed her cheek. "I feel the same, Mama. Get some sleep." Turning on the video baby monitor she kept by the bed, she confirmed that the receiver she carried with her was working before she left the room.

Once she was downstairs, Carrie double-checked the locks and poked her head into each room, doing a quick sweep to look for messes before heading to the kitchen. There, she set the monitor on the counter and pulled the cork from a bottle of red wine. As soon as she filled the glass, she focused on getting out a Dutch oven to make another batch of yogurt.

As she did, her mind wandered back to her husband. She had loved Mike so much, she thought her heart might burst. Carrie's father had hinted that she and Mike were too young to get married, but Carrie had known, without a doubt, she would never love anyone the way she loved him. They were only nineteen when they'd wed, but they'd had a lavish event in the gardens of the inn. Mama had cut the perfect flowers for the bouquet and baked the most delicious cake. Carrie had practically been family from the day she'd come to work at the inn. The wedding had made it official.

She frowned as she considered that she would probably never find that kind of happiness again. That was depressing as hell. She refused to believe her best days were behind her, even though it felt that way most of the time. Someday, she'd have time to breathe and she could return her attention to the dreams that she and Mama had talked about so many times.

Mama had wanted to open a restaurant at the inn. Cooking was her passion. Running her home as a bed-and-breakfast had been a means to an end, not the dream she'd always felt was too far out of reach. Carrie disagreed. She knew they could turn Gable Inn into a successful tearoom. If only they'd had the means. Unfortunately, Mama's medical expenses had drained what little savings they'd had.

"What's that?" Will asked, pulling Carrie from her thoughts.

She followed his gaze to the monitor. "Keeping an eye on Mama from afar."

Carrie hated that she felt the need to do so, but Mama had taken to wandering. When the house got too quiet, Carrie would panic. After running up the stairs one too many times, only to find Mama sound asleep, Carrie decided investing in the monitors would save her from constantly fearing the worst. For a moment, she recalled far too vividly the fear she'd felt the first time Mama had gotten out of the house unnoticed and disappeared.

He tilted his head and narrowed his eyes as if trying to see through her. "Are you okay, Carrie?"

"Yeah. Of course," she said, returning her attention to the milk she was warming.

"You know, we only met yesterday, but I've already learned something very valuable about you."

Confused, she furrowed her brows. "What?"

"When you say 'of course,' you really mean anything but."

"What, exactly, is anything but 'of course?'"

"Well, just now, it meant 'not really.' And when you say it to Donnie, it sounds like you mean 'kiss my ass.'"

Carrie chuckled, mostly because he wasn't wrong.

Will smiled. "And when you say it to Juliet, that means 'fuck you.' Pardon my French," he said as she laughed, "but that is what you mean, isn't it?"

She simply grinned, neither confirming nor denying his observations. After turning off the flame and setting a thermometer into the warmed milk, she gestured toward the bottle of wine. "Would you like a glass?"

"Yeah, I would. Thank you."

He sat at the island as she filled a glass for him. He lifted his glass, surprising her with a toast, but she clinked her drink to his before taking a sip.

Leaning against the counter, Carrie considered her words before speaking. "Juliet is...challenging."

"Yeah. Try working with her," Will muttered.

Carrie tried to hide her smile, but she couldn't. "Donnie is..."

"A schmuck," Will offered.

Taking a breath, she opted not to confirm that she agreed with his assessment. "I'll work harder at hiding my displeasure."

"Oh, don't. I find your underlying snark quite entertaining."

Widening her eyes, Carrie gasped. "Am I snarky? Because I don't mean to be."

"Nobody else has noticed."

"Even so," she said, "I don't mean to be disrespectful."

He considered her words for a few moments before shrugging. "Personally, I think it's good for them to have someone who doesn't fall at their feet. They need to be reminded they aren't as special as they think."

"That's not my place," Carrie said. She took a drink before realizing his glass was already empty. She hadn't even noticed him finish his drink but didn't hesitate to pour him another.

"Can I be honest with you about something?" Will asked quietly as he stared at his glass.

"I guess."

He looked up at her with his gray eyes, and for a moment she saw pain and vulnerability there. Her heart tripped in her chest with the uncertainty of what he was about to confess. The look only lasted for a moment before he blinked the agony away and smirked. "This wine is terrible."

Carrie laughed lightly. "Well, it does the job."

Nodding, he focused on his glass again, and she was tempted to try to pry the truth from him. Clearly the wine wasn't what was on his mind. She sensed something heavier weighed on him, but she didn't think it was her place to pry, any more than it was her place to make Donnie and Juliet realize their egos were obnoxiously large.

"Being here reminds me of home," he said. He glanced at

her in a way that made her think he was uncomfortable sharing that but couldn't stop himself.

She understood that. There were so many times she didn't want to complain about what Mama had been up to, what messes she'd made, or how tired she herself felt, but sometimes she couldn't stop the words from coming. Sometimes, when she and Natalie were alone, those quiet moments turned into venting sessions that Carrie couldn't control.

"Your home is comforting. Being here…it's comforting. That doesn't make sense," he said with a smile. "But it's true."

He shifted for a few seconds before flicking his gaze to her. When he did, she smiled softly, the same kind of smile she gave to her mother-in-law when she started feeling overwhelmed by something. Moving around the counter, she sat next to him. "You're from the Midwest, aren't you?"

"Indiana," he confirmed.

"Well, that explains it. Returning to the quiet of rural living after so much time in the city feels familiar," she said.

"I guess," he said and took a big drink from his glass. He winced as he set his glass down. "Remind me to order some real wine."

She chuckled. "I'll have you know that comes from a local winery. It's won awards."

"It's an acquired taste, then."

"Perhaps."

Will finished his drink and nodded toward the stove. "What are you making?"

"Oh." She jumped up and rushed to check the temperature of her milk. "Yogurt."

"You won't forget my biscuits and gravy, right?"

She glanced back and grinned at him. "Not a chance."

He creased his brow. "Am I making more work for you by asking?"

Focusing on her task, Carrie shook her head. "You didn't ask. I offered."

"Because I asked—" he started.

"I don't mind," she said. The truth was, had Juliet demanded it or Donnie insisted, Carrie would have felt put out. She would have resented the request. But the way that Will's eyes had lit with the hope of having a homemade breakfast had made her want to make biscuits from scratch.

"Well, can I help?"

She stopped stirring her starter batch into the warm milk. "Help...what?"

He shrugged and then smiled. "I don't know. I felt like I should offer."

Laughing, she shook her head. "You're lucky I haven't kicked you out of my kitchen yet. Guests aren't usually welcome here. There's absolutely zero chance that I'll let you cook *anything*."

"One of those controlling types, huh?"

"Only in the kitchen," she said lightly. The words had barely left her mouth before she realized they could easily be taken out of context. Rather than look at him to see if he'd caught on to that, she focused on putting the yogurt into the oven to incubate.

"Well," he said when she turned around. "If I'm going to be hanging out in here with you, I'm definitely buying better wine."

Carrie chuckled as he bid her a good night. Once he was gone, she took a drink from her glass. "It's not that bad," she muttered to herself.

CHAPTER 3

Laughter filled the living room as Mama finished telling one of her stories. Three days into their stay at the inn, and sitting in front of the fire listening to the elderly woman talk about her past had become one of Will's favorite parts of his stay in Iowa. He was amazed that she could recount something so vividly that happened forty years ago but, according to Carrie, couldn't remember that her son had passed away three years ago.

When the laughter faded, Carrie set her wineglass down. "Mama, it's getting late."

Doreen sighed. "That means she'd like me to go to bed and leave you young people alone."

"That's right. You're embarrassing me," Carrie teased. She stood and waited for Doreen to rise beside her. The pair bid the group good night and headed upstairs.

Will admired the way Carrie patiently walked next to the slower woman. An unexpected flash of guilt hit his gut. Several years ago, his father had been diagnosed with kidney failure. Will had paid the medical bills and hired a nurse to help his parents. He'd felt that had been enough. Watching Carrie take such good care of someone who wasn't a blood relative stirred something inside him that didn't sit well.

He'd been in the middle of a film when his father had become ill. His older brother had assured Will there was nothing he could do, and Will had accepted that at face value. He hadn't been there when his father's health took a sudden turn for the worse. The next time he'd seen his dad was at the man's funeral.

He should have been there. Film budget and deadlines be damned. He should have rushed home and spent time with his father while he could. Though his mom assured Will it wasn't his fault, the guilt Will felt weighed on him more and more with each passing day. Seeing Carrie with Doreen seemed to magnify all that.

Will had chosen his career over his family. His mom could reassure him all she wanted, but Will knew it and his brother knew it too. Their relationship had never been the same since. Brian hadn't come out and said what he was thinking, but the rift that had always been between them had grown into an uncrossable chasm.

Will was yanked from his thoughts when Grant announced it was his bedtime as well. Left alone, Will reached for the script he'd been reading when the gathering started and began leafing through the pages. The lines were as flat as the page they were printed on. He frowned as he tossed the papers aside.

Rising from the sofa, he walked to the mantel to look at the photos resting there, many of which were obviously originals from decades prior. A picture of Carrie and a man dressed for their wedding caught his attention. Carrie's smile was genuine in the picture; the happiness she felt radiated from her. As he took in the soft curve of her oval face, he thought she was one of the most beautiful women he'd ever seen. Even on her wedding day, she hadn't caked her face with makeup. She was clearly comfortable with her looks, which was something he didn't see much of in his line of work.

"Still up?"

Will looked over when Carrie walked back into the room. "You were a lovely bride."

She smiled as she moved to look at the photo he was holding. He swayed slightly when she leaned in close enough for him to inhale her scent—a sweetness that unexpectedly stirred something inside him. He glanced at her, but she was focused on the photo. She seemed completely unaware of the effect she'd had on him.

When she did look up and catch his gaze, she scrunched her nose a bit. "I look so damn young in that picture. It wasn't that long ago. Life certainly has a way of changing quickly, doesn't it?"

Her smile faded, and Will sensed sadness come over her.

"Are you going to be up long?" she asked before he could point out the change in her. She stepped away from him and started straightening the pillows on the sofa, fluffing each one and setting them in a row.

"Uh, I've got a pretty long scene to prepare for tomorrow, but those lines..." He frowned at his script lying on the sofa. "I can't get them. They aren't resonating with me."

She put the last pillow in place and then started gathering glasses. "I don't know how you can possibly remember all that. I'm lucky to know my name half the time."

"Would you help me?"

Her eyes filled with curiosity. "Help you what?"

"Read lines with me."

"No." She laughed quietly and shook her head. "I don't think so."

"Please," he all but begged. "I need help."

"Really, Will. The only time I even attempted to act was in a sixth-grade rendition of *Snow White*. It didn't go well."

"I'm not asking you to act. I only need you to recite the lines."

Carrie shook her head. "I'd only confuse you more."

"I am completely lost already." He swiped his script from where he'd left it. "It would help me tremendously."

"Can't you *act* like you know your lines?"

He smiled at her teasing before holding the pages out to her and giving her his most irresistible smile. Few people could defy him when he put on his charms. For a moment, he thought she might be in the minority, but then she gave in with a dramatic sigh.

"Fine," she muttered, putting the glasses back onto the coffee table. "But I'm not going to be much help."

"All I need you to do is read what's on the page and tell me if I get something wrong."

Taking the papers from him, she cleared her throat as she eased down onto the couch.

"Start here," he said, tapping at a line on the page.

Carrie inhaled deeply before reading. "So here you are again, Mr. Jennings."

"No, no. You have to sound flustered."

She lifted her brows at him. "Flustered?"

"I'm chasing after you, and you find it incredibly annoying."

"You just told me I don't have to act."

"This isn't acting," he said with a chuckle. "It's enunciation."

She knitted her brows together into an exaggerated scowl. "So here you are again, Mr. Jennings."

"Much better."

She glanced up at him from the script in her hand. "That is not your line."

"Oh, right." Will scratched his temple lightly, as if that might trigger his memory, and then laughed. "I can't remember."

"Alas, it would appear the fates have—"

"This is terrible," Will said, cutting her off.

She scoffed and lowered the pages. "I told you I'm not good at this."

"The script," he corrected. "The script is terrible. The *movie* is going to be terrible."

Carrie lowered the paper onto her lap. "Then why are you doing it?"

Will didn't know the answer to that. He knew what he was supposed to say. "The hottest director, the hottest actress. Put a little life back in my career. At least, that's what my agent said. But honestly, I don't know. Things haven't been going well for me lately, so I thought signing on to this film would give me a much-needed boost."

"Even though you hate it?" she asked.

"I don't *hate* it." His denial didn't sound the least bit convincing. He exhaled heavily and tried again. "I'm unmoved by it. This script makes no sense to me."

Carrie scanned the words on the page. "It's a romantic comedy?"

"Yeah."

"Did you expect to find deeper meaning in it?"

He laughed softly, but it wasn't with humor. His laugh held a sad kind of acceptance. "No, I wasn't looking for deeper meaning. I've been at this a long time, you know. It used to feel like I was doing something with my life. I thought I was making a difference somehow. I've come to realize that was very presumptuous of me."

She was silent for several long moments, clearly processing his confession. "Why do you say that?"

"Did you see the last film I made?"

She grimaced, and he knew she had. He'd jumped at a project in a futile attempt to stay busy. His agent had warned him against it, but Will had been determined to do the indie film. That was just one mistake in a long string that had plagued him since his father's death.

"It was awful," he said so she wouldn't have to.

"It was"—she paused—"lacking something."

Will grinned as he repeated her assessment. "Lacking something?"

Blushing, she looked down. "So you're making a movie you don't like because you no longer trust your instincts?"

"I didn't…" He stopped when he realized her assessment wasn't completely off the mark. "I guess. I wonder sometimes if I've overstayed my welcome. Maybe it's time for me to look into a new career."

She widened her eyes before hesitantly asking, "Such as?"

He shrugged. "Other than a few shitty jobs to feed myself, I've never really done anything else. All I know is that this isn't what I was hoping it would be."

"The job or the lifestyle?"

Again, she seemed to have been able to see through to the heart of the issue when he was still trying to deny the truth. "Both, I guess," he admitted softly.

"What would you like to do?"

Will tried to imagine what he could do. He didn't have any

skills outside of the industry, none that would give him the ability to start over. He was staring down forty years old. That was hardly the time to be reevaluating his entire existence. "Maybe something behind-the-scenes. I could direct or...write. I've always wanted to write."

When he refilled his glass of wine, she picked up her glass from earlier in the evening and held it out to him. Will smiled, happy that she was asking for more. He'd given Donnie a list of wines he wanted sent to the inn, and they'd magically appeared that morning. He'd picked out a few bottles of red for the sole intent of proving to Carrie that her local winery wasn't as good as she insisted. "This wine is better than that bottle we shared the other night, isn't it?"

Carrie laughed. "Much better. Do you think that will give your projects more meaning?" she asked as he filled her glass.

"Maybe," he said so quietly, he doubted she heard him. He didn't like where this conversation was heading. He'd spent far too much time trying to avoid his inner demons to simply lay them bare so easily. "What about you? You must have some plan for life after this."

Creasing her brow, she asked, "Life after what? You mean after Mama?"

"Not to sound callous," he said hesitantly, "but yeah. Are you going to keep running the inn?"

"I don't know." She looked into her glass as if in contemplation.

"I ask because... Well, to be honest, you don't seem to enjoy it much."

Carrie laughed, and that blush returned to her cheeks. "It shows?"

He held up his fingers with as much space between them as he could manage. "Just a little."

"I'll have to work on that," she said as the color in her cheeks deepened.

"Why are you doing it?"

"It's not the work, Will. I don't mind the job. It's…everything else. I came to work here when I was eighteen. It was more than a job. My mom passed away when I was young, and my dad, hard as he tried, never really knew what to do with a daughter. Doreen took me in and taught me how to run this place. When Mike and I got married, she really did become my mother. It wasn't long after Mike was gone that I noticed her starting to forget things. Within a year of his death, she got her diagnosis. It's up to me to care for her, but it's also up to me to care for this old house. It gets to be a little much sometimes, that's all."

He nodded. "I imagine it does. That's a lot for one person to tackle alone."

"I want to keep her here as long as possible," Carrie said as she swirled her wine. "That, unfortunately, takes money, and I'd stopped taking on guests some time ago. Donnie's offer came at a time when I really needed it."

"But it's a lot of work," he offered.

Carrie laughed lightly. "Yeah. It's a lot. But don't worry," she said, darting her eyes to his. "I can handle it."

"It's wonderful what you're doing for her. Very noble."

"Noble?" she asked.

"Yeah. It is." He debated how much of his own struggles to share. She'd already figured out that he wasn't keen on making this movie, but that was minor compared to the secrets that really pressed on his soul. "My father was ill for quite a while before he passed away. I didn't make time to go see him."

Carrie sat quietly for a few moments before gently saying, "It's not easy to see someone you care about struggling."

"No. But that's not why I didn't go home. I...I was working, and that seemed more important."

"You regret that," she pointed out.

Will nodded. "Yeah. I made a mistake."

"We all make mistakes," Carrie said softly. "We're human, Will. It's what we do. We screw up and we learn and then we do better. Hopefully."

"Hopefully," he said.

Will hated seeing the sadness in her eyes, but he'd noticed it from the moment they'd met. Now, he was starting to understand why he felt so connected to her. His grandfather had told Will a million times when he was growing up that everyone was fighting a dragon nobody else could see. Will had only just begun to really understand what his grandfather had been trying to teach him.

After a moment, he reached out and gently squeezed her hand. "I'm sorry. This isn't the most uplifting conversation we could have."

She shrugged as if to dismiss his apology, but when she looked at him, the depth of emotion in her eyes let him know he'd hit on a topic she didn't want to delve into. "It's not like I don't think about it from time to time. Life changes. You gotta roll with it, or it's going to take you down. Why put it off, right?"

"Right. Why put it off? So, uh, what was that line again?"

She laughed as she picked up the script. "This really is terrible."

He grinned as the misery on her face eased. "I know."

———

CARRIE SAT STRAIGHT UP in bed. There was nothing worse than the high-pitched screaming of a smoke alarm in the middle of the night. The irritation the sound caused lasted only a moment before fear kicked in.

The smoke alarm was blaring in the middle of the night!

Kicking the blankets off her suddenly energized body, she jumped out of bed and ran to her bedroom door, jerking it open.

"What's going on?" Grant asked.

"Go," Carrie instructed. "Get out." When she started to go the other way, someone grabbed her arm and pulled her to a stop. She looked back to find Will staring down at her. "Mama!"

While everyone else headed for the stairs, they went to the end of the hall. Doreen's door was wide open with no sign of the woman inside the room.

"Oh, God." Carrie turned, pushing past Will and running to the stairs. *Please, please, please...*

She was certain that Mama had done something to set the house on fire. Carrie had feared this for a long time. She'd hidden matches, lighters, and replaced all the candles with battery-operated imposters. Doreen couldn't be trusted with open flame. She was too forgetful. Too clumsy. Too untrustworthy. But now the house was on fire.

As she feared, the closer Carrie got to the first floor, the stronger the smell of something burning became. She followed the scent to the kitchen, where a thick haze had filled the room, originating from a pan on the stove. Flames were leaping, not quite touching the cabinets above them, but the white paint had begun to bubble at the extreme heat.

Grabbing the fire extinguisher from a bracket on the wall, Carrie pulled the pin and aimed the hose at the stove while Will climbed onto a chair. He pulled apart the blaring alarm. Once the fire was out and the kitchen was quiet, Carrie hurried out of the room, calling for her mother-in-law. She found the old woman sitting on the couch in the den, her head lying to the side, illuminated by the images on the television.

Her heart nearly seized in her chest. Oh no.

"Mama!" Carrie grasped Doreen's arm, shaking the woman roughly.

Doreen opened her eyes with a start and instantly scowled. "You scared me half to death, Carolyn!"

"Not half as much as you scared me."

"What?" Reaching into the pocket of her robe, she pulled out a small hearing aid and pushed it into her ear. "What'd you say?"

Carrie didn't know if she should laugh or cry. The sound that left her seemed to be a mix of both. "Are you okay?"

"What's wrong?"

"Come on. It's late." Holding Mama's hand, Carrie helped her off the sofa and led her from the room. Seeing Will standing by the doorway, she apologized with a sad smile. "Would you mind—"

"I'll let them know they can come in."

Carrie guided Doreen up the stairs as the woman told her about the old *I Love Lucy* episode she'd been watching before falling asleep. Carrie, all the while, silently reminded herself that no one was hurt and no permanent damage had been done. She tucked Doreen into bed and smiled. The woman was so unaware of the panic she'd caused, Carrie couldn't hold on to the frustration she felt. Instead, her heart ached at how very oblivious Mama was. "Sleep tight, Mama."

"You too, honey."

She stroked Doreen's hair and waited for her to close her eyes before easing off the bed and heading downstairs. She thankfully made it all the way to the kitchen without running into anyone. The incident had shaken her to the core, and she didn't know if she could handle being chastised by some Hollywood elite. Walking into the kitchen, she paused at the door as Will stretched above his head, putting the alarm back in place.

"You don't have to do that," Carrie said.

Will looked down at her. "I don't mind."

She moved to the stove and scoffed at the smoke-covered paint on the cabinets. It was going to take her hours to clean this up. Frustrated, she reached for the stove knobs and yanked them off, making it impossible to turn on the burners. Why hadn't she thought to do this before something happened? Mama could have burned the damn house down.

"How is she?" Will asked.

"Sound asleep." Carrie opened a drawer and dropped in the knobs. "How was everyone else?"

"Fine."

Carrie returned to the stove for the pan. "I'll apologize to Donnie in the morning."

"It was an accident, Carrie. He'll understand."

"Right." She looked at the black blobs in the pan. "What do you suppose she was cooking at this hour?"

Will hopped off the chair and moved to her side. "Green eggs and ham?"

She laughed quietly, but her smile faded quickly. She wished she could dismiss the episode so easily. "What a mess."

"Are you okay?"

She wasn't, but she figured she'd dumped enough of her

problems on a man she barely knew. She'd had a hard time falling asleep as she'd replayed their earlier conversation. He was being kind, and she'd just opened up and said much more than she should have. "I'm fine," she said with a forced smile. "Thank you for turning off the alarm."

"Do you need help with anything else?"

"No. You should get back to bed, Will. You have an early morning tomorrow."

"So do you. Are you sure you're okay?"

"Don't I look okay?" She moaned as soon as she asked the question. "Please don't answer that."

"You look stressed."

"I said please."

"And very tired."

She turned and playfully narrowed her eyes at him. "Manners go nowhere with you, huh?"

"Not really. No." He smiled, and she couldn't help but chuckle along with him.

She had almost managed to relax thanks to Will's kindness when the kitchen door swung open. Will opened his mouth, but he didn't have a chance to speak before Donnie snapped at Carrie.

"This kind of thing cannot happen again, Miss Gable."

"Of course," she replied softly.

"If Doreen—"

Carrie cut him off. "It won't happen again." The clip of her tone held a warning that she had not meant to vocalize. Her exhaustion had weakened her censor, and she'd unintentionally made it clear that she wasn't going to have him attacking her mother-in-law. "It was an accident," she said, trying to be understanding. "It will not happen again."

Donnie turned to Will, as if asking him to verify that he'd

heard the way Carrie had snapped at him. When Will said nothing, Donnie eyed Carrie again. "Very well. William, you have to be in makeup in less than three hours. I'd suggest you get some sleep while you can."

When Donnie was gone, Will turned to Carrie and gently rubbed her arm. "Are you okay?"

"Yeah." She forced a smile. She had to smile so she didn't break down and cry. Now that the adrenaline was wearing off, she could feel the fear settling over her. Fisting her trembling hands, she insisted, "I'm fine."

"Really?"

"Really."

"Okay. Do you need help with anything else?"

"No. Go to bed. I'm fine."

"All right. Good night, then."

She managed to hold her fearful tears at bay until the door closed behind him.

CHAPTER 4

"What a bunch of jerks," Natalie said as Carrie scraped loose paint from the cabinets above the stove.

"Well, it *was* the middle of the night."

"So what?" Natalie barked. "Shit happens. It wasn't deliberate."

"She was sleeping when you checked on her, right?"

"Snoring." Natalie was quiet for a moment before clearing her throat. That was something she did before treading on dangerous territory.

Carrie knew her well enough to recognize the sign, and her defenses instantly went up. "Don't."

"Don't what?"

"Say that I'm in over my head. Don't you dare say it."

"Okay, I won't. As long as you know it."

Carrie frowned. Of course she was in over her head. She'd been in over her head for months before the house was filled with guests. "Yes," she said with a slight pout. "I know it."

"Maybe it's time to hire someone. I don't mind helping," Natalie quickly said, "but I can't be here every day. I have to go to my job sometimes."

"I know you do. I really do appreciate all you've been doing."

"Get someone to clean in the mornings. That will free you up to do something exciting, like sleep."

"I don't know, Nat. I don't think the superstars would appreciate some unknown gathering their dirty sheets and scrubbing their toilets."

"You have to take care of yourself."

"I take care of myself."

"Really?"

"Yes. This morning I stayed in the shower long enough to actually wash my hair. Yesterday, I washed my body."

"You damned slacker. What the hell are you complaining about, then?"

"I'm not complaining. You are." Carrie stepped back to check her work. Seeing another bubble, she used the tool in her hand to scrape it away. "It's not that bad. I get things done."

"I know you do. I know you keep up. But with these people invading your house, you get absolutely no downtime."

"What's this? Hmm? I'm chatting with you in the quiet of the kitchen."

"Because these are the servant's quarters. Your house no longer belongs to you."

"It's an inn, Natalie. We've had guests coming and going for as long as I can remember."

"That was before," Natalie said. "Before" was in reference to a time prior to Mama's diagnosis. Prior to Mike's death. Prior to everything falling apart.

Carrie grabbed a sheet of fine grit sandpaper she'd been using and smoothed out a spot on the cabinet so she could slap a layer of paint on the wood and call it done—at least until spring. "They're not even here. Well, most of them."

"I need food," came one of Juliet's snotty demands, as if Carrie's comment was her cue. She looked between the two women when neither moved. "Well?"

Carrie smiled as nicely as she could. "I don't serve lunch. I serve breakfast and dinner on weekdays. Lunch, snacks, and weekends are on you."

The woman was clearly confused. "What are you saying?"

"There're several restaurants in town that deliver," Carrie said. "Or you could go to the store."

A half laugh left Juliet's perfectly lined and pouty lips. "I don't think so, Ms. Gable."

Carrie inhaled deeply, slowly, cursing herself before she even spoke. "Shall I heat up some leftovers?"

Juliet stared with hard and cold eyes before turning to leave the kitchen, the door swinging behind her.

"I'll take that as a no," Natalie said.

Carrie shook her head. "Great. Looks like Donnie is going to have to have another talk with me."

"Don't cave," Natalie warned her. "You can't handle three meals a day, plus snacks, plus cleaning, *plus* Mama without help."

"I'm not going to cave," Carrie insisted.

Natalie rolled her eyes. "Please. You will be whipping up lunch for that life-sized, soulless doll before the hour ends."

Natalie wasn't wrong. As soon as she'd left to go back to work, Donnie had come storming in to demand Carrie alter their agreement and feed Juliet Ramirez a midday meal.

Within an hour, Mama stood next to Carrie, a scowl

causing the lines around her mouth to deepen. "They shouldn't push you around like that."

Carrie continued taking out her frustrations on the carrot she was peeling. "It's fine."

"No, ma'am, it is not."

"Mama." She exhaled before looking at her mother-in-law. "I can handle it."

"I don't think you can."

"Oh my God," Carrie whispered, silently wishing Mama and Natalie would get off her back and let her do what she felt was best. She knew they were both trying to protect her and look out for her, but she'd done what she'd known was best.

"If I were you, I would—"

"Mama."

The woman smacked her lips closed and then started again. "I was going to say, I read in a magazine that Ms. Ramirez has a weakness for sweets. She avoids them at all costs."

"So?"

"So, I make some pretty mean desserts. Pies, cakes, tarts, breads. You name it, I can bake it. They are irresistible."

Carrie looked at her for a moment before her anger gave way to a disbelieving chuckle. "Are you suggesting we make her fat?"

"I'm suggesting we kill her with kindness, and if her size-two waist expands a little, so be it."

"You have been spending too much time with Natalie."

"I like Natalie. She's got spunk. Not like you. I don't know where you get this pushover attitude. Certainly not from my side of the family." Mama shook her head.

Carrie raised her brows, passing on the chance to remind Doreen that they were not blood relatives. "I'm not a pushover. But I'm not going to bite the hand that's paying the bills."

"Some things aren't worth the money they pay, Carolyn. Being pushed around in your own home is one of them."

Carrie thought of the hefty check the production company had agreed to pay her to add cooking on a whim for Juliet Ramirez to her list of duties. When combined with the first large sum they paid for staying at the inn, it would easily pay off Mama's incurred debt. It would also go a long way in supporting the two of them for some time after the star-filled inn had emptied. "I'm not being pushed around."

"What are you doing right now?"

Carrie ground her teeth. "I negotiated a higher rate in exchange for lunch on the days when it is requested of me."

"Because the High Priestess demanded it."

Carrie reminded herself that Mama had no idea how close she was to losing her home. If the woman had even the slightest understanding that she'd been on the verge of being homeless before Donnie called, she'd be kissing the ground the man's overpriced designer shoes walked on.

"What kind of pie should we bake?" she asked instead.

Doreen hooted as she got off her stool. "I have all the fixings for Dutch apple. It doesn't get any sweeter than that."

Will stepped into the kitchen and smiled wide. "Did I hear the words Dutch apple?"

Carrie glanced over her shoulder. "Why are so many of you here? My schedule says you wouldn't be back until dinnertime."

"Never trust an actor's schedule, Carrie." He walked into the kitchen and glanced at the lunch she was making before sitting at the island. "Talk to me about this apple dish."

"Um, Mama wants to bake a pie."

He smiled. "I love pie."

"I hope so. You and I will probably be the only ones who'll eat it."

"You don't eat pie, Mama?" Will asked as she came out of the pantry with a stack of ingredients.

"I have diabetes," she said, easing containers onto the counter.

"Luckily," Carrie said, "she can remember that."

"That's not fair. That she doesn't eat what she bakes, I mean."

He grinned and winked, and Carrie very nearly swayed on her feet. All her life she thought women swooning was another of those figments of men's imaginations, but she'd be damned if every cell in her body hadn't wanted to throw themselves into William Walker's arms in that moment.

Carrie cleared her throat and drew a deep breath as she returned to making lunch. "No, it's not fair. She's done nothing to help my figure, I can tell you that." She cringed. She hadn't meant to say that aloud.

Will winked as he stood. "I think she's done just fine."

Carrie looked at him through surprised eyes. A sly smile curved his lips as he threw out another of those devilish winks.

She laughed when he lifted a bottle of water to salute her and then turned to leave the kitchen. "Thanks," she said quietly, not certain how to take his comment.

———

THE DISGUST on Juliet's face was out there for everyone to see, but Will did his best to ignore it. He refused to allow her downturned mouth and wide eyes to ruin what was probably the best meal he'd ever eaten. The pot roast was so tender it nearly melted in his mouth and soaked in a thick, rich gravy that was perfect for sopping up with the homemade bread. Not to mention the perfectly tender vegetables. He couldn't remember the last time he'd had such a hearty home-cooked meal, and he was thankful that Carrie had so easily settled into the habit of cooking extras of her meals and sparing him and a few of the other guys the horrors of the Hollywood diet.

He'd be damned if the carb-deprived princess next to him was going to take the enjoyment from him.

"Oh, you boys need more gravy," Mama said as she refilled Will's iced tea.

She leaned over the table to pick up the half-full boat of brown gravy. Her hand trembled as she lifted, and before Will could reach out to help, a dollop splashed over the side and landed on Juliet's plate.

Time seemed to have stood still. Everyone knew what was coming. The diva was about to have a fit.

Juliet's mouth dropped open and her eyes widened as the gelatinous substance oozed onto her lettuce. "Oh my God!"

"Whoopsie," Mama said.

"Whoopsie?" Juliet's head snapped up to glare at the woman. "*Whoopsie?*"

Will set his fork down. "For heaven's sake, just remove the piece of lettuce from your plate. It was an accident."

Pushing herself back, not caring that she bumped her chair into the older woman, Juliet stood and stared at her plate. "The hell it was." She was storming out in a full-force march when Carrie came around the corner, carrying a tray with several slices of pie on it.

Putting her arm up, Juliet blocked the tray from hitting her, sending two slices of pie to the floor while the rest squished against Carrie's chest. Juliet didn't even stop. She didn't apologize or acknowledge what she'd done. She simply took a moment to correct her trajectory before continuing out of the room.

Will looked at Donnie, who was already calling out to his starlet as he jumped to his feet and followed her.

"We'll discuss this later," Donnie snapped at Carrie.

She lifted her face, her eyes filled with confusion and her clothes covered in pie filling and broken crust. Her mouth was open, her brow creased, as Donnie rushed after Juliet.

"Are you all right?" Mama asked, using her apron to scoop pie from Carrie's chest. "That woman!"

"What happened?" Carrie asked Doreen.

Doreen frowned. Will wasn't certain if she couldn't remember or if she was too frustrated to speak. He sat back and sighed, pissed as hell that despite his determination, Juliet had managed to ruin his dinner. Not only his, it seemed. The room remained tense and quiet the rest of the meal. Even Mama's smile had faded, and when she came to clear plates and refill glasses, her mood was somber. There wasn't a hint of sparkle in the woman's eyes.

Carrie had disappeared for some time, and when she'd returned, she silently mopped the floor. Once she walked into the kitchen, she didn't reappear. This was the first time Mama had been the prominent presence during what remained of dinner.

The women hadn't even joined the actors in the den for what had become the customary nightcap. After everyone else had gone upstairs, Will could no longer deny the need to check on Carrie. He found her in the kitchen, scouring the countertops with enough vigor that he was tempted to warn her about ruining the surface. He kept his comment to himself though. The scowl on her face implied she wasn't in the mood for teasing.

When she finally noticed him, she stopped scrubbing and stared, clearly waiting.

"You okay?" Will asked.

"Fine."

Will had been in enough relationships to know that a clipped response of "fine" was anything but. He didn't blame her for being angry. Even if it hadn't been Juliet's intent to cover Carrie in pie, her behavior over the last week had been atrocious enough for everyone to know she likely didn't regret how things had turned out.

"The pie was delicious," Will offered.

"Thank you." Her tone was still flat. Angry. Warning him to give her space.

He never had been good at heeding warnings. "May I make myself some coffee?"

"Sure."

He moved to the coffee machine and was immediately confused as he looked at the buttons. The options seemed endless—from size to flavor to temperature. "Um..."

She pulled a mug from a cabinet and slid between him and the machine. "Decaf?"

"Please."

He watched as she masterfully scooped beans into the grinder, filled the filter, and started his coffee brewing. "Anything else?"

"LA is a different world, Carrie," he said in response to her question. "Juliet is pretty sure that she's the only person on the planet who matters. Don't let her get to you."

"It's easy to tell someone not to feel like a doormat when you're not the one getting stepped on."

"I know," he admitted. "But I think it's important for you to know she acts like that because deep down she's as insecure as everyone else."

She scoffed. "I don't care. She chooses to behave like that. It's a choice. *Her* choice. I don't care why. I care about how her behavior impacts my mother-in-law and me. She is a spoiled brat, and you *all* enable her."

Will held his breath. The fiery anger wasn't unwarranted. This situation wasn't his fault, but he hadn't spoken up when Juliet acted out. He hadn't put her in her place and told her she was out of line. "You're right," he said as shame bloomed in his chest. "I'm sorry. I'll talk to Donnie about her. I'll tell him to get her in line."

She relaxed slightly. "That won't help anyway. He's so far up her ass, I don't know how he can breathe."

"Well," Will said with a hint of a grin, "she's awfully full of hot air."

His comment lingered for a few seconds before Carrie chuckled.

"Yeah," she said, "she really is."

"Would you like some coffee?" Will asked. "I think I've got this thing figured out, if you'd like to have a seat on the patio and relax for a few minutes."

"Am I that much of a mess?" she asked as the edges of her frustration softened.

"Nah," he said. "You're doing great."

"I would have thought an actor would be a better liar,"

Carrie said. "You don't have to make me coffee. I can do it myself."

"Well." He looked at the machine. "I'm pretty lousy at building a fire, so I thought if I sent you out there first, you could do that."

Carrie sighed, but her smile widened. "Okay. Decaf, please. I take it black."

"I can handle that." Or so he hoped. While Carrie was outside, likely starting a fire without issue, Will hesitantly pressed buttons until her coffee started to brew. Finally, he made his way outside carrying two mugs with him as flames danced in the firepit. "I never could have done that."

"All you need is lighter fluid, dry wood, and matches. I'm sure you could figure it out." Carrie added another log to the cast-iron pit before she put the mesh top on and eased into the chair next to him, accepting a cup once she was settled. "What made you want to become an actor?"

Will focused on the burning logs. "I didn't have a lot of ambition to do anything else."

"Oh, come on," Carrie said with an air of disbelief. "It takes a lot of hard work to get to where you are."

"Or dumb luck."

"You *are* talented," she insisted.

Will considered how to answer that. Talented by some standards, he supposed, but by others, he was starting to realize he really didn't have what it took. "I used to think so."

"You heard me reading lines," she said with a laugh. "It was truly terrible."

He fell quiet as he stared at the dancing flames. After a long silence, he admitted, "I wasn't very good at much else. I dropped out halfway through the first semester of college, threw what I could in my car, and headed for LA. I've been there ever since."

"You've been successful."

"That depends on how you measure success."

She tilted her head as she looked at him. "What are you thinking, Will?"

He grinned. "That you make a great fire."

"You're unhappy," she pointed out.

The bottom of Will's stomach dropped out. He hadn't expected her to call him out so bluntly. "I don't know when it became not enough, but it's not. It hasn't been enough for a long time. I tried to break away from it. I took time off last year. I thought I was ready, but being involved in this project... Something is missing. I don't know what it is." He looked into his mug before casting a quick glance at her. Though she seemed genuine in her concern, embarrassment flared in his chest. "This can't be interesting to you."

"Why do you think that?"

"It's very boring."

She stopped lifting her mug before it reached her lips and furrowed her brow at him. "Are you kidding? It's nice to know the rich and famous have midlife crises too." Carrie took a sip of her drink as he chuckled. "I've been thinking about opening a restaurant," she said. "Here. At the inn. Like a tearoom."

"That would be nice."

"Mama would like that. It would keep her occupied. She needs something to keep her busy."

"So do it."

"If it were only that simple." Carrie eyed him like he didn't have a clue what he was saying.

"It is."

"*No*, it's not."

"Why?"

She held his gaze for several seconds before explaining, "Maybe you don't have to concern yourself with things like bills and living expenses, but I do."

He laughed a tense, uncomfortable laugh. "Right."

"The only reason you and your friends are staying here," Carrie continued, "is because I had to find a way to pay property taxes, medical bills, and the utilities. If I had the money to invest in a restaurant, you wouldn't be here. I'm trying to keep that woman in her home for as long as possible."

"I apologize," he said.

Carrie shook her head as she looked at the fire. "No. I'm sorry. I didn't mean to snap."

Will looked up at the dark sky. "I'm sure it seems like I have everything, but it's not easy living your life on the front page of the tabloids. Reading headline after headline about how your career is over and having details of your life exposed and exaggerated. Poor Mr. Celebrity, right?"

"I wouldn't like it either," she said. "But it is part of the life you've chosen. Just like maintaining this house is part of my life. I might not like it, but I could walk away if I chose to. I could convince Doreen to sell. And you could find another way to make a living. We're where we choose to be, Will."

"I've been in this business for over twenty years," he said thoughtfully. "I think I've grown weary of it. Do you know that this is my big comeback?" He faced her, but Carrie didn't respond. "It's been over a year since my last film, which, by the way, was the last in a string of unbearable flops. Taking a break wasn't all by choice. Finding someone who wanted to put my name on their work isn't as easy as it used to be, but that was my chance to stand back and figure things out. I needed to recharge, regenerate, and remember why I wanted to be here, but I haven't been able to figure that out yet. I don't remember why I wanted this life. It seems so shallow and unimportant now."

"What would you do if you weren't acting? You mentioned the other night maybe something behind-the-scenes?"

He stared into the pit and pressed his lips together, as if debating if he should share. "I think I'd like to write."

"Write what?"

"I don't know." He shook his head and hoped they could drop this line of thinking. He tended to get depressed when he thought about his life too much. "How do we end up in these conversations?"

"Beats me, but I find them exhausting."

"Me too."

She looked up at the stars. "Doreen walked into the kitchen one day about eight months after Mike had been gone and asked where he'd gone to. I didn't know what to say. I stuttered around until she moved on to something else, but a few weeks later, the same thing happened. I took her to the doctor and found out she'd been struggling more than I'd realized. We spent months getting test after test. When we finally sat down to get a diagnosis, she only asked one thing of me: that I never put her in a home. I agreed, but I didn't take into consideration that I wouldn't be able to keep up with her and running this place. We had to cut back on guests and events. Two months ago, I didn't know how I was going to keep her here, but I knew I had to. This is her home. She was born here; she wants to die here. I couldn't bear the thought of being the person who took it away from her. So...now you're here and I've bought us a little bit more time."

Will could see a sheen of unshed tears in her eyes, and the

underlying depression he'd detected so many times suddenly made sense. "She loves you for what you've done for her."

Carrie nodded. "I know. I love her too. My mother passed when I was young, and I'm not close to my dad, so in a way, Mama is the only family I have left. She's always taken care of me. She was my rock after losing Mike, even though I know she was hurting too."

"How did your husband die?"

Carrie lowered her gaze. "Some kid walked into the convenience store where Mike had stopped for cigarettes and ended up shooting the three people inside for the hundred bucks in the register. They all died."

"I'm sorry."

"Well," she said with a shrug, "I'd been telling him for years that smoking was going to kill him. I'm okay," she said when he didn't respond to her sad excuse of a joke, "for the most part. Days like this—"

"I'm going to talk to Juliet," Will offered.

"Oh, don't. It's not her. Well, it is, but I can handle it. It's just...everything else."

"What is everything else?"

"Losing Mama a piece at a time, being in the house Mike grew up in with daily reminders that he's dead, taking on the burden of this place. It's more than I bargained for sometimes." Carrie rolled her head, looking at him for a moment before laughing. "My God, that sounds so pathetic."

"No, it doesn't. You're doing great, Carrie. You really are." Will reached out, putting his hand on her forearm and giving her a gentle squeeze. The simple act seemed to have them mesmerized as they both stared at where they were connected.

"The fire is burning out and it's getting late," Carrie said softly. "I should get to bed so I can get up in time to fix break-fast. I'd hate to disappoint the great Juliet Ramirez yet again."

Will frowned. "I didn't mean to upset you."

"You didn't, I promise. I'm just tired."

He was tempted to push because he suspected that wasn't the entire truth. He felt connected to her for some reason, and when he'd touched her, he was certain she felt the same. She wasn't exactly running away, but she was setting a clear boundary. He wanted to point that out, but she stood and snagged the nearby garden hose to douse the fire.

As she did, Will took her cup and stood by so he could follow her into the house and right to the dishwasher.

"Thanks," she said as she accepted the mugs from him. She dumped the contents into the sink and then opened the dish-washer. After placing the dishes inside, she turned and jolted, as if surprised to see him still standing there.

Suddenly the room seemed too small, the air too thick. He was certain she noticed the shift between them too. She was no more than six inches away. Close enough that he could touch her. That same comfort that he'd felt sitting with her in the kitchen discussing wine while she made yogurt washed over him. Something about her felt like home to him, and warmth started to spread throughout his chest. The tempta-tion to pull her to him so he could bask in that feeling was strong and unexpected. However, something stopped him.

When she cleared her throat and slipped around him, he realized that thing was common sense.

"Thanks for tonight." Her words came out quickly, forced.

Oh, yeah. She'd felt something too. He grinned. "It was nice."

She gestured behind her toward the door. "I am never

going to be able to get up if I don't get some sleep. I'll see you tomorrow."

"Right. Sleep well," he said.

She made it to the door before turning to look back at him. He was still watching her, and when she caught his gaze, she smiled too. "Don't stay up too late, Will."

"I won't."

She disappeared before he forced his breath out with an audible sigh. Well, that was a surprising turn of events.

CHAPTER 5

"Shit," Carrie hissed as she rushed down the stairs. "Shit, shit, shit."

It was nearly five in the morning. People would be getting up at any moment, eager for their breakfasts, and she had yet to get anything started.

She'd spent half the night tossing and turning, thinking and rethinking the evening she'd spent with Will, and slept through her alarm. Sighing with relief at the smell of coffee brewing, she bolted into the kitchen.

"Thank you, Mama," she said to the woman already cutting up fruit. Walking to a cabinet, Carrie pulled a mug from the cupboard and filled it while she explained. "I couldn't sleep last night. I didn't even hear my alarm go off. What needs doing?" She turned, finding the old woman looking crossly at her. "I'm sorry. I overslept."

"What are you doing in my kitchen?"

"Making breakfast?"

"No, you are not." Mama angrily wiped her hands on her apron as she moved across the room. "Guests do not fix meals.

Not at my inn." Taking Carrie by the elbow, Doreen started guiding her toward the door. "Go. Sit. Enjoy your coffee in the dining room. I'll bring breakfast out when it's ready."

Carrie started to protest. She wanted to deny being a guest, remind Doreen that she lived there, that she was married to Mike who had been at the store for the last few years, but the words caught in her throat as a harsh reality crashed down on her.

Mama didn't recognize her.

Tears burned the back of Carrie's eyes. "Mama?" The word came out as a broken plea.

Doreen pointed over Carrie's shoulder. "Go. I'm perfectly capable of handling this."

She forced her lips into a smile. "I know that. I wanted to help."

"I don't need help. I'm an old hand at this." Doreen returned to the island to finish what she'd been doing.

Swallowing the emotion that was threatening to choke her, Carrie passed by the dining room and headed straight for the small room that served as her office. Even though she knew she'd get the answering service, Carrie pulled her cell phone from her pocket and called Mama's doctor.

She left a message requesting he call her as soon as possible and then put the phone back into her pocket. She stared out the window at the still-dark sky. In her mind, she could see Doreen cutting fruit and wiping her hands on her apron before spreading the food out on a platter, creating a perfect presentation. Carrie had watched her do it a thousand times before.

When she was younger, helping Doreen during the busy summer months, she had thought it odd how much work the woman had put into simply laying out food. She'd spend nearly as much time putting out the food as she had spent preparing it.

When asked, Doreen had explained to Carrie the importance of presentation, showing pride in her work, even if it was simply slicing fruit. Mama had instilled a work ethic in her that had pushed Carrie through school and kept her going in her culinary career despite the long, crazy hours and insane demands put upon her.

It was in that kitchen, under Mama's watchful eye, that Carrie had fallen head over heels in love with a boy in ripped jeans and a baggy T-shirt.

Carrie stood there for a long time reliving the past, snapping out of her thoughts only when she sensed someone standing behind her. Clearing her throat, she blinked her tears away and turned around. Will stood in the doorway, his features shadowed by the lights from the other room.

"Do you need something?" she asked after a moment.

"Are you okay?" When she didn't answer, he stepped into the office. "What is it?"

"Mama," she whispered. "She doesn't know me. She..." She swallowed when her voice cracked. Lowering her face, she closed her eyes, but a hot tear slipped down her cheek before she could stop it.

"I'm so sorry," Will whispered.

He only hesitated for a moment before he pulled her to him.

Carrie didn't even pause. She didn't think twice about accepting his comfort. She needed support, and she didn't care who offered it. Resting her forehead on his shoulder, she sank into his embrace as she finally let go of the emotions she'd been fighting.

WILL SPENT MORE of his day worrying about what was happening at the inn than on the set. Carrie had started occupying more and more of his mind, but usually those thoughts were about the conversations and light teasing they shared. This day, his mind was consumed with worry for her and wishing he could be at the inn to help her through what he was certain was a tough day.

As soon as the shoot wrapped for the day, he headed straight back to the house to check on Carrie and Mama. He found Carrie in the kitchen and looked behind him to make sure no one was following him into the room before letting the door swing shut behind him.

He found her staring out the back door, seemingly unaware that he'd walked into the room. Her shoulders, which she usually held back, sagged as if they held the weight of the world, and rather than a neat braid holding back her long brown hair, she'd pulled the strands into a messy bun. She hadn't even looked at him, but he was certain she'd had a hell of a bad day.

"Hey," he called when Carrie continued to stare out the back door. He swallowed when she jolted and spun around. He had never seen such sadness and raw desperation on the face of a person who wasn't acting.

Her eyes were so sad, he had to physically stop himself from rushing across the room to her.

She forced a laugh as she turned her back to him. Though she was clearly trying to hide her actions, he knew she was roughly wiping at her cheeks. "You scared me. I didn't hear you come in."

"Sorry. Are you okay?"

She dried her hands on her jeans. "I'm fine."

"You're crying."

Inhaling again, she gave him an unconvincing smile. "I'm fine, Will."

When he'd first come to the inn, he'd had the urge to defend her. This wasn't so different, only rather than defend her, Will wished he could solve all the problems in her life so they could sit with a glass of wine and casual banter. That wasn't possible, however. All he could do was try to make this easier for her. "What happened?"

"Oh," she exhaled, "the usual." Pushing past him, she walked to the counter as she glanced at the clock and cursed. "Where did the day go? It's almost dinnertime, and I haven't even started anything."

She was trying to change the subject, but he wasn't going to back down that easily. She clearly wasn't okay. "It must be heart-wrenching to see Doreen fading away like that."

Carrie's face sagged. "It isn't easy."

"It's a lot of work trying to keep up with her."

"Sometimes." She walked to the refrigerator and scanned the menu. She looked at the clock again and laughed bitterly. "Well, I won't be slow roasting chicken tonight, will I?"

"I'm worried about you."

"About me? Why?"

"This is a lot for one person to handle."

She barely acknowledged his observation. "I'm fine."

"You keep saying that."

"Because I am."

"Carrie," he coaxed gently.

She turned from the fridge, her gaze pleading. "What do you want me to say, Will?"

His heart broke for her, and again, he wanted to hold her

and make everything right in her world. "You can start by telling me how you are doing."

"How the hell do you think I'm doing?"

He took in the deep creases on her forehead and the puffiness of her eyes. "Not nearly as well as you'd like everyone to believe."

"Falling apart is not an option right now."

"Well, burying your hurt isn't either."

Carrie opened her mouth as if to argue with him, but after a moment, she stepped back, putting space between them. She pulled out a Dutch oven and carried it to the sink to fill with water.

Moving to her side, he looked down at her. "Talk to me. Tell me what you're thinking."

"What I'm thinking?" She laughed humorlessly. "I've spent the last two years pretending that my husband is at the grocery store." She set the pot on a burner. "Returning insane purchases, picking her up from all over the county after she's driven off to some place that no longer exists, if it ever did exist, but somehow her disease didn't seem real until today."

"The Alzheimer's—"

"I know. I know what it does. But I've never really felt it. Pretending Mike is running errands, taking away her access to money, hiding the car keys, that all seemed so ordinary. Laundry? Check. Dishes? Check. Lie to Mama? Check."

Fresh tears glimmered in her eyes before she turned toward the drawer where she'd hidden the knobs for the stove. She tried several times to get the knob in place, but it refused to fit. He moved closer, intending to help, but she cursed under her breath and slammed the plastic handle down. "I've read the books," she said with a broken voice as she faced him. "I've done the research. I've talked to support groups and doctors, but nothing they said could have possibly prepared me for that." The tears that had made her eyes shine fell down her cheeks. "Nothing could have prepared me for her not knowing who I am."

"I'm sorry," he whispered as he reached out to her, no longer able to stand by without comforting her. When he wrapped her in his arms, she leaned into him and buried her face in his chest. He hugged her close and lightly kissed her head as he tried to soothe her. A sob escaped her, shaking her shoulders, and he softly whispered how sorry he was and ran his hand over her back. "I'm so sorry you're going through this."

She leaned back after several minutes. Wiping her cheeks dry, she inhaled deeply. "I appreciate your concern, Will, really I do, but there isn't anything that can be done. We'll get by for as long as we can and then..."

"What?"

She closed her eyes and shook her head. "I don't know."

"Let me help you," he all but begged as he put his hand to her face and wiped her tears with his thumb. The sense of helplessness he felt was almost all-consuming. He couldn't explain the need, but he couldn't deny it either. He had to do something to make this easier for her.

"What can you do?"

"I don't know," he admitted.

"Nothing," she said on her breath. "There isn't anything you can do. I really have to get dinner started."

"No, you don't."

"Yes, I do. They do not want to be kept waiting," she said, reminding him of what Donnie had told her that morning as she'd sat heartbroken among the guests while Mama insisted on serving breakfast alone.

"I'm taking care of dinner tonight."

"Oh no. I told you already. You won't be cooking in my kitchen."

He smiled warmly. "No, I won't. I'm ordering in. My treat."

"Will—"

Putting his hands on her shoulders, he gently squeezed them and held her gaze. "You do not need to be taking care of all those people tonight."

"It's my responsibility to take care of them."

"Not tonight. Let me do this for you. Please."

Once again, the need to help was more than he could refuse. Ordering dinner wasn't much, but it was something. It was one thing he could do to make her life easier.

Before she could answer, the kitchen door swung open and Donnie stopped, taking in the scene of William Walker standing intimately close to their hostess, his hands on her shoulders, before saying, "Juliet is wondering what is for dinner this evening."

"Chinese," Will stated. "I'm treating. Why don't you find out what everyone wants and call it in, Donnie?"

The man's mouth opened, but he didn't argue with the star. "Sounds great."

"You do eat Chinese?" Will asked Carrie.

"Sure."

"What do you want?"

"Um, beef with broccoli. Mama and I can share."

"I'll have the same." Will's tone dismissed the location manager. When Donnie left, Will smiled down at Carrie, feeling a great sense of accomplishment. "See?" he asked, proud that he'd done something to help ease her burden. "Dinner is taken care of."

———

AFTER DONNIE HAD BEEN SENT to order dinner, Carrie wondered if Will had any idea of the wrath his actions were going to bring down upon her. Clearly he didn't. He thought he was helping her. So, instead of pointing out his error in judgment, she had smiled and thanked him for looking out for her, knowing she'd deal with the fallout later.

She didn't have to wait as long as she'd thought. She was scraping uneaten Chinese food into the trash can when the kitchen door was thrown open. Turning around, she frowned at the fury on Donnie's face.

His jaw was set like stone as he narrowed his dark brown eyes at her. "What the hell do you think you are doing?"

Carrie lifted the dirty plate. "Cleaning up dinner."

"William Walker is way out of your league, lady."

She stared at him, wanting to laugh. Instead, she gave him a sweet smile. "I'll remember that."

"Don't make a fool of yourself, Miss Gable."

"Mrs. Gable." Her tone came across far icier than she'd intended. "My husband may be dead, but I am still his wife. I am not after Will, Donnie. He saw that I had a bad day, and he was kind enough to try to make it better. There is nothing more to it than simple human kindness. I do appreciate you putting me in my place, though."

His cold glare eased somewhat. "I am showing you human kindness by saving your dignity. You aren't the first rural pumpkin to throw yourself at a famous actor on location, and you won't be the last. I'm trying to save you the humiliation of rejection. He will never see you for more than what you are—an innkeeper."

Before she could respond, he turned and marched out of

the kitchen with great flair. "'Rural pumpkin'?" she asked the empty room. "What the hell is... Oh." She snickered. "'Country bumpkin.' What an idiot."

Opening the dishwasher, she loaded the dirty dishes and cleaned up the counters before heading upstairs to check on Mama. The woman was already in her nightclothes. Carrie hesitated, wondering if she was going to have another bout of not knowing who she was. Easing into the room, she smiled, waiting to be recognized. Once she was, Carrie closed the door behind her. "Tired, Mama?"

"I don't think I like the way that young man was looking at you over dinner tonight." Mama walked to the bed with her knitting in her hand.

"Which one?"

"I can't remember their names. The one giving you the evil eye."

Carrie nodded. "Donnie. He doesn't like that we ate with the stars tonight. He thinks we should stick to the servants' quarters."

Mama's mouth fell open as she sat next to Carrie. "Did he say that?"

"Not in so many words."

"I don't like them. I don't want them here."

Carrie gave the woman a sad smile. "It's just for a little while longer."

"There are other places for them to stay."

"Mama," Carrie gently pleaded.

She was so tired of everyone trying to solve her problems. Natalie's pressure to refuse the guests, Will's determination to ease her stress, and now Mama's frustration—it was all more than Carrie could deal with. She had gone into this knowing full well that it would be challenging, but she'd also understood it was the best option.

Instead of arguing, she pulled the blankets back for the woman to climb into bed. "Remind me again how many presidents have stayed here."

CHAPTER 6

The moisture in the air clung to Carrie as she jogged. The sky was gray with the threat of rain, but that hadn't been enough to dissuade her from trotting down the stairs and across the yard. The path would lead her along the perimeter of the property, around the old fields, and back again. The humidity was becoming stifling, though.

She'd worn a path long ago, back when Mama could be trusted not to burn down the house and she didn't have guests to cater to at any moment. With most of the cast gone and Mama sufficiently alert, Carrie had some rare time for herself and a head that needed clearing, so she'd thrown on a T-shirt, shorts, and an old pair of running shoes.

The jog quickly turned into a sprint as her mind raced with the thoughts that she'd intended to escape. Memories of what Mama was like before she started forgetting things were fading, and Carrie was having a difficult time remembering the person Doreen used to be.

She used to be a bouncing ray of sunshine. She called everyone "darling" or "dear" but not in a way that sounded superficial or condescending. She said the endearment with love and admiration that made each person feel they were special to her. She could solve any problem, fix any issue, or mend a broken heart over one cup of coffee.

When Mike had died, the two women had taken turns being the strong one so the other could fall apart. No one else, not even Natalie, had seen the depth of Carrie's grief. No one else could have possibly understood. How unfair that this rock could crumble right before her eyes.

With every step she took, Carrie's heart raced faster and her breathing became more labored. When her mind moved on to other subjects, Will included, the sprint quickened into a run.

What was going on there? Nothing, a voice in her head insisted. He was handsome and seemed to be genuinely concerned about her and Mama, but nothing was going on. So what were those long stares all about? And why the hell did they pull her in until she couldn't think straight?

And Juliet. What was her problem? She walked around like everyone should be grateful that she was alive. Impossible to please, never satisfied, and very content to tell everyone how they didn't live up to her expectations. People like that had always irritated Carrie, but when that attitude came from Juliet Ramirez, Carrie felt like razors were cutting at every nerve in her body.

Like her run, the rain began at a calm, steady pace that quickly became faster. Puddles began to form, splashing dirt onto Carrie's ankles and calves as she stepped in them. She didn't notice the water that soaked her socks through the mesh sides of her shoes or the clothes that began to cling to her skin. She put all her energy into escaping her thoughts, even though they kept coming after her.

Moving down the path, Carrie was going as fast as her legs could carry her, her fury being beaten out with every step she took until a bright flash of lightning and a sharp crack of thunder snapped her out of the daze she was in. Slowing to a trot, Carrie finally felt the ache in the lungs that were lacking sufficient air intake and the heart that was pounding in her chest to keep up with the demands of her muscles.

Coming to a stop, she hunched over and put her hands on her knees, gasping for air as raindrops and sweat mixed into beads that fell from the tip of her nose.

"Hey." Will trotted to her and bent over in much the same way. "Man, you're fast."

She stared at him, taking a few seconds to find her voice. "What are you doing?"

"I wanted to join you for your run. I didn't realize what I was getting into. Hold on." He took a few more breaths, forcing them slower and deeper into his lungs.

Carrie focused on the darkening sky when thunder rumbled again. "We should head back before the weather gets worse."

"Wait." He gently grasped her arm when she took a step, stopping her from walking away. "You've been avoiding me since dinner two nights ago. Why?"

"I haven't—"

"Was it Donnie or Juliet?"

Carrie debated whether to answer and what kind of hell she'd have to pay if she did. However, looking at Will, she saw the fire in his eyes and knew there would be hell whether she answered him or not. She decided she'd much rather have some egotistical greasy-haired location manager mad at her than Will.

"Donnie valiantly swooped in to save my pride by

informing me that I'm not the first—how'd he put it?—'rural pumpkin' to throw herself at you, and I won't be the last."

"Rural pumpkin?"

"I think he meant 'country bumpkin,'" she said.

Will nodded, but then he narrowed his eyes. "Donnie's an ass. He's looking out for his investment in this movie, nothing more."

"How does our"—she struggled for the word—"friendship impact his movie?"

"The thing about achieving even the slightest bit of success in LA is, you convince yourself everyone else wants to be you. I'm sure that in his mind, you are trying to use me to wriggle your way into his world."

"Fat chance." She laughed. "My life is exciting enough, thank you very much."

"He has no say in what I do, Carrie. He doesn't dictate my life. If I want to befriend some bumpkin, that's my choice."

She chuckled when he used the term that she had rolled over and over in her mind. "Will, please, I want to get through these next months with as little turmoil as possible. So far, that seems like an insurmountable feat, so I'd like to cause as few ripples as possible."

"That's fine, but I am going to let him know that I won't have him sticking his nose in my business. Whatever happens between you and me is between you and me and nobody else."

She looked up at him, searching his face for the meaning of his words, but his gaze was still hard with anger. The thunder rumbling again gave her a reason to look away, and she took it, turning her face up at the dark clouds.

"We better get back before this breaks." She didn't wait for his response before heading back toward the house.

With another flash of lightning and a loud clap of thunder,

the steady downfall turned into a pouring rain. Big, heavy drops surrounded them with a loud drumming. They were running, side by side and soaking wet, when Carrie called out over the sound of the rain for Will to follow her as she veered off to the right.

The trek was more difficult, more uneven than the beaten path they'd been following back to the house, but they trotted along until Carrie pointed out a small building that had been built many years ago to house one of the various farm workers.

Until recently, the building had been run-down and full of old tools and cobwebs. The producers had brought in a crew to refurbish it for one of the scenes they were filming in the coming weeks. Instead of being filled with dust and old junk, the small cabin had a fresh coat of white paint and usable furniture.

Will reached it first, pushing the door open and stepping inside as he waited for Carrie to join him. She cursed as she made it to him as another clap of thunder caused the world to quiver.

Once inside, they both took a moment to look around. A metal cot frame was covered with a thin mattress and a vintage blue and red quilt. A small table with two wooden chairs sat in the middle of the room, and the old potbelly fireplace had been cleaned and painted with a fresh coat of black heatproof paint. Along one wall, a tall oak hutch stood, filling much of the space. Though the cabin was only a few hundred square feet, the space had been converted into a cozy space that would be used for the film.

Gasping for oxygen, Carrie pressed her palms to the small table in the center of the room, finally feeling the chill in the air as the storm front pushed the warmth of the last few days east. When she could breathe again, she swiped the soaked strands of hair from her face and turned to Will, who still had his hand against the door, trying to steady his breathing. His T-shirt stuck to him like a second skin as water formed streams over his face.

Heat twisted her belly, but she pushed the sensation away. "You okay?"

He turned his face to her, and Carrie found that she wasn't the only one who noticed how wet cotton tended to mold to the person wearing it. Will clearly took a moment to skim the outline of her body, letting his gaze linger over her breasts, before he looked at her face and nodded a little. "You?"

She pretended she hadn't noticed the path of his gaze and managed to nod her head the same as he had. Outside in the rain, running for the nearest shelter seemed like the best thing to do, but after taking in the one-room building with a made-up cot on one side, Carrie realized hiding out here was the worst decision she could have made.

Seeing a blanket spread on the small bed, she snatched it up and brought it to her face, blotting away some of the water, only to have more run into her eyes. Hearing the sloshing of Will's water-filled shoes as he moved to stand next to her, Carrie turned her gaze his way. What was supposed to be a glance turned into one of those long stares they'd seemed to find themselves locked in from the moment they'd met. He'd brushed his hair back from his face, but a wayward strand fell, sticking to his forehead and sending a band of water down his cheek.

The urge to brush it away was irresistible, and Carrie started to lift her hand, stopping midway with the realization that touching his face would be inappropriate. She put her hand to her own hair, squeezing water from her ponytail, all the while feeling the proximity of his body.

"This is crazy," he said over the pounding on the tin roof.

Carrie's heart thudded against her chest. She looked at him, shocked that he dared to put voice to the insane attraction that she seemed to have, but she realized he was referring to the fact that he was soaked. She watched him grab the bottom of his shirt and pull it up, exposing his chest. Turning away, her eyes wide, she listened to water splattering on the floor as he wrung out his clothing. She'd only caught a glimpse of his bare skin, but it was enough to convince her that he did indeed have a perfect body.

"I haven't seen a storm like this in a while," she said.

"How long do you think it will last?"

"No way to know, really."

"Great."

She turned back to him, and her mouth fell open to find him dropping his shorts. "Will!"

"What?"

This time, she spun away from him. "You're in your underwear. In front of me."

His laugh sounded a bit too self-satisfied for her liking. "I'm sorry. I forgot how innocent you country bumpkins can be."

She couldn't resist the urge to glance over her shoulder, hoping he had the decency to pull his pants back up. Instead, he yanked the sheet that was on the bed free. Wrapping the material around himself, he smirked. "Better?"

She faced him. "Yes. Thank you."

"You might want to do the same. You look a little cold." He let his gaze lower for a moment and then looked into her eyes and smirked.

Carrie dropped her face and noticed her nipples pressed

against her shirt. When she looked at him again, he raised his brows and his grin widened.

"I'm going to try to start a fire."

She watched him in front of the potbelly stove for a moment before turning her back on him. She glanced over her shoulder one more time to make sure he wasn't watching and then whipped her wet shirt over her head. Hurrying as she focused on the sound of him stuffing logs in the stove, she kicked her shoes off and pushed her shorts down. Still wearing her sports bra and underwear, she quickly wrapped the quilt around her and gathered her wet clothes, draping them over the edge of the table so they could dry faster.

"You have to, uh..." Carrie gestured toward the stove. "You need twigs, paper, things that will burn long enough to catch the wood."

Looking around, Will frowned. "There isn't anything."

Moving closer to the fireplace, her face sagged as well. "Apparently, there was no intention of starting a fire."

"Shit." Looking impossibly cute with the sheet haphazardly wrapped around him, he started opening drawers in search of something to start the fire. "Aha," he announced when he found some old newspapers. "This is from 1983. Wow. Maybe we shouldn't burn these."

Carrie stepped beside him to look at the papers. "It's that or freeze. I vote for burning."

He agreed and moved to the fireplace. A few minutes later, he stood back proudly as the fire whooshed to life and spilled a glow into the room. "Look at that."

"I'm very impressed." Carrie smiled as she moved next to him. Pulling the band that held her hair back, she ran her fingers through the damp strands and stared into the fire. Though she saw him turn his face to her from the corner of her eye and felt his intense gaze, she forced her focus to remain on the small fireplace. She was tempted to ask what was on his mind, but decided that, for as long as they were hidden away in a tiny cabin, it was probably best she didn't know.

———

CARRIE SMILED a little as she stared into the flames, but it faded quickly. Will was amazed how easily he could read her emotions. He might not know exactly what was going on inside her head, but he'd figured out the difference between her genuine and faked smiles. He'd also noticed that she seemed to save her real smiles for him. And when she gave them, her eyes seemed to soften.

He'd watched her desire building over the last few weeks—he refused to believe he was imagining the connection between them. When she looked at him now, he sensed she was struggling with what to do next. He'd been having that struggle himself.

He was attracted to her. He couldn't deny that, nor had he tried. He admired her strength and how giving and understanding she was. In fact, he couldn't think of much he didn't admire about her.

She must have felt the weight of his stare because she looked at him and held his gaze. He noticed that her lips parted slightly, as if she wanted to stay something but didn't know what. The uncertainty in her eyes made him want to pull her to him and kiss her so she had no doubt how he was feeling, but he didn't know how she'd react to that. He was still debating when lightning struck outside, and she turned her gaze to the window.

"Why do you do that?" Will asked when she continued to stare out at the rain.

"Do what?"

"Divert. Look away. You do that whenever we look at each other," he clarified when she hesitantly returned her gaze to him.

Her lips curved slightly. "You stare. Intently. It's...disturbing."

"Disturbing?"

"It feels like—"

"Like what?"

"Like you're trying to read my mind."

"I am." Will shrugged his shoulders slightly. "I seem to have developed a fascination for you that keeps me from thinking about much else. I am more attracted to you than I have been to anyone in a very long time. However," he said hesitantly, "I'm beginning to wonder if it's one-sided."

Carrie held his gaze for another few heartbeats before looking away.

Will sighed heavily at her unspoken rejection. "I know that you have enough on your plate with Doreen. I don't mean to add to it."

"You didn't."

"I did."

"It's not one-sided," she answered. "It's just that right now —I don't think it's a good idea to act on this."

"Because of Doreen?"

"Because of a lot of things. I don't need a broken heart."

Will moved closer, standing close enough to smell the sweetness of lavender rising from her body. "I don't want to break your heart, Carrie."

"But you will. I'm not exactly a summer... Well, in this

case, an autumn fling type of girl. I'll get attached to you, and then you'll leave, and I'll be watching you in your next movie, wondering what the hell I was thinking."

He exhaled, knowing her assessment was probably more logical than his shortsighted desire to act on his lust for her. "This wouldn't have to end because I left. There are telephones, computers, social media. The United States Postal Service."

She lifted her brows. "Long distance? That doesn't really work, does it?"

"It can."

Carrie exhaled slowly. "Honestly, Will, I don't know that I'm up for that. I'm spread so thin with Doreen. I don't know that I could do that. And I have to wonder if you could either. I don't think it would be fair to either of us."

"I'm not proposing here, Carrie. I'm just... I like you. A lot. I want to know you better. And before you ask—yes, I do mean in a possible romantic relationship kind of way."

She sighed, but her lips curved back into one of those soft smiles that seemed to warm his heart. "I like you too. A lot. More than I should."

"You probably think I do this all the time—"

"God, I hope not. You don't—"

He put his fingers to her lips to hush her. "No. I don't. I was about to say that I actually make it a point to keep my distance. People tend to befriend me for all the wrong reasons. You're genuine. I can see that you're genuine. That means the world to me, Carrie. Maybe that's why I feel like I need to take this chance and try to be with you. I don't meet very many genuine people in my life. I try to keep the ones that I do."

Carrie returned her focus to the fire. "Mama couldn't

possibly understand me seeing someone, Will. She thinks Mike is still alive."

"We don't have to tell her."

She looked up at him and attempted to look cross. "Do you have an answer for everything?"

"I try."

"Donnie?"

"Donnie isn't an issue."

"Oh, but he is. He doesn't like me, and he certainly doesn't like that you do."

"You let me deal with Donnie."

"I'm not sure it's that simple where he is concerned."

"It is. It really is. It's all a game, a very high-stakes game. And I trump him." Seeing that she was still hesitant, Will ran his hands up the cool flesh of her bare arms until he was cupping her face. "I'm not going to push this. I've told you how I feel. But you need to know that this thing between us isn't going to go away."

Searching her eyes in the flickering light of the fire, he saw a longing that gave him the courage to lean down to her. Her eyes drifted shut, and his breath mingled with hers, heating the whisper of space between them.

With his entire body reacting to the seductive teasing, Will slid one hand behind her head, tangling in the wet strands of her hair. He wrapped the other around her waist and gently but firmly pulled her body against his. He captured her mouth with his, kissing her hard, showing her how much he wanted her. She answered his demanding mouth with her own, brushing her tongue over his when he parted his lips, moaning deep in her throat and raking her fingers through his hair.

His stomach didn't simply flutter. It completely turned

over, sending waves throughout him, settling in a knot of longing low in his gut. She clung to him as the fire inside him flared, escaping in the form of a passionate kiss. Even though the rain had left them both chilled, he could have sworn that her bare skin pressed against his was scorching him, and he wanted more. He wanted to tear the quilt away, press the length of his body to hers. He wanted to pull her with him to the cot and let her warm him from the inside out.

Running her hand down his bare back, she gripped his hip as she ground against his erection. He returned her movement, tightening his arm around her waist, holding her closer. Pulling back, on the verge of going further than he suspected she wanted, Will panted to catch his breath. "My God," he whispered, feeling the shock of their exchange pulse throughout his entire body.

With her head on his shoulder, Carrie drew a deep breath. A moment later, she brushed her nose along his bare chest, followed by a few light kisses. His hand tightened in her hair as she kissed her way up his neck.

"We shouldn't be doing this," she breathed in his ear.

He would have taken that as a sign to back down if she weren't pressing herself against him and clutching his sheet-clad hips so tightly. Instead, he pulled her closer to him. "We're not hurting anyone." He dipped his head down and caught the cool skin of her neck with his hot mouth.

Her head rolled as he suckled her there.

She sighed and laughed softly. "It's just been so long."

"Too long."

His mouth covered hers again. Her lips instantly parted and her tongue pushed between his lips. He let her deepen the kiss, loving the feel of her hands running up his back. She was so passionate, so hot against him, he nearly lost all his sense.

Finally, she broke the kiss and looked up at him. "I think we should stop this while we can."

"Yeah." His disappointment sounded in his tone. "Let's." Wrapping his arm around her waist, he pulled her against him and nuzzled his nose into her hair. "Tease."

She chuckled. "You started it."

"That I did."

They were silent for a moment, each lost in their own thoughts, before she said, "The rain has stopped."

Sure enough, he realized, the constant drumming on the roof had gone silent. Frustration settled over him. He didn't want this time alone with her to end. "I guess we should head back."

"Probably." She sounded as unenthusiastic about returning as he had. "I'm worried about Mama. I've been gone too long."

He held on to her as she started to pull away. When she looked at him, he gave her one of those longing looks, moving his hand to her face, gently stroking her cheek before dipping down and putting his lips to hers.

The kiss was soft and sweet, much more tender than before, but he felt the passion simmering below the surface. He had no doubt that he was going to make love to this woman, and when he did, he expected it was going to set him afire. Leaning back, he smiled at the blush on her cheeks.

"You are so beautiful," he whispered and watched her smile spread. He brushed his thumb over her lips. "And incredibly sexy." He grinned when she laughed.

"While I could stay here and listen to this all day, we really do have to leave."

"Fine." He sighed dramatically as he slipped his arms from around her. "But you remember, as you're putting those cold, wet clothes back on, I was willing to keep you nice and warm."

She picked up her shirt and took a breath before stretching it over her head. As soon as the material hit her skin, she squealed. "Okay, that is freezing!"

"Told you." He smirked.

After dressing, Carrie closed the flue and the door on the fireplace so the fire would smother. "Do you think we should clean that out?"

Will shook his head. "I'll tell Donnie I got rustic. He'll have someone clean it up before we film here."

"Just don't tell him I was with you. I'm pretty sure that I'm already on his shit list."

"So I shouldn't tell him that you brought me here to seduce me in the rain?"

A blush tinted her cheeks at his teasing. "No."

"And I shouldn't tell him that I wanted you to?" he asked, losing the taunting in his voice.

"You're going to get me in so much trouble," she whispered and then bit her lip.

"But it's going to be so much fun."

"I'll bet. Get dressed."

"*Fine*," he said with an overly dramatic flair. He reached around her to grab his shirt. He put his damp shirt on, shivering as it clung to his skin.

When he was dressed, he draped his arm over her shoulders, and they exited the building. "Forget about Donnie and all his bullshit. I'm bored out of my mind. I have spent the last few weeks penned up in this house—not that it isn't lovely, but if I don't get out of here and do something, I'm going to go insane. What do you suggest?"

"What do you want to do?"

"Anything."

She clearly debated before extending an invitation. "I have

to go to the farmer's market before all the good stuff is gone, but we could go to Des Moines after that. Mama has said a few times that she'd like to go to the art center."

Will nodded. "The art center it is."

"After the farmer's market."

"But of course. Race you back to the house?"

"What?"

But he'd already started running.

"Cheater," she yelled as she picked up her pace.

CHAPTER 7

"I am completely disgusted by this," Carrie said when yet another vendor at the market refused to take payment for the goods they had selected.

"What can I say?" Will chuckled. "People love me."

"Take advantage while you can." Mama looped her arm through Carrie's. "They usually overcharge."

"You can't put a price on fresh produce." Carrie echoed what Mama used to say when Carrie had whined about coming to work so early on Saturday mornings. "They"—she nodded toward a booth that held handmade and antique jewelry— "overcharge."

"Just buy it, Carolyn," Mama insisted, as she did every week.

Will looked in the direction where Carrie was staring longingly. "Buy what?"

"She's had her eye on a bracelet for months," Mama said.

"Which one?"

"It doesn't matter," Carrie said.

He headed for the booth. "Show me."

"No. Will." She held on to Mama so she couldn't follow.

Doreen smiled up at her. "He's a nice boy."

"We still need apples."

"I'll bet your father would approve."

Carrie wasn't sure if Mama was referring to Carrie's biological father or Doreen's deceased husband. These conversations were never clear until they carried on a little further, but for this particular talk, it didn't matter. "We're just friends."

"Does he know that?"

Carrie turned to watch Will talk to the starstruck woman behind the table. She wished she could tell Mama what had happened earlier and how confused she had been since, but there was no way of knowing how Doreen would react. The urge reminded Carrie how much she used to rely on Mama for advice on everything from cooking to matters of the heart and how far gone Doreen really was.

"Oh," Carrie cooed, pointing to a sign several tables down to divert her attention as well as Mama's. "They have Honeycrisp apples. Let's get those. Come on."

"What about Will?"

"He'll catch up." Carrie led Doreen through the growing crowd. She looked back, watching people pointing and staring at Will, and wondered how he could stand it.

It hadn't bothered him one bit that people had stopped and stared as soon as he'd climbed out of Carrie's car. He didn't seem at all put off by posing for a picture for every girl who ran up squealing and gushing about how amazing he was or signing everything from napkins to shirts as Carrie and Mama squeezed through the crowd to do their shopping.

Looking over the apples, she wondered how he could want a life with no privacy, no anonymity. She even wondered if he'd meant what he'd said about not wanting all the attention fame had brought him. He certainly seemed to be lapping it up.

Turning back to where she'd left him, she pushed her annoyance aside and took a closer look at him as he posed for another picture. She noticed how stiff he was, how forced his smile appeared, and how tense his hugs were until he finally waved and dismissed the group and then pushed his way through.

"That's it," Carrie told the vendor before Will could get to their booth.

"Is that William Walker?" the woman behind the table asked, ignoring Carrie.

"How much do I owe you?" Carrie pressed.

"Oh my God." The woman ran her hand over her hair. "It is."

When Will approached and flashed a smile, Carrie thought the woman might pass out. A strange feeling filled her. Not jealousy, but something unsettling. This was the first time she'd seen one of her guests out of the privacy of the inn. She didn't know why she was surprised at the reaction people were having, but more than that, she was surprised at the reaction *she* was having. Seeing people fawn over Will was to be expected. What Carrie hadn't expected was the underlying sense of resentment she felt—not at having other people notice Will, but at how he drew their attention to her.

As he stopped next to her and put his hand on the small of her back, Carrie couldn't help but feel like a spotlight had been aimed at her. She didn't like that feeling.

"Oh, apples," Will said, seemingly oblivious to how everyone was watching him. "I love apples. Did you get some of these?"

"I did. How much?" Carrie asked the woman.

The vendor stuttered as she pushed the bag of fruit toward Carrie. "No charge."

"Come on," Carrie protested. "How much?"

"Really. On the house."

Carrie frowned as they walked away from the booth, another bag of free produce in the cart she was pulling behind her. She cast Mama a disapproving look when the woman laughed and clapped her hands.

Will smiled at the old woman. "Don't you think it's nice of these people to let us shop for free?"

"Why, yes," she agreed mischievously. "I do. Lord knows we've spent enough of our money here over the years. It's time they let us have something in return."

"This is how many of them make a good portion of their money," Carrie informed the duo with more frustration than she'd intended. Stopping her forward march, she waited for Will to look at her. "It isn't right to take handouts from them."

"She's right." Will gave Mama an exaggerated scowl that made her giggle.

Carrie shook her head at them. "I'm serious. These farmers struggle to make ends meet. Don't take things for free, even when they offer. The very least you can do is make a donation in exchange."

Will's smile faded, and Carrie thought she'd overstepped, but then his casual smile returned. "Well, there is one booth that didn't hesitate to take my money."

Carrie's mouth sagged when he held up the bracelet she'd admired a hundred times but refused to buy.

"Since you wouldn't tell me which one," he told her, "I had to point you out. She knew exactly what you wanted."

"You bought it?" Carrie asked softly.

"Yeah. And this." He held up a necklace in the other hand. "I thought you'd like this," he said to Doreen.

"For me?" She blushed. "How sweet!"

He draped the long string of colorful beads around her neck before turning to Carrie. "A thank-you. For bringing me with you today."

Sunlight danced off the various charms on the bracelet he held open for her. "That is a very expensive thank-you for bringing you to the farmer's market."

He gave her one of those deep, searching looks. "For everything else too."

"I can't—"

"When someone gives you a gift, Carolyn," he playfully chastised, "you say 'thank you' and graciously accept it."

"It's been a while since someone bought me a gift that cost so much, William."

He smiled and winked at her.

"Put it on," Mama encouraged. "You've wanted it for so long."

Carrie hesitated a few more seconds before holding her arm out to Will. He clasped the antique charm bracelet around her wrist and then ran his fingers over the charms, brushing her skin as he did. The light touch caused her breath to catch.

"You shouldn't be buying me gifts," she whispered.

"I wanted to," he softly said in return.

She fought the urge to touch his face, to kiss him gently, but she couldn't stop herself from taking his hand and holding his gaze. "Thank you."

"Was that so hard?" He grinned before stepping back and turning toward Doreen. "I have to say, that necklace looks lovely on you, Mama."

Carrie didn't hear more of their conversation. She was too busy evading the stares of all the people looking at Will and, she suspected, wondering why he was putting jewelry on two strange women. Several of them had their phones aimed at Will, obviously taking photos or video of him hanging out at the farmer's market.

Those videos would end up on social media somewhere, and Carrie's unease grew. The last thing she wanted was to be picked apart online because she happened to be standing with Will in public.

"I think we have everything we need," she announced as her discomfort grew, bordering on panic.

"Are you still up for the art center?" Will asked.

"I most certainly am." Doreen put her arm through Will's. "I can't remember the last time Carolyn and I did something for the fun of it. She's all business these days."

"That's a shame." Will gave Carrie a wink and a smile. "We'll have to see what we can do about that."

"Don't encourage her," Carrie warned as they headed back to the car.

———

THE ART MUSEUM was small compared to some others he'd been to, but Will was enjoying the displays as they walked through the galleries. More than that, he was enjoying being out of Gable Inn. Sitting still for too long made him feel twitchy. He liked to be on the move, and the little town where the cast had been staying, while quaint, didn't offer much entertainment.

However, he had to admit the quiet was giving him time to think and see his life a little more clearly. Or maybe that was the woman standing beside him. Carrie thought her life was a mess, but Will suspected she was more put together than she realized. Now *his* life…that was a mess.

Ever since his father had passed away, Will felt like he'd lost direction. The wake-up call had come too late, and Will still hadn't come to fully understand what it meant. All he knew was he'd been spiraling for too long, but being with Carrie made him feel grounded in some unexpected way.

She was an anchor he hadn't known he was looking for and one he couldn't explain. He wanted to be there with her more than he wanted to be anywhere else in the world, because being next to her reminded him he was real. He was more than a name or a brand or product to be sold. He was a person, and though he'd long ago lost touch with who that person was, she made him long to reconnect with the side of himself he'd tucked away into the shadows years ago.

Looking at her now, he wanted to wrap her up and hug her close, to feel connected to her. Luckily, his train of thought was derailed by the other woman standing next to him.

Mama tilted her head, peering at a sculpture. "I don't get it."

"Me either," Carrie said.

"It's art," Will explained, clearing his mind of his deeper reflections. "It's been left open to interpretation."

"Interpretation, my ass," Mama said, making Will laugh. "I prefer landscapes and portraits. Give me something I can identify and admire. This contemporary *art* is garbage. Anybody can put a bowling ball in a toilet."

"But only one person did so and gave it a name," Will said.

Mama blew a raspberry and waved her hand. "It's junk."

"I'm with Mama." Carrie moved on to the next piece. "I prefer Van Gogh, Monet, Renoir."

"Picasso?" Will added hopefully.

Carrie scrunched up her nose. "Not so much."

"I like Morisot," Mama said. "She did lovely portraits."

"She did." Carrie nodded.

"I think you two are missing out on something special." Will laughed when Carrie dismissed his observation with a roll of her eyes. He gestured to the next piece. "This expresses the torment the artist has endured. This is a reflection of his pain and inner demons."

Carrie and Doreen looked at him with unimpressed expressions. They might not have been related by blood, but they certainly shared a lot of mannerisms, including the pressed lips and one cocked eyebrow.

"Come on." Carrie took Mama's hand. "Let's move along."

"We haven't seen everything yet," Will stated.

"I've seen enough," Carrie said, and Mama agreed. They entered the next exhibit, where huge frames adorned the walls with skillfully painted landscapes inside. "This is much better," Carrie said.

Will frowned, even though Carrie and Mama looked much more impressed by what they were viewing.

"Look at that." Mama pointed to a painting filled with flowers, wispy clouds, and a colorful sky. "That is art."

"It's a field," Will said flatly. The lack of inspiration it took to copy landscape wasn't something that excited him much. Yes, the artist had undeniable skills, but no imagination. He found the image with the common colors and even more common setting to be boring despite the artist's talent.

"Look closer," Carrie said. "Imagine being there with the sweet scent of all those flowers in the air, the breeze cooling you down from the hot day." She smiled and sighed. "It's beautiful."

He turned to her. The subtle spreading of her smile was the only sign she gave that she knew he was watching her. "*You're* beautiful."

Carrie hesitated before turning her attention to him. "You're staring at me again."

"I can't stop thinking about kissing you," he confessed under his breath. He leaned a bit closer. "I'm going to have start plotting ways to get you alone."

Carrie glanced to where Doreen had stopped several paintings down. "We have to be very careful, Will."

"I know." He put space between them. "And we will. We'll be very careful."

"I don't just mean her." She subtly pointed behind him. "That couple hasn't stopped staring at you since we walked into this room. That's not something I want, Will," she whispered. "Not for me and most definitely not for Doreen."

Will's heart dropped to his stomach. He wasn't quite certain what she was saying, but he understood enough to know she was drawing a boundary. A boundary few people in his life ever drew. Most people enjoyed the attention. Most people tried to use it to get something in return—social media following or the attention of an agent. Few people shied away from being seen with William Walker, even after his starlight had started to fade.

In fact, the last people to draw those boundaries and insist their lives were private had been his family, who had insisted his father's funeral go unannounced to avoid any "unnecessary chaos" Will's attendance would bring. His brother had gone to great lengths to point out that because of Will, they hadn't been able to invite members of their church or friends of their father. Because of Will, they'd had to treat their father's funeral like a dirty little secret that was only exposed well after the fact.

Rolling his shoulders back, Will forced a smile to his face. "I guess we'll have to be more careful," he said and left her standing there as he approached Mama. Certainly being seen with a sixty-plus-year-old woman at an art museum couldn't attract too much attention.

CHAPTER 8

Carrie pulled the blankets down on Mama's bed. "Good day?"

"Very good. Will is a very nice young man."

"Yes, he is."

Climbing under the sheets, Mama snuggled down in her bed. "It was nice of him to take us out to such a fancy restaurant tonight."

"Yes, it was."

"And he bought you that bracelet you've been wanting and me that beautiful necklace."

"Yes."

Taking Carrie's hand, Mama squeezed it. "Mike would want you to be happy, darling. He wouldn't want you wasting your life taking care of me."

Carrie stared at her, startled by the moment of clarity. "I know he would. But I'm not wasting my life, and Will is a friend."

"He could be more."

"I'm not sure that's a good idea. He lives in California. He spends his life surrounded by perfect women who don't mind people staring at them all the time. He flies around the world filming movies and attending award shows. Everybody knows him. I'm just... I'm just a rural beatnik from Iowa, Mama. I don't think things could work between us."

"Oh. That's disappointing, isn't it?"

Carrie nodded before leaning in and hugging Doreen tightly. She couldn't remember the last time Mama knew what was going on. It filled her heart and broke it at the same time. "It is disappointing, but I've accepted that."

"You should reconsider that. Good men are hard to find. It took me years to find your father."

And the clarity was gone.

Disappointment tugged at Carrie, but she squeezed Doreen a bit tighter before leaning back and putting a kiss on the woman's cheek. "Good night." She waited until Doreen settled under the covers before standing up.

Carrie walked downstairs and into the kitchen, intending to open a bottle of sweet red wine and sit on the patio by the fire to quietly end her busy day. She slowed to a stop when she found Will standing at the island, filling a glass with the very wine she had planned on sipping.

He smiled bashfully. "I thought we could sit by the fire." He looked at the wine when she simply stared at him. "I wasn't ready to say good night."

"And you knew I'd be back down?"

"You're a little predictable."

"How so?"

"Well, every night, you put Doreen to bed, and then you come back downstairs to clean and sit in the den or outside, usually with a glass of wine or a cup of decaf nearby. I chose wine tonight."

She sighed. "My God, I am predictable." Taking one of the glasses, she stepped around him and out onto the patio.

"It's not a bad thing." Will followed her.

"No?"

"I enjoy your predictability."

"Really?"

"It's refreshing in my world of chaos."

"Well, I'm glad I can help."

While he added wood to the pit, Carrie stuck in some kindling and started the fire.

Sinking into a chair after the fire roared to life, she sipped her wine and tried to not be so aware of Will sitting next to her. Watching the stars flicker had almost relaxed her when he reached out and covered her hand with his as casually as he would with a longtime lover.

"I had a really good day," he said quietly.

"Me too." Her voice had an unexpected tremble at the feel of his thumb lazily dragging back and forth over her hand. Taking a drink, she noticed how difficult breathing had become and couldn't help but wonder how her body would react to something more than a simple holding of her hand.

She could very vividly recall how it had felt to have his arms around her earlier in the day, how hard he had been, how nice it had felt to lean on someone, and she couldn't help but want it again.

"You look like you're a million miles away." He gave her hand a gentle squeeze.

"Mama remembered that Mike was dead." She listened to the silence before continuing. "It was like she'd always known."

"I'm sorry."

"No, it was good. It was more than I've seen in a long time.

I think it was good for her to be out of the house today. I'm going to try to plan more outings."

"You're amazing with her. She's really lucky to have you looking out for her."

"She looked out for me for years. I owe her."

"It's more than that," he said gently. "It's family."

Carrie looked into her glass before voicing something that had been nagging her most of the evening. "I hurt your feelings earlier."

"You did?" he asked lightly.

"At the museum, when I told you I didn't want the attention being with you brings. I think that came out wrong."

Will shook his head. "No, I get it. I do."

"I upset you."

He stared at the fire. "I wasn't upset. I was reminded of... Not everyone appreciates the circus that tends to follow me around. I understand that, but you have to understand that I can't control it. I can't control the media or how people respond when they see me. I can't tell them to piss off, as much as I want to sometimes."

Carrie nodded. "I know, but I don't want to be dragged into that, Will. Especially not when I have to answer to Donnie."

"You don't."

"I do," she insisted. "He's paying the bill."

"The production company is paying the bill, Carrie," he clarified.

"Well, he represents them, and he's made it very clear he doesn't want this—whatever this is," she said, gesturing between them, "to happen. If pictures of us get out, if people start picking me apart because I'm with you...nothing good will come of that, Will. Not for either of us. I'm sorry, but I have to be aware of that."

"This life has consequences that reach beyond me. I know that. My brother and I have barely spoken since my father's funeral. He blames me for having to keep the service a secret out of fear that the press would have shown up or fans would have stalked us at the cemetery. I wish I could have told him that his fears were unfounded, but they weren't. Either I didn't attend the funeral, or we treated it like a top-confidential event. We chose the latter, and my brother resents it." Will laughed lightly. "You know what he doesn't resent? He doesn't resent that I'm putting his kids through college or that Dad's medical bills are paid or that Mom doesn't have to worry about losing her house. *That* he doesn't mind."

Guilt filled Carrie's gut. Will was obviously hurt by his brother's treatment. "It's hard for us common folk to understand, I guess," she said softly.

"I know," he said flatly as he stared into the flames. "I respect your desire to stay out of the spotlight, but you have to know that could put limitations on..."

"Us," she finished for him. "There are already limitations, Will. I don't know what's happening here, but I do know it needs to stay between us. Whatever *this* is, is not something to be shared with the rest of the world."

He focused on her and smiled sweetly. "No, it's not. This is between us." Putting his fingertips on the charm bracelet he'd bought for her, he said, "I should have asked before I bought this. I didn't mean to offend you."

"I'm not offended." She laughed lightly. "Mama wasn't joking when she said I'd been eyeing this thing for a long time. I couldn't justify the expense." She toyed with a dangling heart. "I always wished that my mother had at least one piece of nice jewelry to pass down to me when she'd died. My father is a handyman. He helps around here quite a bit when needed, but he's never made more than a living wage. If I ever have kids, I'll be able to pass this down with the story of how the famous William Walker bestowed it upon me at a farmer's market." She laughed lightly, and his smile returned. "It will be the pride of the family for generations to come."

"Are you going to have kids someday?" he asked.

She shrugged. "I don't think so. My life revolves around Mama right now. Hard to know what the future holds. You?"

"Same. Not the part about my life revolving around Mama," he added lightly as he entwined their fingers. "But not knowing what the future holds." He looked down at their hands. "Sometimes I think this might be it. This might be the last big movie I ever make. A year ago, that statement would have terrified me. Now, I find it comforting in a way. I find not knowing a lot more appealing than I thought I would."

"I think you're struggling more than I realized."

Grinning, Will said, "I think I'm struggling more than *I* realized. It's been a long time since I've been surrounded by so much quiet. The peace brings clarity, doesn't it? I see why you want to protect your space here."

"It's not for me, Will. Mama's mind is slipping more every day. I can't invite chaos into her world."

"I know that. I wouldn't ask you to. But I would like to ask," he said hesitantly, "that when we're alone like this, you try to forget that I'm William Walker and all the things that go with that title. When we're like this, I'd like to be just your average guy having a midlife crisis."

She laughed. "I like that guy."

"Yeah?" he asked, with an underlying hint of insecurity.

"Yeah," she said honestly. She did like him. She liked that

UNFORGETTABLE YOU

he seemed to be as lost and confused as she was. She liked that he was doing his best to get through his life and wasn't so full of himself that she had to tiptoe around him and diminish her own existence to get his approval. She liked that he was real. As real as someone in his position could be, anyway.

"You know," he said, "I'm finding it very difficult to keep my distance from you right now."

The heat that filled her was not from the fire. Now that she'd cleared the air and made certain he understood her comfort level with exposing their relationship—if she could call it that—she felt like a barrier had come down between them. She didn't have to be so guarded now. He said he understood her need for privacy and the need to protect Doreen. Carrie believed him, she trusted him, and without those defenses in place, she found herself much more open to wanting him. "What are you going to do about that?" she asked softly.

A slow smile curved his lips. "Come with me." He helped her stand and guided her away from the house and into the shadows of a nearby tree.

Pulling her to him, Will searched her eyes in the dim silver moonlight illuminating their hiding place. His intense stare caused her insides to twist with desire, and she thought that even when his face was distorted by the shadows, he was the most handsome man she'd ever seen.

"I'm in so much trouble," she whispered.

"Good," he said quietly as he leaned down.

His mouth covered hers as his arms went around her. Digging her fingertips in his shoulders, Carrie melted into him as he kissed her deeply. His tongue brushed against hers as their mouths worked together. Instead of easing the desire that had been building in her all day, the kiss only seemed to

111

add to the need she had for him and she pulled him even more tightly against her.

After several moments of exploring his mouth, she leaned back to catch her breath and accept that being with him like this was yet again leading them to a place they shouldn't go. Swallowing, Carrie pressed her lips to his one more time.

"I should go," she said against his mouth.

He moaned a plea for her to stay, causing her to put her fingertips to his lips to hush him. It wouldn't take much to convince her to stay and let him kiss her like that all night. But if she did, she would want more. She already did. For now, she had the sense to stop before she went further than she knew she should. Leaning forward, she kissed him softly and tasted the wine on his lips one more time before heading inside alone.

———

WILL WOKE the next morning and, as they had been so many times in the last few weeks, his first thoughts were of Carrie. Before he'd even cleared the sleepy fog from his mind, he wanted to jump up and find her. Kiss her. See her smile at him. He hadn't had a crush in a long time, but he was pretty certain he had a thing for the innkeeper.

After rushing through the shower, he trotted down the stairs, whistling as he went. However, as he walked into the kitchen, his excitement dimmed a little when she glanced up but barely acknowledged him before returning her attention to the pile of fruit in front of her.

"I'm running behind," she said. "Could you take this juice out to the dining room?"

"Yeah, of course," he said and grabbed the pitcher. He

found several people already at the table, a few of them mumbling about the lack of offerings on the usually over-flowing buffet. "Breakfast is on the way," he reassured them, ignoring the frown on Donnie's face.

"Maybe you should order in for everyone," Juliet barked. "We'd certainly get fed faster."

Will smirked. "Maybe you should throw food all over the floor during another one of your famous tantrums. That certainly helped matters."

Juliet narrowed her eyes. "Maybe you should—"

"Maybe you both should stop," Grant stated from where he sat. "Jesus, it's too early for this. Someone text me when there's more to eat than oatmeal."

"Here," Carrie said, carrying a platter in. "I'm so sorry. Here's the fruit."

"And the yogurt?" Juliet asked.

Carrie's hard stare only lasted a moment before she plastered on a warm smile. "It'll be here in a minute."

"That's what you said fifteen minutes ago," Juliet said.

Will watched Carrie rush from the room before sitting. "Calm down, Juliet."

"Enough," Donnie warned. "From both of you. I don't want to hear another word. From anyone until we get on set. *If* we ever get on set," he added, causing Will's defenses to spike again.

Rather than comment, he sat silently while everyone else got their breakfast and Carrie darted in and out of the room looking flustered. Once everyone else had gotten what they wanted, he went to the buffet and sighed at the lax offerings. This was the first morning there hadn't been biscuits and gravy available since he'd made the request. Juliet had pouted until Donnie nixed the sausage and eggs. Apparently, the smell made her sick.

But he'd compromised and allowed the other two dishes to remain a staple. Will was about to settle for oatmeal when Carrie stepped beside him and presented his coveted breakfast food.

"Sorry," she whispered. "Mama's still in bed. I'm on my own this morning."

"Everything okay?"

She smiled, but the dark circles under her eyes and the frustration of her morning betrayed her attempt at reassuring him. "Yeah." Then she disappeared again.

After covering two hot biscuits with gravy, he sat at the table and ate in silence, as did everyone else. The clinking of silverware and sipping of drinks was almost enough to drive him mad, so when his plate was empty, he didn't stick around. He rushed upstairs to brush his teeth again, grab his script, and get ready for the day.

By the time he returned downstairs, everyone was gone, but the mess of their breakfast was still on the table. Mama and Carrie would be cleaning things up by now. Something was definitely off this morning. When he didn't find Carrie in the kitchen, he went to her office and gently pushed the door open.

She looked up, and the tension on her face eased. "Sorry about breakfast. It was a bit of a mess today."

"Don't worry about it. What's going on?"

She focused on her computer screen. "Mama had a bad night."

"I'm sorry."

"She was up and down until about three o'clock, waiting for Mike to come home."

"How do you deal with this?" Will asked. "I mean, when she comes at you with things like that, how do you handle it?"

"Just roll with it," she said sadly. "I used to try to correct her, but that only upset her. Distracting her works well most of the time. Lie to her," she said, sounding guilty for her confession. "It seems to be getting worse. I'm wondering if it's the new medication she's on."

He moved around the desk to where he could see the screen. "So you're looking it up?"

"Trying. It's hard when there are so many variables."

Leaning over her shoulder to see what she'd been reading, Will asked, "Like what?"

"Like everything." After a moment, she tilted her head back so she could see his face. "Are you really interested in this?"

"Of course I am. I want to know what's happening so I can help."

Carrie turned her chair, bumping into him so he had no choice but to step back. "I wasn't sleeping well even before Mama woke me up. I kept thinking about us."

Will didn't like the look of doubt on her face. "You're not dumping me before we even start dating, are you?" he asked as lightly as he could.

"You have to admit that this is insane."

"Why?"

"Because," she said.

"Because?"

"Yes. *Because*."

He couldn't seem to be able to stop the corners of his mouth from moving upward. She looked absolutely worn out. She looked frazzled. But more than that, she looked like she needed him to scoop her up and hug her tight.

"You are a huge star, Will, and as Donnie so eloquently put it, I am but a mere innkeeper."

The lightness he'd been feeling faded, and anger started to boil beneath the surface. "Did he say something to you this morning?"

"I don't need Donnie to tell me that we live in two completely different universes."

He noticed that she didn't answer his question. However, before he could press, she continued.

"How in the hell are we supposed to—*whatever* when our lives are so completely incompatible?" she asked.

"Our situations aren't ideal at the moment," he said, "but those could be altered if we wanted. This doesn't have to be decided today, Carrie. I thought we were in agreement on that last night. What changed?"

She sank back in her chair and shrugged. "I'm feeling very unsure of myself these days. I don't know if I'm doing the right thing for Doreen. I don't know if I'm making the right decisions for her. It's all starting to feel very overwhelming."

Cupping her face, he brushed his thumb over her cheek. "You can lean on me as much as you need to. I want you to."

She gave a half-hearted laugh. "I'm so tired of taking on the world all by myself, I might take you up on that."

Grasping her hands, he yanked her to her feet and into his arms. He hadn't realized how scared he'd been that she really was ending things before they'd started until she didn't. Holding her close, he inhaled deeply and slowly released the fear with his breath. "Whatever you need," he promised, holding her against him, "I'll be here."

"Thank you."

"You're welcome."

"I'm sorry I'm so flustered," she said.

"It's okay," he reassured her as he dipped his head down. Their lips barely touched before they jerked away from each other like sneaky teenagers at the sound of someone approaching.

"Hey, Care." Natalie skidded to a dramatic stop inside the office. "Whoa. Um, yeah, so I got here as soon as I could, but it looks like breakfast is done. So...should I clean up?"

Carrie nodded. "Yes. Please. I'll be there in a second."

"Should I close the door?" Natalie started backing out of the room.

"*Go*," Carrie insisted.

Natalie smirked and winked. "Just askin'."

"Great," Carrie moaned when she and Will were alone.

He didn't want to laugh, but the sound slipped from him anyway. "Is she going to give you a hard time?"

"She wouldn't be Natalie if she didn't."

Tucking her hair behind her ear, Will waited for her to look at him. "I meant what I said. Anything you need."

"Thank you. I appreciate it."

He took advantage of the moment they had alone and put his mouth to hers. While it was more comforting than passionate, like the kisses they had shared the day before, it still made his stomach tighten and his heart flip. Carrie had teased him the night before, saying she was in trouble. In that moment, Will realized she wasn't the only one.

CHAPTER 9

C arrie stared blankly at Donnie. On a whim, she and
Mama had whipped up peach cobbler after they'd
finished serving dinner for the day. Apparently, that
displeased someone. If Carrie had to guess, it was Juliet.
Because *everything* displeased Juliet.

"Stick to the menu, Miss Gable."

"The peach cobbler was for me and Doreen. I offered it to
our guests to be polite. Ms. Ramirez could have said no."

"I expect, going forward, you and your mother-in-law will
keep your unhealthy food choices in the kitchen and out of
sight." He sighed heavily, as if he was exhausted from trying to
explain the situation to her. "I'm asking that you take the
eating habits of your guests into greater consideration."

"It seems to me that most of the guests are happy with the
food that I've been serving."

Donnie tilted his head back, literally looking down his
nose at her, clearly trying to determine if she was intentionally
being difficult or if she really didn't understand. "I made it

clear to you that Ms. Ramirez and Mr. Walker are your top priorities. While you seem to have figured out that all William needs is a pretty smile and batting eyelashes, you have a long way to go before Juliet is pleased with her accommodations."

Carrie couldn't help the smirk that tugged at her lip. Not only had he gotten in another jab at her for befriending Will, but he'd also managed to make the laughable suggestion that Juliet Ramirez was able to be pleased—and all in one sentence.

"I'll try harder," she said.

"Please do." He left, closing the door behind him.

Carrie exhaled some of the frustration that had built over the course of the conversation. Her patience was wearing thin with Donnie.

She recognized that a great deal of her low tolerance was the stress of Doreen's increased delusions, but his demands didn't sit well with her. Reminding herself to be calm, Carrie tore the Donnie-approved grocery list free from the notepad, unlocked the drawer where she kept the inn's checkbook and her car keys, and dropped them into her purse.

She expected to find Doreen in the den watching the movie she'd been glued to when Donnie had come in. The den was empty, but the television was still on. Grabbing the remote, Carrie turned the cooking show off and headed toward the kitchen, checking to make sure Mama wasn't in the half bath on her way.

Finding the kitchen abandoned as well, Carrie looked through the back window. She decided the woman wasn't outside on the patio, nor was she on the front porch swing when Carrie checked there. Heading up the stairs, Carrie made it to the landing before she found Doreen looking out the window.

"Mama?"

When Doreen didn't respond, Carrie put her hand on her shoulder.

"No." Doreen shook her off.

Startled by the outburst, Carrie pulled her hand back. She hated when Doreen got agitated; that was the most difficult part of dealing with this disease. The anger came from nowhere and usually for no reason and disappeared as quickly as it had appeared.

"What are you looking at?" Carrie asked softly, hoping to ease her bad mood.

"Go away."

"I need to go to the store. I'd like you to come with me. Mama?"

When Doreen responded by muttering under her breath as she continued to stare out the window, Carrie rolled her head back and looked at the ceiling. *Not now*, she silently begged. *Please, not right now.*

Carrie put a gentle smile on her face and tried again. "Mama, we have errands to run. Come with me, and we'll stop for lunch on the way back. Anywhere you want." Still receiving no response, Carrie reached for the curtain to pull it open so she could see what had the woman so intrigued.

Carrie jumped back when Doreen grabbed her wrist and jerked her hand away. "Mama," she squealed as the woman lifted her hand, preparing to swat her if she tried to touch the curtain again. "Stop that!"

"Where's Mike?" Mama demanded before Carrie could get a grip on what was happening.

"He's at the store." She watched Doreen's eyes move back and forth as if she were processing the information. Carrie needed to get Mama to focus on something other than whatever was upsetting her. "We can stop at the fabric store and pick up some material for the new quilt you've been wanting to start."

"I want my son."

"Me too." Carrie wished with all her might that he were there to help her with his mother.

"Where is he?"

"At the store, Mama."

Eyes narrowed, Doreen glared at the woman she said she had always considered a daughter. "You lying little bitch. Where is my son?"

Carrie looked at her, again with her eyes wide and mouth hanging open. "That's enough!"

"Where is he?"

"He's out."

Setting her jaw with determination, Doreen stepped around Carrie and headed for the stairs. She ignored Carrie's plea to stop until the younger woman reached out and grabbed her gently by the upper arm. Turning, Doreen lifted her hand and brought her palm down across Carrie's face.

"Where is he?" she asked in a voice that quivered with anger.

Carrie held her stinging cheek as tears started to burn her eyes. The knowledge that Mama would never slap her if she were in her right mind didn't take away the pain of what she had done.

Doreen's lip quivered. "You took him from me."

"No."

"You made him leave."

"That is not true," Carrie said with disbelief, forgetting

that she was arguing with a disease rather than the woman she'd known for years.

"I want him."

Carrie couldn't stop her lip from trembling as tears dripped down her cheeks. "He's gone, Mama."

"No."

"I wish he weren't, but he is."

"No."

"I'm sorry," Carrie whispered.

"No!" She put her hands on Carrie's shoulders, pushing her with all the strength her petite body could exert.

Gasping with surprise as she stumbled back, Carrie threw her hand out, scrambling to grip the bulky solid oak banister that lined the stairs. She thought she had caught herself, but gravity proved stronger. Her weak hold pulled free with a jerk that caused pain to shoot through her arm as her upper body turned awkwardly. A scream involuntarily escaped her and echoed through the stairwell and down the hallway as she fell backward.

The air in her lungs was forced out with a gush when her back slammed into the stairs. Her body painfully flipped and twisted as she rolled. Her shoulders and knees scraped along the carpeting while her head repeatedly hit the hard edges, and her hands reached aimlessly for something to stop her fall before hitting the bottom seconds after stumbling at the top.

———

PULLING HIS BEDROOM DOOR OPEN, Will listened, only to hear silence. He'd been rehearsing his lines, trying to nail a scene before morning, when he'd heard a terrified scream.

When the door across from him opened, he stared at his cast-mate. "Did you hear that?"

Grant nodded, wide-eyed. "What was it?"

"It didn't sound good."

"I think somebody got hurt."

Will headed down the hallway with Grant right behind him. He slowed when he noticed Doreen at the top of the stairs looking down at the floor below, her hands covering her pale face. He called out to her but didn't hear her choked response as he realized why she looked so horrified. His chest tightened at the sight of Carrie curled on her side at the bottom. The contents of her purse littered the stairs and floor around her.

"I'll call 9-1-1," Grant said as Will pushed past Doreen and ran down the stairs, taking them two at a time.

Kneeling next to Carrie's unmoving body, Will pushed her hair from her face, gently calling out to her. "Can you hear me? Carrie? Carrie, wake up."

"What happened?" Donnie demanded, entering from the back of the house. "Holy shit. Do we need an ambulance?"

"Grant's calling." Will stroked Carrie's face again.

"Don't move her."

"I know that. I just want her to wake up."

"Maybe it's best if she doesn't until the paramedics get here."

"What the hell happened?" Will looked back up the stairs at Doreen standing at the top of the stairs and realized how far Carrie had fallen. His stomach tightened anxiously. The high ceilings demanded that the staircase be longer than normal, adding considerable distance to her tumble.

He remembered the day he'd arrived. He'd commented about how long the staircase was. What was it that Carrie had said? *"Try not to fall down it. I'd hate to have to call all the king's horses."*

"Jesus," he breathed. "Do you think she fell all the way down?"

Will glanced at Donnie and noticed that he was looking up at Doreen, his eyes filled with suspicion.

Slowly standing, Will held his hands out reassuringly. "She's okay, Mama. Why don't you go to your room for a while? I'm going to call Natalie and have her come over to sit with you."

The old woman didn't seem to hear him. She started down the stairs, moving slowly, clinging to the banister. Will didn't want to have to deal with however Mama would react to seeing Carrie unconscious. However, she appeared to be too shocked to do anything as she eased down the stairs.

"You don't think Doreen pushed her, do you?" Donnie whispered so as not to be heard by the older woman.

Will barely glanced at Donnie as he knelt next to Carrie again. "Go check with Grant to see how long before the ambulance gets here."

"They're on the way," Grant called down as Donnie passed Mama on the stairs. "She okay?"

"She's not dead," Donnie said. "That's a good sign."

"Anybody see her cell phone?" Will asked.

When Grant bent down and snatched it off the stair in front of him, Will held out his hands for it to be tossed down to him. He scrolled through Carrie's contacts until he found Natalie's number.

"Hello, darling," Natalie sang into the phone.

"Natalie. It's Will Walker. There's been an accident. Carrie's hurt."

"What? What happened?"

"She fell down the stairs. An ambulance is on the way."

"Tell her I'll meet her at the hospital."

"I need you to come to the house and stay with Doreen."

"What?"

He glanced up, noticing that Donnie and Grant were clearly debating what had happened while Mama stood three steps from the bottom, clutching her hands together as she stared at her daughter-in-law. "She's pretty upset."

"Bring her to the hospital."

"I don't think that's a good idea. I think it's best—"

"Bring her to the hospital."

Will sighed when Natalie ended the call. A groan rose from beside him and the conversation with Natalie was forgotten.

"Hey," he said soothingly. "Carrie?"

She made a soft, painful noise in response.

"Don't move. There's an ambulance on the way. It'll be here any second."

She made another noise, this time scrunching up her face a bit, letting him know that she was feeling the pain of her fall.

"What the hell happened?" came a demanding voice.

Will sighed. "She fell."

"Is she okay?" Juliet asked, not sounding very concerned.

"Go open the front door so the paramedics can get in. Now," he said more forcefully when she didn't move.

The paramedics arrived several agonizing minutes later, and Will told the two men what little information he knew about Carrie and the accident. It distressed him to realize that wasn't much. He asked Mama a few questions, but she didn't respond. She was completely focused on what was going on, not understanding that her help was needed in obtaining Carrie's medical history.

Stepping back to give the medics plenty of room, Will

gently put his arm around Doreen's shoulders and assured her that Carrie would be okay. From where he was standing, Will could hear the paramedics asking questions but could only assume Carrie was answering. The medics masterfully slipped a neck brace on their patient and rolled her onto a backboard, strapping her down so even if she were able, she couldn't move. Will was startled at the bruising that was already becoming evident on the side of her face, and he began to understand how hard she had hit the solid wood floor where he found her.

"She's going to be okay, right?" he asked in a voice that didn't sound much stronger than Carrie's.

"We'll get her to the hospital as quickly as we can." The medics lifted her onto a cot. Within seconds, they extended the legs and were rolling her out.

Will walked behind, not looking at the actors who had formed a small gathering on the porch to watch their hostess being taken out on a stretcher. When the medics stopped to lift her into the ambulance, Will looked down at her face, but she was motionless.

"We'll see you there," he said. "You're going to be okay."

If she heard him, she didn't respond. The medics lifted her into the ambulance, shut the door, and drove away. Will headed back inside, ignoring the questions the other actors asked as he walked past them.

Several feet from the staircase, he found the keys to Carrie's sedan. Seeing Mama sitting on the stairs, staring at the floor where Carrie had been minutes before, he followed her gaze, noticing the charm bracelet that he had bought for her. Bending down, he scooped up her jewelry and put it in his pocket before kneeling in front of Doreen. "The ambulance took Carrie to the hospital. We should go too."

Doreen stared at him for a long moment. "Did I do that?"

"She fell," Will said, unable to confidently answer her question. "It was an accident."

She looked at him with confusion, but Will didn't have a clue what else to say to her.

"Come on," he said. "We need to go."

CHAPTER 10

The sounds of the hospital waiting room seemed to fade away as Will sat with Mama tucked between him and Natalie. They had barely spoken since they'd been instructed to sit and wait. As they did, Will's mind faded. This fear, this agony, must have been what his family had gone through the day his father had a kidney transplant. Hours and hours of sitting and waiting, worrying, and wondering. Hoping. Dreading.

His heart pounded in his chest as his mind bounced between worrying about Carrie and the remorse he felt for not being with his family when he should have been. No, he couldn't have done anything more than he had by being on the other side of the world, but he still should have been there. He should have been holding his mother's hand like he was holding Doreen's. He should have occasionally offered reassurances to his nieces as he'd done to Natalie.

He hadn't been there, and that had always bothered him, but sitting in this emergency room waiting room now, he thought he could almost drown in the guilt.

"What is taking so long?" Natalie whispered to Will while Mama stared at the beige linoleum of the waiting room floor. Though Natalie had always come across as gruff to Will, he saw through her now. Her fear was right there in her eyes. The pushiness he'd sensed in her before suddenly became transparent. She wasn't nearly as rough around the edges as he'd assumed—she was a protective friend who hadn't cared for the imposition placed on Carrie.

Will checked his watch and counted the minutes that had passed since arriving at the emergency room. It was closing in on ninety, and they had yet to hear a word out of the medical staff. "You're sure they know we are here for Carrie?"

"Yes. You try."

"Try what?"

"Getting us some answers. Go," she insisted when he didn't move.

Rising from one of the uncomfortable plastic chairs, Will approached the window and gave his warmest smile to the nurse. As he'd expected, her eyes widened and she fumbled with the pen in her hand when she recognized the man standing in front of her. "Hi."

"Hi," she squeaked out.

"I don't suppose you could find out about my friend, could you? Carrie Gable. She was brought in about an hour and a half ago."

"Well, I..." Her hand lamely gestured toward Natalie, but one more look at William Walker and she caved. "I'll see what I can do."

"Thank you very much." He returned to his chair and gently squeezed Doreen's hand. "She's going to see what she can find out."

Natalie sighed. "You should have asked a long time ago."

"I brought her here soon after she and Mike started dating," Mama said out of nowhere. "She bumped into a cookie sheet that had just come out of the oven and reached out to catch it. Burned her hand something fierce."

Natalie sighed. "I remember that. She was useless for days."

"I don't know what I'd do if—"

"She's going to be fine," Natalie interrupted. "A few bumps and bruises. That's all."

"If that were all," Mama muttered, "they'd have finished with her by now."

Will frowned, not having anything to say to the contrary. "They're taking care of her. She'll be okay."

Another eighteen minutes went by before a young man in green scrubs came through the doors and headed for the trio, introducing himself as Dr. Pallot. "Your friend had a pretty nasty fall. She's not really clear on what happened. Was anybody with her when she fell?"

Will put his hand on Doreen's before the woman could speak. "There was so much confusion. No one is sure what happened."

"Well," the doctor said, "amazingly enough, nothing is broken. Her right elbow was dislocated, probably from trying to catch herself. That's pretty common in that type of injury. We got it back in place and everything is working fine. She'll want to avoid heavy lifting and overexerting the joint for a few days, but it will be fine. Her arm will be in a sling for a day or two. She'll need to get it moving as soon as possible so her elbow doesn't get stiff, but since she's right-handed, I want to stabilize her injury for now. The rib cage on her right side is pretty tender and will probably cause her a lot more pain than her arm, but none of her ribs are broken."

"She was unconscious when I found her," Will said.

"She has a concussion and a very bad headache. She may have some bouts of confusion to go with it. That can last for a few weeks, unfortunately. We're going to keep her overnight for observation, but other than the fall, her memory is fine. Her speech is clear, and her eyes are reacting normally. I think she'll be ready to go home tomorrow, as long as there's someone around to keep an eye on her. She shouldn't do too much until the pain eases up. I'll prescribe some painkillers to help her through the next few days. She's going to be fine, guys."

"That's it?" Natalie gawked at him. "She'll be fine?"

"I want her to see her regular doctor in a few days to follow up, but I don't expect any long-term issues. We'll go over all of that when I release her, hopefully tomorrow."

"Can we see her?" Will asked.

"Yes, but don't wear her out."

Natalie stood, pulling Mama with her, and then fell into step behind Will and the doctor. Will glanced back and slowed down as well, not giving Natalie enough distance from him to talk to Doreen alone. He'd seen the suspicion in her eyes, and he didn't want her quizzing Mama.

When they arrived at Carrie's room, the doctor stepped inside and smiled at his patient, even though she barely lifted her gaze to look at him when he spoke to her. Natalie stepped in and gasped at the sight of Carrie limp in the bed, one side of her face severely discolored.

"Oh my God." Seeming to forget that she had been holding up Doreen, Natalie rushed to Carrie's side. "What happened to you?" When Carrie quietly mumbled her response, Natalie turned to the doctor, accusation in her eyes. "What is wrong with her?"

"She's on some pretty strong pain medication right now. Give her a minute to focus. She's fine."

"So you keep saying." Natalie sat in the chair next to the bed. "Care? Are you okay?"

"Mama?" she asked in that muttered, slurred voice.

"She's right here. Do you want to see her?" Without waiting for an answer, Natalie gestured for Doreen. "Mama, come let her see you."

Doreen moved closer to the bed and let out a sob. "Oh, baby." Leaning down, she took Carrie's left hand in hers—the other was being held to her chest by a sling—and kissed the top of her head. "Are you okay?"

"Yeah," she said, her voice clearing a little. "Fuzzy."

"The doctor says it's the drugs," Doreen assured her.

"Good drugs." Carrie gave a lopsided, dopey smile. "You okay?"

"Me? I'm fine. You're the one lying in a hospital bed."

"Let me have one more look at the patient before I leave." The doctor moved around to the other side.

Doreen and Natalie obediently moved back. They all watched him flash a light in front of Carrie's eyes and talk to her softly. After a moment, Natalie's attention drifted to where Will stood at the foot of the bed. She hesitated before stepping away from Mama.

"You can go," Natalie told Will. "I'll see Mama home."

He looked at her for a moment, reminding himself that under her grouchy approach was a worried and protective best friend. "I don't mind staying."

"I appreciate your calling me and bringing Doreen over, but I've got it from here."

Will smirked slightly. "I feel like I'm being dismissed."

"You can see that she's fine. We shouldn't overwhelm her."

"I agree. As soon as I get a second to talk to her, I'll take Doreen home."

"I'll take her home."

"I'm headed that way anyway."

"So am I," she said firmly. "I'll be staying with Doreen tonight and probably for a few nights after that to make sure Carrie is okay."

"That's a good idea."

"Another good idea would be for you and the rest of the people in the house to clear out. She doesn't need to be taking care of you right now."

Will looked down for a moment before sighing heavily. He had been wondering if, on top of her protectiveness, Natalie was suspicious of Carrie's fall. This seemed to confirm it. "I appreciate that you want to look out for your friend and do what is best for her, but whether we stay or go isn't up to you. It's up to Carrie. The last thing I want is to make her life difficult, so if she feels that she can no longer handle having the cast at her inn, I'll make it my personal mission to find us another place to stay. But until Carrie asks us to leave, we're not going anywhere."

"I want to know what happened," she said quietly but with enough force to let him know that she didn't believe Carrie's fall was an accident.

"I told you—"

"You found her at the bottom of the stairs," she said angrily. "But I have to wonder what Doreen would say if you would actually let her answer."

Will locked gazes with her, his hard, hers heated with anger. After a moment, he looked over at Carrie and watched the doctor talk softly to her as he pressed on her abdomen while Mama held her hand. Will took Natalie by the elbow and steered her toward the door.

In the hallway, he looked both ways before facing Natalie and leaning down slightly so he could speak without being overheard.

"I don't know what the hell happened. I heard a scream, and when I got to the top of the stairs, I found Doreen looking down at Carrie unconscious on the floor."

Natalie stared at him for a long time. The suspicion in her eyes faded to something else—a sad recognition perhaps. "Are you saying that—"

"I don't know. Doreen doesn't either. She doesn't remember what happened, and I don't think we should push her to try. Carrie wouldn't want her upset."

"Carrie isn't thinking clearly where Doreen is concerned." Natalie voiced a fear Will figured she had kept to herself for too long. "All she sees is Mike's mother. She doesn't see that Mama isn't who she used to be."

"Has she been violent before?"

Natalie shook her head. "No. Not violent, but she can get very agitated. Carrie handles her mood swings like a champ, but eventually it's going to become too much. Maybe it already has. Shit. If Doreen lashed out, and Carrie got hurt... I don't know how either of them would handle that."

"We don't know anything. Carrie may have missed a step and fallen."

"Right." Natalie sounded less than convinced.

"Carrie thinks the new medication that Doreen is on is causing her issues. She was planning to talk to the doctor about it."

Natalie looked at him, questioning him with her gaze.

"I walked in while Carrie was researching it," he explained

as if he knew what she was thinking. "That's what we were talking about in the office when you walked in."

Natalie narrowed her eyes. "Is there something going on between the two of you?" When he simply stared, Natalie's mouth dropped open. "How do I not know this? She tells me everything."

He stepped back when the door opened and the doctor came out, glad that the doctor's presence gave him good reason to end the conversation. "How is she?"

"Good. You guys can visit for a few minutes, but don't stay too long. She needs to rest."

"Thanks." Natalie watched the doctor walk away before looking back at Will. "I don't think we should tell Carrie that Mama may have pushed her."

"I agree."

"I do intend to stay at the house until Carrie is better. I'll help take care of the guests. But I'm telling you right now, if Juliet Ramirez looks at me cross-eyed one time..."

Will lifted his hands in surrender. "I promise not to stand in your way."

"Thank you." She smiled half-heartedly before losing her amusement. "I've been really worried about Carrie. She's taken on way more than she can handle but refuses to ask for help. It seems like she's let you in a little. I'm really glad about that. That said, you'd better take it easy on her. She doesn't need any bullshit."

"Nor do I."

"Good." Pushing the door to Carrie's room open, Natalie walked in and headed straight for the bed. "Well, the doctor says you're going to be dancing on the ceiling in no time."

Carrie's gaze was slow to leave Doreen and meet Natalie's.

Natalie gave her a slight smile. "You look tired, kid."

"I'll send Mike over with some clothes in the morning." Doreen continued the conversation she'd obviously started before Natalie and Will walked in. "The doctor said you'll be here through midmorning. Would you like him to bring something to eat so you don't have to suffer through hospital food?"

"Sure," Carrie said, still looking at Natalie.

Natalie put an arm around Doreen. "Hey, Mama, how about we go get her a snack from the cafeteria so she has something for later?"

"Oh, that's a good idea. We'll be right back, sweetheart."

Will stood back, watching them leave, before moving to the side of the bed they had vacated. Carrie gave him a lazy smile as he sat next to her and took her hand.

"Hey," she slurred.

"Hey yourself. You scared the shit out of me."

"That was my intent."

He smiled at her sarcasm. "Was it?"

"Hmm," she half moaned, half sighed in response. "How's Mama?"

"She's fine. Don't worry about her. We'll take care of her. How are you feeling? Really?"

"The drugs are good."

He softly laughed at the way she dragged out the last word. "Are you in pain?"

"More discomfort than pain."

Reaching into his pocket, he pulled out her cell phone and showed it to her. "I programmed my number in here. You call me if you need anything. I don't care what time it is."

She smiled as much as the drugs would allow. "Wow, my very own gofer."

Leaning forward, he gently put his lips to her forehead. "Do you remember what happened, Carrie?"

She closed her eyes, and he suspected that she wanted to say something, but then he thought that perhaps he was hoping she would.

She finally sighed and looked up at him. "I'm really tired."

Reaching out, he brushed her hair back from her temple, taking a good look at the skin that had grown dark around her eye. "It's the drugs," he said, allowing her to change the subject. "Go to sleep. We'll be back in the morning to take you home."

"Make sure Mama takes her meds."

"I will," he promised as he held her hand in his, still wondering exactly what had happened before she'd gone plummeting down the stairs.

CHAPTER 11

The next morning, Carrie stood in the bathroom of her hospital room, examining her face in the mirror. The bruise that started on the bone above her right eyebrow now encompassed her eye and cheekbone in a dark purple shade that seemed right for how much her face hurt. She touched her skin gingerly, wincing at the wave of pain that shot through her. The doctor had said that she was lucky nothing was broken, but looking at herself, she had to wonder if he had forgotten to check her face for fractures.

Hearing the door to her room open, Carrie expected her doctor. Instead, Will called out her name, and she looked at the door with horror. Not only did she look and feel like hell, but she was wearing a cheap hospital gown with her ass hanging out.

"Just a sec," she called out miserably.

Her right arm lay useless in a sling, leaving her to fight through the pain of her stiff muscles to clumsily pull her gown more tightly around her. Once she did, she realized she didn't have another hand to open the door. Giving up any attempt at having dignity, she cracked the door and peered out at him. Her spirits lifted as she watched him pulling breakfast from her favorite coffee shop out of a bag.

"Hey," she said.

Will turned and his smile fell. "Wow. The stairs definitely won that fight."

She chuckled, and her abdomen instantly reminded her that sudden movements hurt, and her head throbbed in agony. "You gotta turn around."

"What?"

She imagined that her entire face was turning a shade of red that rivaled the dark bruise around her eye. "I'm in a hospital gown. They aren't exactly..." She paused to search for the word. "Conservative."

Laughing, Will walked around the table and looked out the window. After several minutes, he looked over his shoulder. "Do you need help?"

"No. I'm just taking my time."

"Probably a good idea."

"Well," she said, shuffling toward the table, "I can't really take credit. My body refuses to move any faster."

Will turned. "Let me help you."

"Unless you have morphine or a shotgun, there isn't a lot you can do. Now turn around and let me have what is left of my pride."

While he wasn't looking, Carrie closed her eyes and gritted her teeth as she eased herself into the chair closest to her. Her breath left her in a hiss when every muscle and several joints screamed in protest to the movement.

"Have they given you anything for the pain this morning?"

"Yup." She grunted then took a few more breaths before

opening her eyes. "There, I'm good now. You can turn around."

Taking the blanket off the bed, Will carried it with him and placed it over her lap as he pressed his lips to the top of her head. "I brought coffee and scones. I hope you like scones."

"I like anything that isn't made in mass quantity in the hospital kitchen."

"Good."

Carrie sat while he served her a pastry and then took the seat across from her. "I don't really remember much of what happened last night." She saw him hesitate, taking a moment to sip his drink.

"You scared the shit out of me, that's what happened." He scanned her wounded face again. "I found you unconscious and stayed with you until the ambulance got there, and then I hung out here until you fell asleep."

"That's all?"

"Sums it up pretty well."

He took a bite of his breakfast and wiped his hands, but Carrie wasn't as prepared to move on as he was. "Was Doreen here?"

"Mm-hmm."

She paused, creasing her brow. "I don't remember. It's so fuzzy."

"You hit your head pretty hard. Several times, probably."

She wished she could say that wasn't it, but her body agreed with him. "Right."

"And they gave you painkillers. You were very groggy."

"I still am a little confused, I guess. And, oh my God, my head hurts."

"I know it does," he said softly. "Hey, look what I found." He held out her broken charm bracelet.

She slowly stretched her hand out to run her fingers over the chain, fingering the link that had snapped during the fall. "Damn it."

"I'll get it fixed. This time," he added with a faux stern tone, "but the next time you decide to take a tumble down the stairs, you had better take this off first. It's fragile."

Half a smile curved her lips. "I'll do that."

Will put the bracelet in his pocket and nodded toward her breakfast. "You don't like it?"

"It hurts to eat."

"Do you want me to get your doctor?"

"No. I'm sore. Like, put-through-a-meat-grinder-and-pounded-into-burgers sore."

"You look like someone tried to pound you into burgers."

She attempted to give him a playful glare but couldn't quite pull it off with her head aching and one side of her face still throbbing. "Are you trying to sweet-talk me?"

"Trying." Will smiled. "How am I doing?"

"Not very well. Did Natalie take care of things this morning?"

"Not with your finesse, but she did make breakfast and managed, with Doreen's help, to get everyone served and off to the set on time."

"Good. I was worried about that."

"Don't. Everyone understands that you're hurt."

"Everyone?"

He opened his mouth and then closed it. "Almost everyone. Those that count. Don't worry about anybody else."

Leaning up from his chair, Will put his lips to Carrie's. Though she was too sore to react beyond puckering enough to call it a kiss, she would have been happy to have him stay there forever. However, the door opened, and he pulled back to see who had entered.

"I'm so sorry," a nurse said apologetically.

"No problem." Will sat back in his seat. "She's really uncomfortable. Is there anything you can do?"

Carrie sighed and was glad that she was in too much pain to turn and look at the woman. She imagined she was fumbling with whatever she was doing, as that seemed to be the customary response to seeing William Walker.

The nurse said to Will, as if Carrie weren't there, "She had something a little bit ago. It might not have taken full effect yet." Finally, she moved so Carrie could see her. "Do you think you're okay to go home today, hon?"

"I'm fine. Just a little stiff."

"Well, that's to be expected after a fall like that. It must have been a nasty one."

"I don't really recall. How long before I can be released?"

"The doctor is going to want to look at you one more time and then go over your release instructions with"—she looked at Will—"your friend." The nurse's gaze lingered on Will before she turned and smiled at Carrie. "I need to take your blood pressure. I'm going to clip this to your finger. I know you're hurting." Carrie and Will watched her in silence until the machine she was holding beeped and she jotted something down. "Okie dokie. Can I get you anything else?"

Carrie barely looked up. "Anything that happens here is under patient privilege or whatever, right?"

"Of course."

"Good. Then I'm fine."

"Your doctor will be in soon."

The nurse closed the door behind her, and Carrie sighed.

"She's going to tell anyone that will listen that she saw William Walker kissing one of her patients."

"If anyone asks, I'll swear it was the dying wish of a ninety-year-old woman to be French-kissed by a terrible actor."

Carrie chuckled and then closed her eyes. "Stop making me laugh."

"I'm sorry." He took her hand in his and squeezed it gently. "I'm sorry."

"We have to be more careful. That could have been Mama walking in."

He nodded. "I wasn't thinking."

"Me either."

Will looked at the door when it opened again. This time it *was* Mama, with Natalie right behind her. Will smiled and greeted them before meeting Carrie's gaze. She suspected he, too, was silently acknowledging the irony of their timing.

———

WILL HOVERED RIGHT behind Carrie as she slowly moved from the car to the house. The doctor had assured them that with adequate rest, her muscles would heal in no time and she'd be moving as easily as she had before the accident. Will had made a mental note to make sure she took the doctor's advice and took the recommended downtime.

For now, she was moving so slowly, he was beginning to think they wouldn't make it inside before her body forced her to rest.

Finally, they entered the foyer and Will had to hold back a laugh. Yellow caution tape wound around the banister of the staircase. A sign that said Danger Zone was sitting on a free-standing pole at the bottom and an outline of a body had been drawn on the floor.

"Oh my God," Carrie said, closing her eyes as she softly giggled.

Natalie took in the scene and let her laughter roar. "They must have done this after we left."

"You okay?" Will asked, focusing on Carrie so he didn't join in Natalie's laughter. Carrie had told him how much laughing hurt, and he didn't want to contribute to her pain.

"Oh, those pranksters," Doreen said. "They are always up to no good. Wait until Daddy sees this mess."

"I'm more concerned about where they got these props," Natalie said. "I'm guessing there is a construction site somewhere missing a few things."

"If that's the case," Will said, "they're probably in jail by now."

"Who's in jail?" Grant walked in from the kitchen. He let out a low whistle as he looked at Carrie. "Damn, girl. You better ice that eye."

"A little late for that, I'm afraid. This is"—she gestured to the tape decorating the stairs—"interesting."

Grant stood back and admired the display. "We were concerned that you may have forgotten where the stairs are."

"I see that." She smiled, but Will recognized the effort she'd put behind it. She was in pain and toughing it out to be nice.

"We got pizza out back," Grant said. "You guys want to join us?"

"Oh, I think I'm going to have to pass," Carrie said. "I'm due for one of those fabulous pills and a little rest."

Will was glad she'd recognized the signs so he didn't have to coax her into it. Being overbearing wasn't really his thing, but he was prepared to do battle with her if necessary. He suspected she wasn't going to take care of herself without someone pushing the issue.

"Want me to bring something up for you?" Natalie asked.

"Take Mama," Carrie said. "Will can help me upstairs."

"Okay," she said in a singsong voice, turning to Doreen. "Come on, Mama, let's go eat some pizza."

Mama looked between Carrie and Will for a moment, as if uncertain about trusting him to care for her, before letting Natalie pull her away. She almost looked suspicious, but Will resisted the urge to explain that Carrie needed help up the stairs.

"Here's the deal." Dread strained Carrie's voice. "There is no way in hell I'm walking up those stairs right now. So, I can either lie in the den on that incredibly uncomfortable couch and wake up feeling worse, or you can carry me up to my room which will, without a doubt, be extremely painful but hopefully worth it in the end."

Will closed the gap between them and kissed her forehead. "Ready?"

"No."

"Okay." He scooped her up in his arms, ignoring the pained sounds that came from her. He climbed the steps quickly without jarring her too much and eased her onto her bed. "Sorry," he whispered, knowing the effort hadn't been as painless as either would have hoped.

"I'm good," she grunted between clenched teeth.

"Don't move."

"Okay," she responded in the same pain-filled voice. She lay, eyes closed, as he closed the bedroom door and then returned to her side.

"How are you doing?" he asked with a whisper.

"Shoot me. Please. End my misery."

Will smiled and brushed her hair back from her face. "How about I drug you up instead?"

"If that's the best you can do."

"It is." He dug the prescription bottle out of his pocket and tapped out her prescribed dosage. After handing her the pills, he held out a glass of water and watched her take the medication. "Give those a few minutes, and you'll forget you ever fell down the stairs."

"Right." She closed her eyes and let out a long breath.

"You look terrible," he informed her.

A grin twitched at the corner of her mouth. "Thank you. I appreciate that."

"You're welcome."

"Did the doctor say how long I have to wear this stupid thing?" She lifted her arm to indicate the dark blue sling.

"Until the swelling in your elbow goes down."

She made a miserable sound. "This stinks."

Will brushed her hair from her face again and kissed her forehead. "I know. As soon as you feel better, I'm taking you out."

"Really?"

"Yup."

Opening her eyes, she finally smiled. "Like a date?"

"Like a *real* date. Dinner and everything."

"That sounds nice."

Will nodded and ran his hands along her cheeks. "I'm sure there's a McDonald's around here somewhere, right?"

She attempted to give him a playful glare. However, it didn't quite work when half her face was bruised.

"I'm kidding." He took her left hand in his. "Does this hurt?"

"No, it's good."

"Is it okay if I stay with you for a while?" he asked. He was so worried that she might need something and no one would be around to help her. That wasn't a new concern. He'd been restless the entire night before, worried that she wasn't being taken care of in the hospital. Will would never consider himself to be the nurturing type, but he'd had to fight the urge to take her car and go back to the hospital to oversee her care.

"More than okay." Carrie watched him for a moment before chuckling quietly. "I'd really like to kiss you, but I can't move."

"Allow me." Will leaned down and put his lips to hers. After a soft, lingering kiss, he grabbed the quilt from the foot of her bed.

"Thank you," she whispered when he carefully draped it over her.

Sitting in the chair next to the bed, he took her hand again and debated pressing the other issue that had kept him up half the night. "Can I ask you something?"

"Hmm?"

Will hesitated before asking, "Do you remember what happened? When you fell."

Her eyes fluttered open, and she stared at the ceiling. "Vaguely."

"Was it Doreen?"

Carrie took her time before saying, "She was agitated. She wanted Mike and knew I was lying when I said he was out. She tried to push me out of her way. I couldn't right myself fast enough, and I just went flying." She was quick to add, "It was an accident. She didn't mean for me to fall. She would never hurt me."

"I know."

"It's the medication," Carrie continued. "It has to be. It's aggravating her."

Will ran a soothing hand over her hair. "We'll call the doctor and let him know she's been more confused than usual. I'm sure he can find something else to put her on."

Carrie's lip trembled and a sheen of tears appeared in her eyes. "Aren't you going to tell me to put her in a home?"

"No," he stated, "but I am going to tell you that you need to make sure her doctor understands the extent of her episodes lately and that you need to listen to his advice and do what he tells you. Doreen wouldn't want you hurt. Physically or emotionally."

"I know. I'm so tired," she said quietly. "This is so exhausting."

That unexpected urge to take care of her hit him again. He wanted to solve every problem she ever had but knew that wasn't possible. Or even reasonable. "We can find help. We'll hire someone to come in and take care of her a few hours a day so you can get a break."

"I feel so guilty doing that. Like she's a burden."

"You can't do it alone," Will reassured her. "Nobody expects you to. We can start looking for someone now, and when you're feeling better, you can make the final decision."

She exhaled heavily but didn't argue. "I can't keep denying that I'm in over my head," she whispered.

"We can get a few people lined up and see how she reacts to them," Will continued. "We don't have to rush into someone. We'll check their credentials and references and make sure they are qualified to care for her. Sound good?"

"Natalie probably already has a list," Carrie said. "She's been pushing me to do this for months."

He smiled. "Probably."

The tears that had been building leaked from the corners of Carrie's eyes. "I feel like I'm failing her."

Will leaned closer and kissed her head. "You aren't. There is only so much you can do on your own."

"I know that in my head, but I can't let go of this need to make everything okay for her."

He wiped her cheeks dry. "Nobody can do that. She's ill and she will continue to get worse. As she does, your ability to help her decreases."

"God," Carrie said as she closed her eyes, "you sound like one of those pamphlets I've read."

Smiling, Will confessed, "I may have done some research last night."

"Ugh. That was a terrible idea."

"Why?" he asked.

"I don't need a counselor," Carrie said. "I need someone to listen to me whine without judging me."

"I can do that." He kissed her head again. "Anytime you need."

"Thanks. Just don't let it be too often. If I start incessantly complaining, push me down the stairs."

"That's not funny," he said, despite the smile that curved his lips. "Get some rest. We'll talk more later."

"Without the benefit of your research, I hope."

Will shrugged. "I might have to throw something out there every now and then. I thrive on sounding intelligent."

"Poor you," she teased, and his smile spread.

CHAPTER 12

Though she was still feeling the stiffness of her fall in her muscles, Carrie had managed to sit on a stool at the kitchen island and look over page after page of résumés. "No," she said, pushing another one away.

"What's wrong with this one?" Natalie asked, obviously aggravated by Carrie's inability to agree to any of the people she had suggested.

"It should be a woman. Women are more patient and understanding."

"He's a registered nurse. He knows what he's doing."

"I think Mama would do better with a woman."

"Fine." Natalie thumbed through the résumés she'd collected, pulling out two and setting them aside. "What about hair color?"

"What?"

"Do you have a preference on hair color? Height? Weight?"

"Go ahead and be a bitch," Carrie said with as much frustration. "You don't have to live with this person."

"You don't either, Care. This is someone coming in a few

hours a week to help take some of the pressure off you. Stop being so damned picky."

"It has to be someone that Mama will get along with."

"She doesn't get along with men?"

"There are things that she isn't going to want a man helping her with. What if she needs help going to the restroom, changing, bathing? She may have dementia, Nat, but she still has some dignity."

"Okay," she said, "no men."

Carrie watched her read over a page and frowned. "This is a bad idea."

"No, it's not. It's the best idea that you've had for a long time. Not that it was *your* idea, but I'll give you credit since it took so long for you to agree to it."

"What if Mama reacts badly to having someone care for her? What if it upsets her?"

"You don't have to tell her that this person is here to take care of her. Let her start helping in small ways and then take over more. Or tell Mama that you are still hurting too much from your fall to do those things for her. Which isn't a lie."

Carrie sighed, looking down at the sling that still held her right arm. "I hate this."

"I know, babe. But until your arm feels better, the doctor doesn't want you to overdo it. The only way to stop you from doing that is strapping you in."

"I meant the situation," Carrie said. "Needing help from a stranger."

"It was going to happen eventually."

"Right." She exhaled heavily.

Natalie cleared her throat. "William Walker seems pretty concerned about your well-being."

"He's very nice."

"Mm-hmm. Is there something going on there?"

Carrie exhaled as she rejected another applicant. "I don't know."

"You don't know?"

Carrie contemplated her answer. "What would you think if there was?"

"Are you kidding? He's nice, sexy. Rich."

"He also lives in California."

"So?"

"So, I doubt Iowa is high on his list of places to reside. Especially since there isn't much of a demand for multi-million-dollar actors here."

"There are these things called planes. They make traveling to Iowa so much easier than the covered wagons you're used to."

"I'm serious."

"So am I."

"He's leaving in a matter of weeks, two months at the most. What then?"

"Long-distance relationships aren't unheard of."

"But they don't work well."

Natalie frowned. "They do for some people. Don't be so quick to end something that could be great for you. He cares about you. I saw that plain as day when we were waiting to hear from the doctor. He was terrified for you, and he went out of his way to comfort Mama."

"I don't think I'd fit in his world, Nat."

"What does he think?"

"I don't know. We haven't really talked about it."

"How did this happen?" Natalie asked with amazement. "I mean, he's *William Walker*."

"Yes, I know who he is."

"And he is interested in *you*."

Carrie lifted her gaze to her friend, taking in the confusion on Natalie's face. "Thanks."

"I don't mean it like you aren't worthy, because you definitely are. It's just that he is *the* William Walker, and he is interested in *you*."

"Stop saying that. You make it sound like I'm a band geek dating the quarterback."

"Honey, you kind of are."

Carrie laughed at Natalie's comparison and the realization that, in a way, it was true. He was known around the world. She was barely noticed in her own town.

"I don't know how it happened. We spent a lot of time talking and, you know."

"No, I don't know, but I am trying to find out."

"He's very easy to talk to, and he is very sympathetic toward Doreen. He has a really good sense of humor. It's been a long time since someone has made me laugh like he does."

"Are you dating?"

Carrie scrunched up her nose. "What exactly is dating? We've never gone out, but he did ask me to dinner."

"Nice."

"He seems interested in pursuing some kind of relationship."

"And you are seriously considering turning him down?"

Looking at a résumé without really seeing the words, Carrie shrugged. "I don't want to get caught up in something that isn't real. I don't need that right now. I keep wondering if he's going to get back to his life and realize how uninteresting I really am."

"You aren't."

"I am." She locked gazes with Natalie. "Compared to the

women he's used to, compared to the people he's usually around, I'm extremely uninteresting."

"Well, something turned his head."

"Midlife crisis."

"He said that?"

"No, of course not," Carrie said. "But that's what I've determined by overanalyzing every word he's ever said to me."

Natalie gave her a sideways glance as she continued to examine the papers in front of her. "Have you kissed?"

Carrie felt her face instantly burn to a bright shade of red. "I'm not discussing that."

"Oh my God, you have! I mean, I thought that's what was going on in the office, but I wasn't sure."

"I mean it. I'm not talking about that."

Her refusal caused Natalie to gawk before breaking out into a full laugh. Carrie tried to resist, knowing it would hurt, but she couldn't help but laugh as well.

Doreen walked into the kitchen. "What is going on in here? You two are as giggly as schoolgirls."

Natalie turned in her seat to look at Mama. "We are looking for some part-time help. Carrie can't handle it all anymore, so we're going to get someone in here to take over a few things."

Carrie eyed her friend, not appreciating the way she threw the idea of having someone else in the house out there without consulting her first. "Just a few hours a day."

Doreen smiled brightly. "I think that's a great idea. She doesn't believe me when I say she can't take on the world."

"I knew you'd approve." Natalie smiled cockily at her friend, causing Carrie to roll her eyes and return her attention to the résumés.

———

"DECAF." Will set a mug in front of Carrie. Though she was doing much better, he still found himself taking a few extra steps to look after her. She didn't seem to mind as much now as she had the first few days. He was glad she was letting him do small things for her now. That was the least he could do considering all she had on her plate.

She looked up and smiled. "Thank you."

He looked over her shoulder, scanning the résumé she was reading. "Have you decided on one?"

"I don't know." She let out a long, dramatic sigh. "This is so difficult."

"May I look?"

She handed over the pages and picked up her mug, taking a sip. "They're all perfectly qualified to help with Mama, but I can't seem to accept that any of them could do a decent job."

"Why don't you call them in to interview them?"

"All of them?"

"Sure. Why not? Anyone can look good on paper. It's a lot more difficult to look good in person if you are a complete screw up."

She chuckled at his assessment. "True."

"Do you want help?"

"Interviewing?"

"Yeah. I can sit back and give them the evil eye."

"Somehow I don't think that will have the same effect coming from you."

"I don't look scary enough?"

"Not really." She accepted the papers when he held them out to her and set them back on the counter, fiddling with them instead of looking to where he sat, next to her.

"You're moving better today," he observed. Before long, she'd be back to running the house, and Juliet and Donnie could quit complaining about how Natalie and Mama weren't proficient enough at serving food, cleaning up, and everything else they'd come to rely on Carrie to do.

"Feeling better today."

"Did you talk to Doreen's doctor?"

She nodded. "We have an appointment the day after tomorrow. Which is good timing, since that's when I go back in to see if I can stop wearing this stupid sling."

"If you would stop using your arm," he pointed out, "the swelling would go down faster."

"Yes, I heard."

"From?"

"Natalie."

"Bossy, isn't she?"

Carrie chuckled and nodded. "And nosey."

"Nosey?"

She inhaled as she absently turned the mug that he'd put in front of her. "She's curious what's going on between us."

Will couldn't blame Natalie for that. He was curious himself. He hadn't quite been able to pinpoint what he was feeling, but he knew he felt something for Carrie. A protectiveness that had become dominant in the last few days, a sense of intrigue because she wasn't like the women he'd come to know in the movie industry, and more than anything else, the attraction that he couldn't deny. "And what did you tell her?"

"That I don't know." Leaning back in the chair, Carrie held his stare. "Are you really interested in something beyond the next few weeks, Will?"

"Yes," he said softly.

"You aren't going to get back to LA and wonder what the hell you were thinking?"

"No. I'm not."

She exhaled slowly. "I don't want to let myself care about you just so you can disappear."

Reaching across the counter, he covered her hand. "That's not going to happen, Carrie."

"It scares me how different our lives are," she admitted. "I can't leave this place, and I don't think you'd want to be here."

"I agree that there are things we can't ignore forever, but they don't have to be resolved right now. We may decide a month from now that this isn't what we want. But right now, tonight, I can't imagine that happening. All I want right now is to get to know you better."

She smiled as she squeezed his hand. "I feel the same."

"That's good. I'd feel like an ass if you didn't."

Carrie laughed quietly. "I'm sorry. I swear I'm not trying to corner you into some kind of emotional guarantee."

"I get it," he whispered. "You've had a hard time lately."

She looked at him with sad brown eyes. "I don't need complications."

"So let's not complicate it." He lifted her hand to his lips and kissed it. "Let's do this thing one day at a time, okay? If we're done analyzing this thing, can we talk about our date?"

"Sure."

"I want to take you someplace really nice. Someplace very fancy." He scrunched up his face as he confessed, "But I haven't a clue where that could be. So, if you have to pick the place and make our reservations, does that still count as me taking you out?"

Carrie laughed. "I'll make an exception and say yes, it still counts as you taking me out."

"Okay. So you pick the place, you make the reservations, you tell me when, and I'll pick you up in the foyer."

"That works for me."

"Good." Will stood, ready to kiss her, when they heard laughter filtering from the other room. "Come with me." Pulling her behind him, he led her outside and into the shadows. "One of these days I'm going to kiss you without being worried about who may see."

"One of these days."

CHAPTER 13

Carrie started down the stairs, still moving slowly, but at least moving. She sighed nervously when she noticed Will standing in the foyer waiting for her. That voice started nagging her, warning her not to get attached, but she pushed it down. One night. Damn it, she was going to have one night without the fear and the dread and the anxiety. Natalie was looking after Mama. Carrie had the evening to herself and was determined to enjoy it with Will.

When he turned and smiled, her heart did a flip and landed with a thud in her chest. God, he had an amazing smile. She didn't have to wonder how or why he'd risen to the top of the movie industry. The world hadn't stood a chance against that smile. Neither had she.

Dressed in light-colored slacks and a button-down shirt that was open at the collar, he looked even more handsome than ever. She couldn't quite believe that he was interested in her, but she'd given him plenty of outs and he hadn't taken a single one.

"You look beautiful," he said smoothly as she stepped onto the wood floor next to him.

She looked down at her casual, knee-length, light yellow sundress and red-painted toes peeking out of her white sandals. Her bruises had faded but were still visible despite her extra layer of foundation. She'd given up trying to hide her war wounds. It wasn't like he didn't know they were there.

Her arm was no longer in a sling, though, and for that she was incredibly grateful.

"Thank you. And you. Wow."

He grinned and gave her one of those longing looks that always set her pulse racing. "Are we ready for our big date?" he whispered in case someone was around to hear.

They had let everyone know they were going out to dinner, but Carrie had made it clear the meal was to thank Will for helping her when she'd fallen down the stairs, hence her insistence on casual dress.

If anyone knew or suspected otherwise, they said nothing.

"Not that way," she said when Will started toward the front door. "Out back."

He eyed her suspiciously. "Do you have a horse-drawn carriage out there?"

"Hardly." She chuckled. "Just come with me."

Will followed her lead, going down the hallway, out the back door, and across the backyard to the jogging path.

It was then that Will finally spoke. "Carrie?"

"Yes?"

"Where are we going?"

"Dinner."

"I'm pretty sure I suggested reservations at a restaurant."

She stopped and looked back up the path, happy that she could barely see the house through the lush, green trees. "I thought about all the nice restaurants that I know in Des Moines. I even thought of a few not-so-nice restaurants, and I came to the same conclusion every time."

"Which was?"

"No matter where we had dinner, fancy or not, we were going to be stared at all night. I know that you had something else in mind, but I want to enjoy a nice evening without feeling any more self-conscious than I would on any other first date, so I made alternate plans."

He smiled after contemplating her reasoning. "I like your plan much better."

"Really?" She crinkled her nose. "Because I was afraid I was being a little bit of a baby."

"Not at all. I'm used to people staring. I don't even notice anymore, but I completely understand that it bothers you."

"So this is okay?"

"This"—he dipped his head down to put a soft kiss to her lips—"is perfect."

"Good." Taking his hand, she started down the path again. "I hope you like what I packed."

"I have yet to be disappointed by your cooking."

"That's a good answer. I like that."

Pulling her closer, Will wrapped his arm around her shoulder and kissed her head as they walked. "So where is this private dinner for two taking place?"

"Well, I thought it would be really nice to sit out and watch the sun setting, but I didn't want to get pestered to death by bugs while we were eating." Carrie lowered her face and her cheeks heated. "I have the food in a cooler at that little cabin where we waited out the rain."

Will smiled at the way she averted her gaze. "Why do you look so guilty?"

"Because," she said, still looking away, "I feel like I'm giving you the completely wrong idea of my expectations for the evening by taking you to an isolated cabin."

"What idea do you think you're giving me?"

Carrie closed her eyes and shook her head. "I hate when you pick on me."

"You love when I pick on you," he countered.

She would have argued, but he leaned in and kissed her sweetly and she did that swooning thing that he somehow always conjured up.

"I'm starving," she said after he broke away. "Let's get there so we can eat."

Will put his arm around her again as they moved along the path, veering off when they neared the cabin. He held her hand, reminding her to be careful as she walked through the higher grass in her sandals. At the cabin, he pushed the door open and stepped aside, allowing her to go first.

As she slid past Will, a quiet chuckle escaped him, causing her cheeks to heat with a blush again.

"Stop it," she said. Inside, she turned her focus to pulling food out of the cooler.

"What can I do?"

"Sit and relax." She walked to the table with an insulated container and filled two bowls with salad and a homemade dressing, setting one across from him. "I hope you like it."

Will swallowed a bite, pretending to contemplate the taste before putting his hands to this throat and making a gagging noise.

She gasped and swatted his shoulder. "You are being awful tonight."

Smiling, he watched her attempt to scowl at him. "It's wonderful. As is everything you serve."

"I think I've changed my mind about you," she said as they returned to eating the appetizer.

"It's too late. You already adore me."

Carrie held his gaze, intentionally filling her mouth with vegetables rather than responding.

His smile widened even further. "Admit it."

"Admit what?"

"That you adore me."

Again, she slipped her fork between her lips, refusing to answer him.

"All right." Dropping his napkin on the table, Will stood. "You asked for it."

"What are you doing?"

"Proving that you adore me." Stepping around the table, he bent so his nose was almost brushing hers. "You made me do it," he whispered before closing the small gap between them and claiming her mouth with his.

Cupping her face with his hands, he gently held her as he pushed his tongue between her lips. When she moaned and gently touched his cheek, Will leaned back and rested his forehead on hers. "Admit that you adore me, or I'll have to do that again."

"You are terrible at issuing ultimatums." She leaned forward, kissing him and then breaking away when the moment intensified. Licking her lips, she shook her head slightly. "This is going to be a very long night, isn't it?"

"I hope so." Will returned to his seat across from her. "It's your fault."

"Really?"

He nodded. "You look amazing. I had to kiss you."

"Hmm, I so frequently have that problem."

"I bet you do." He stabbed at his salad. "This really is very good."

Small talk filled the cabin as they finished the appetizer and then worked together to serve the main course. Will held the plates while Carrie served pasta onto them. At the table, he poured wine into their glasses.

She sat across from him but didn't touch her food.

"What are you thinking?" Will asked.

"Nothing that's appropriate for dinner conversation."

"Come on," he said. "Tell me."

Carrie set her wine down and draped her napkin across her lap. "Actually, I don't want to think about what I was thinking."

His smile faded. "What is it?"

"Even if you leave and I never hear from you again, I'm glad we're here. I'm glad we have this time together."

Reaching across the table, he waited for her to put her hand in his. When she did, he squeezed it. "I'm not going to just walk away."

"But if you did—" she started.

"I'm not."

"But if you did."

Will chuckled. "My God, you're impossible."

"I want to clear the air so there are no pretenses about what's going on here."

"What do you think is going on here?"

Carrie shrugged. "I think two lonely people have found an unexpected way to connect. I think we both have the best of intentions. But I deal with enough delusions with Doreen, Will. I don't need any of my own. I have to stay grounded in reality."

"That makes it really hard to sweep you off your feet."

Carrie smiled. "I'm pretty sure you've already done that."

"Oh yeah? When?" he asked.

"Sometime between sitting by the fire and nursing me back to health."

Will grinned broadly. "Damn. I'm good."

"Yes, you are." Standing, she pulled him to his feet with her. Stroking his face, she searched his eyes before leaning in and kissing him. He wrapped his arms around her, pulling her close as he slipped his tongue into her mouth. Breathless, she broke the kiss and chuckled. "We had better eat before it gets cold."

"I'm not very hungry."

"No?"

"No," he said under his breath, and Carrie's heart started to pound as she realized the banter was about to come to an end.

———

WILL GENTLY CARESSED Carrie's curves, moving over her hips, pulling her to him. She moaned into his mouth and tangled her fingers into his hair as he pushed his face into her neck and started nipping at her skin. When she whispered his name and pulled him even closer to her, he wrapped his arms around her and walked her to the small bed, where he eased her down.

Carrie wrapped her legs around his, and he ran his hands down her thighs. As he moved his hands higher again, he inched her skirt up and his heart raced faster with every inch of her skin he discovered. He planted kisses along her jaw until he found her lips again.

As he pushed his tongue into her mouth, Carrie slid her hands between them and started undoing the buttons of his shirt. She pushed the material open, sliding the shirt down his shoulders, and then lifted her head off the stiff mattress to lick his exposed flesh.

While he pulled away from her to discard his shirt, Carrie grasped the hemline of her dress. Will stood back, watching as she sat up and pulled the material over her head. She tossed her dress to the floor with his shirt and immediately reached for his belt. Within moments, his pants fell. He kicked off his shoes and stepped out of his pants as she brushed her nose along the waistband of his underwear.

"Jesus," he said as she slowly exhaled hot moisture over him.

"There are condoms—" she started.

"Yeah," he said, more than prepared. "I brought some."

She chuckled when he bent down to where his pants had fallen and pulled out a row of six, letting them dangle for her to see.

"Wow," she teased. "That's very ambitious."

He tore one free. "I aim to please."

"Repeatedly, I see," she said, causing him to laugh. Carrie slipped her shoes off and then turned on the bed and lay back on the mattress.

He stretched out beside her on the tiny bed and set the foil packet within reach. As he gently ran his fingertips up the inside of her thigh, he leaned down and kissed her sweetly. The kiss lingered as he teasingly traced the leg band of her panties. "I like these," he whispered, "but they have to go."

Carrie lifted her hips enough that he could slide the thin barrier off. He leaned back as he eased them down her legs and over her feet. As he moved between her legs and hovered over her, he noticed what seemed to be hesitation in her eyes.

"Are you okay?" he whispered.

"Yeah," she said as she looked away.

Brushing a hand over her hair, he waited until she met his eyes again. "I don't want you to think you have to do this."

She put her hands to his cheeks. "I never, not even for a moment, thought you'd expect me to do something I didn't want to. It's just...this is the first time since...you know," she said as her voice faded.

The first time since...Mike. Shit. This was her first time since her husband had died. "Oh, Carrie," Will said as he started to move away from her.

She grabbed his arms and stopped him. "I'm fine."

"You say that a lot, you know."

Wrapping her arms around him, she leaned up and kissed him softly. "That's because I am. Please, Will," she said, giving him a sweet smile. "I want this. I do."

"Are you sure?"

She pulled him down, and he kissed her again. When he leaned back, the hesitancy he'd seen in her eyes was gone. Reaching for the condom, he tore the packet open and sat back to put the protection in place. Moments later, their gazes locked as he slid into her, moving slowly until he was deep inside. He loved the feel of their bodies coming together.

Will planted soft kisses on her face and neck, taking his time as he made love to her. And she didn't seem to be upset that he was making love to her, not just having sex, not just seeking pleasure, but giving it in return. The most unexpected thing was that he didn't mind, either.

CHAPTER 14

As soon as Carrie opened her eyes the following morning, a smile curved her lips. Stretching as she rolled the night before through her mind, she giggled. It had been nearly impossible for her to say goodnight to Will, and he'd told her it wasn't much easier for him.

When they'd reached the house, he'd pulled her into the shadows as he'd done before and kissed her fully on the lips, one more time, before they'd parted ways. Even now, she could still feel his breath on her neck as he'd whispered how much the night had meant to him.

Carrie probably could have stayed in bed all morning, recollecting the evening, engraving every word and every touch into her memory, but she decided it would be much more fun to see him in person. She jumped out of bed and rushed through her morning routine so she could get downstairs.

"You're up early."

Doreen smiled brightly at her. "That nice girl you hired is starting today. I want to make sure everything is in order."

Carrie's mood dipped slightly at the reminder, but she pushed her depression aside. "I'm really glad you like her, Mama."

"Why wouldn't I? She reminds me of you."

Carrie kissed the woman's cheek before heading for the coffee pot. "It's going to be a beautiful day today. I thought we could skip a few chores and go to the nursery and finally get those rosebushes we've been talking about."

"Skip chores? Buy rosebushes? Who are you, and what have you done with my Carolyn?"

Carrie laughed softly as she filled her mug. "I'm easing back into the routine of being an overachiever. I have to take it slow. Doctor's orders."

"Well, I'm glad you're listening to someone. You work too hard."

"I know, Mama. You've told me."

Setting her coffee down, she went to the stove, ready to start preparations for egg white omelets and a side of fruit, which Doreen was well in the process of preparing, as well as freshly squeezed orange juice.

She was beating the eggs when the door opened. She immediately thought of Will sweeping in to say good morning. Her smile froze when she noticed Donnie taking in the scene of breakfast being made. The only time this man dared to venture into the kitchen was when he was walking through to the backyard or when he needed to warn Carrie about going against his wishes.

She knew by the look on his face it was the latter, and she sighed heavily. "Good morning."

"I need you for five minutes. I'm sure she can handle things for that long."

Carrie was tempted to remind Donnie that "she" had a

name, but decided it was too glorious of a morning to start an argument. She'd listen to what he had to say, let his latest complaint roll off her back, and return to her good mood as soon as he was finished.

"I'll be right back, Mama."

Doreen frowned as she glared at the man. "Take your time, honey."

Wiping her hands on her apron as she went, Carrie followed Donnie into her office. He held the door, letting her go in first, and then closed it behind him. She tried not to instantly become angry, but from her experience with him, she knew that he was displeased. When he was, it was usually over something so insignificant that his need to talk the issue over with her was ridiculous.

"What can I do for you, Donnie?"

"First off, let me tell you how happy we all are that you have recovered from your accident so quickly."

He didn't sound happy. In fact, he sounded outright resentful that he had to extend such niceties.

"Thank you," Carrie said, knowing he was setting her up for one of his lectures.

"It was quite a scare for all of us."

"Well, I appreciate your patience with the situation while Natalie and Doreen covered for me."

He nodded, which seemed to heighten the tension in the room. "We need to discuss what happened."

She waited for him to expand on his comment, but he didn't. "I fell."

"Did you?" he asked.

"Well, I didn't jump," she said with a sarcastic lilt to her voice that she hadn't intended.

"Juliet is very uneasy around Doreen. She has been from the start. This has increased her anxiety."

"My falling down the stairs increased her anxiety of elderly people?"

"Do not be contemptuous with me." He stared her down, anger boiling behind his dark eyes. "We'll only be here a few more weeks, a month at the very most. I think it best if, for that time, Doreen found other accommodations."

Carrie leaned a bit closer and tilted her head as she lifted her brows, certain that she had misunderstood what he'd said. "Excuse me?"

"Doreen needs to find another place to stay," Donnie stated.

A bitter laugh escaped Carrie's lips. "Really? Perhaps you have forgotten that this is her home. *You* are the guests here. She has no other accommodations, nor does she need them."

"We will not stay where Juliet is not comfortable, and she is not comfortable in this house with that woman."

Carrie shook her head slightly, not believing the words that were coming from this man. "You arrogant bastard," she whispered. "She is a sixty-four-year-old woman with dementia. She isn't a leper. It isn't contagious."

"She's dangerous."

"To whom?" Carrie demanded with narrowed eyes. "What has she done to that little bitch that makes her such a threat?"

"Do not call my star—"

"You leave." Carrie pointed toward the office door. "You go upstairs right now, and you tell your precious stars, every single one of them, to get the hell out of my house."

Donnie reared back. "*What?*"

"I'll write a reimbursement for what's left of your payment. I just want you gone."

"You dare—"

"Now, Donnie," she said firmly. "Get out *now*."

He stared at her, obviously fuming at her response to his request. "I have never been treated so shabbily before in my life."

"Nor have I." She stared him down until he turned.

He jerked the door open and then slammed it behind him. Once he was gone, she let out her breath, hating that it sounded more like a sob.

Who the hell did he think he was? Telling her to kick the woman who was practically her mother out of her own home? And what kind of person was so scared of a little old lady that she'd want her gone?

"It doesn't matter," she answered herself. "It doesn't matter."

Sitting at the desk, she turned on the computer and irritably tapped her fingers on the desk as she waited for it to boot up. Once it did, she opened a spreadsheet to start determining what she owed the production company.

She was digging for her checkbook when the door to the office opened again. Her anger almost shattered into tears when Will looked at her with concern.

"What the hell happened?" he demanded.

"Donnie wanted me to 'find other accommodations' for Doreen," she said, mimicking his tone as she quoted him.

"He said that?"

"Apparently Mama makes his prized hen nervous, more so after I fell down the stairs. What that has to do with anything, I don't want to know, but under no circumstances am I telling Mama to get out. He can go to hell."

"What are you doing?"

She started taking her anger out on the calculator. "I told

him to leave. I owe him for the room and board that you guys haven't used."

"I'm not going anywhere. So he owes you for me."

"Hey," came a voice from the door. Grant and a few of the other actors were crowding into the office. "What's up?"

Will looked at him. "Juliet strikes again."

"She sucks," Grant said.

"Donnie told Carrie that Mama has to leave, so Carrie kicked him out."

Grant nodded. "Good for you."

"I'm staying," Will told his co-stars. "What about you guys? Do you want to stay?"

Carrie smiled sadly when all but two agreed to stay at the inn. "He's not going to like that."

"Who the hell cares?" one of the actors grumbled.

"You get to tell him," she informed them.

"With pleasure." Grant herded everyone out.

When they were gone, Will closed the door and circled the desk as he opened his arms to her. She immediately rose and leaned into him, exhaling some of her anger as he wrapped his arms around her.

———

THE STRESS WILL HAD BEEN FEELING all day faded away when he walked into the kitchen and found Carrie and Natalie giggling as they stood at the island working on dinner. Seeing Carrie smile made him forget all his worries.

When she noticed him standing in the doorway, her smile widened. "Hey."

"Hey," he responded, a little less enthusiastically. Sitting next to Carrie, he kissed her on the lips, not caring that

Natalie was right there to witness the interaction. "I hope your day was better than mine."

Carrie frowned. "Donnie?"

"Of course."

"What'd he do?"

Will shook his head as he scanned the contents of the countertop but didn't really see them. He was trying to release the frustration that had been building all day. The last thing he wanted was to add to Carrie's problems with his own. "He was an ass all day to everyone who didn't walk out of here with him."

"I'm sorry."

"I'm not. I'd much rather be here. Trust me." He looked across the island, finally acknowledging Natalie. "Hi."

She scrunched up her nose and grinned. "You two are so freaking adorable. I can't stand it."

"Shut up," Carrie said.

"Seriously," Natalie continued. "*Adorable.* I'm going to side-line that mother-in-law of yours so she doesn't catch the two of you together."

When they were alone, Carrie leaned toward Will, giving him another gentle kiss. "So it was bad, huh?"

"Oh," he said, snagging a carrot slice off the counter, "he threw his weight around all day, as if he had any to throw. I already made a few calls about it."

"To?"

"Let's just say that Donnie will find it hard to get some people to work with him in the future."

Leaning back, she widened her eyes. "Holy shit. You're the Godfather of Hollywood."

Will laughed. "If I were the Godfather, he'd be waking up in the morning with Juliet's head on the pillow next to him."

Her laughter filled his soul as she took his hand. "Thank you."

"For what?"

"For standing up for me. It means a lot that you'd stay here despite what he wanted."

Cupping her face, he held her gaze. "I'll always stand up for you."

"That's good to know." She sighed and looked into his eyes as she leaned closer. As her lips neared his, the sound of approaching footsteps caused her to stop. Before whomever was headed their way could enter the room, she stood and headed for the stove. The door swung open and a small group of her remaining guests barged in, asking if Carrie had any champagne. They wanted to toast her for finally ridding them of Juliet Ramirez.

She didn't need more prodding than that. Within minutes, she was setting flutes on the counter as Grant popped the cork. The atmosphere in the kitchen was so much more relaxed than it had been their entire visit that Will couldn't help but join in toasting Carrie. Of course, she insisted she didn't deserve the accolade, but she did appreciate the thought.

With the casual air in the room, Will nearly forgot his relationship with Carrie was a secret. He'd started to reach for her at least twice, catching himself both times, but he also caught a suspicious look on Grant's face. Anyone in the house would have to be blind to not have picked up on the change in Carrie and Will's relationship, but it was important to Carrie that they keep things quiet.

Honestly, it was important to Will too. He didn't want the chaos of his life to touch hers more than it had already. The sense that he needed to protect her grew even stronger.

CHAPTER 15

Will walked into the kitchen the next evening and smiled at the glasses of wine sitting on the counter. "How did you know?"

Carrie glanced up as she finished capping the bottle. "I'm a mind reader."

"Oh, that could be dangerous."

"Could be."

"How did Mama's doctor appointment go?"

Carrie sighed and shook her head. "I started a fire." She eyed him. "Would you like to sit with me and unwind?"

Will put his arm around her shoulder to guide her to the back patio. "This is my favorite part of the day. Just so you know."

Easing into one of the chairs sitting around the fire pit, he brushed his thumb over her hand. "I think Grant is on to us. He was watching us last night."

She sipped her wine. "I noticed that too."

"He gave me a few curious looks today too. I'll talk to him."

After a few seconds, she sighed. "Won't that confirm what he suspects?"

"Maybe."

"So maybe you shouldn't. Let him think it, but unless he says something, assume it's only a suspicion."

He looked at her, wishing the light were better so he could read her eyes more clearly. "I don't think he's the type to spread gossip, but I can't say for sure."

Carrie frowned and looked into the fire. "I'm more concerned about Juliet or Donnie than I am about Grant. We're on both of their shit lists, and something tells me that won't end well."

"They won't come after you," Will said softly. "I'll make sure of that."

She smiled slightly and glanced at him. "Are you sure you're not the Godfather?"

He laughed softly. "Even if I was, I wouldn't admit it."

When she looked into his eyes, his heart rolled over in his chest. Her smile faded, but then she looked away.

"You turned away again," he said.

"You were looking at me like that again," she responded lightly.

"Like what?"

"You know what." She grinned, staring into the fire.

Will thought that was ironic, considering the slight curve of her lips set his insides on fire. "Come with me," he said.

Carrie chuckled when he stood and pulled her up. "I know where this is going."

"Do you?" he asked.

"Mm-hmm. You're about to take me into the shadows."

Will's smile widened. "Why would I do that?"

Carrie feigned innocence. "I have no idea."

When they were hidden in the darkness, Will turned and pulled her against him. Before she could say anything, his mouth was on hers and his stomach flipped over and knotted, a feeling that was becoming increasingly familiar. She wrapped her arms around him, clinging to him as he held her close.

After several moments of passionate kissing, he needed to breathe. Pulling back, he licked her kiss off his lips as she rolled her head back and gasped for air. Will took the opportunity to move his mouth to her neck and then lower, trailing the neckline of her shirt and coming dangerously close to her breasts. She breathed his name as he worked his way up the other side, eventually finding her lips again.

He moved his hand under her shirt to caress her lower back. He wanted nothing more than to feel the warmth of her body. She indulged in his kiss for another minute before leaning back and meeting his gaze. The look in her eyes, even in the darkness of the shadows, let him know that she was thinking the same thing.

They stood in silence, panting to catch their breaths, while Carrie seemed to be holding an internal debate. Oh, this could be so dangerous, he realized. But it felt so damn good.

"Stay here," she said, stepping away from him.

He gripped her hand. "Where are you going?"

"Just...stay."

She left him standing there with his body in knots. He felt like a teenager sneaking around so his parents didn't catch him. He'd laugh at the assessment if he hadn't realized that added an unexpected element of excitement to their relationship.

After what felt like hours, Carrie reappeared with a flashlight and a blanket. "Come with me."

He took the flashlight from her as the previously recognized excitement amped up a few notches. "You sure?"

Instead of answering, Carrie took his hand and started toward the path they'd traveled so many times already. He thought they'd been down it so many times that they probably didn't even need the light.

When they were out of sight of the house, Carrie stopped. "I don't want to get too far from the house. Mama might need me."

He looked around at the overgrown grass and bushes. "Right...here?"

She smirked in the light of the half-moon. "Unless you're afraid of the dark."

Will enveloped her in his arms and kissed her deeply. After a moment, he took the blanket from her, walked several feet from the path, and spread it out. "Are there snakes out here?" he asked.

"Maybe."

He glanced around. "What about raccoons or...fifty-pound rats?"

Carrie laughed as she eased down on the blanket. "I'll protect you."

"Even from a fifty-pound rat?"

Holding her hand out, she gestured for him to come to her. "They are far more afraid of us than we are of them."

"That's what they always say." He lowered his body over hers. "And then somebody gets dragged off into the brush."

Carrie touched her fingertips to his cheek. "You're thinking of serial killers. Serial killers drag you off into the brush. Fifty-pound rodents eat the evidence."

He sighed as she pushed his shirt up. "Oh, you don't have

serial killers in Iowa?" He dipped his head down and captured her neck.

"I don't think so. But just in case..." She pushed him onto his back and straddled his thighs. "You should probably shut up and have sex with me while you still have a chance."

"I love it when you talk dirty."

Carrie's laugh rang out as he pulled her down to him.

———

"THAT IS SOME SMILE," Mama commented when Carrie walked into the kitchen to help with breakfast.

"It's a beautiful morning." Swooping around the island, she kissed Doreen's cheek as she stole a piece of freshly sliced apple.

"Have you looked outside? It looks like rain."

Carrie turned and looked out at the dark clouds. "The world would be a dry, dreary place without rain, Mama."

The older woman chuckled. "I guess that's one way of looking at it. That, or you had a very good night."

Carrie's cheeks warmed and started to ache at the pull of the enormous smile on her face. Filling a mug with coffee, she fought the urge to tell her mother-in-law that last night had been one of the more amazing nights in recent history. "Or I'm in a great mood. Is that so hard to believe?"

"Honey, nothing puts a blush like that on a woman's face except a handsome man and a lot of lovemaking."

"*Mama!*"

"Well, it's about time you and Michael got to working on having me a grandchild."

A cloud as dark as the ones outside instantly loomed over Carrie's good mood. "We'll get there, Mama."

Doreen stopped cutting fruit and focused on Carrie. "Is there a problem? Between you and Mike?"

"No. Everything is fine."

"I can't remember the last time I saw the two of you together. He's always running here, running there. He needs to slow down."

"Yeah." Carrie moved to the pantry to get her apron and ingredients for the morning meal. "I thought I'd add fried potatoes to breakfast this morning. How does that sound?"

"Oh, the boys will like that."

"I'm sure they will." Carrie sighed, depressed by the reality Doreen had showered upon her.

CHAPTER 16

Noon had come and gone before Will had a chance to find Carrie and ask her if she was all right. She'd seemed a little off at breakfast, and he'd hardly been able to concentrate while filming, worried that she was regretting the night before.

He'd hoped all morning that he'd read her wrong. He'd barely been able to sleep after walking her to her room. He'd been tempted to sneak in and hold her all night, but he knew that wasn't an option without even asking.

After showering and heading downstairs, he'd been determined to find a moment to steal a kiss before heading out for the day, but that wasn't meant to be either. She'd seemed disturbed, giving him a forced smile as she served breakfast, leading him to believe she might be feeling guilty.

Searching the house, he found Doreen in the kitchen with Jenny, teaching the girl how to roll out dough. "Honey, I'm home."

Doreen feigned a pout. "Oh, you guys are early. I was hoping to have dinner ready for you."

"That's all right. I'm not really that hungry yet. Where's Carrie?"

"I gave her the evening off. We're cooking dinner tonight."

"All right." He grabbed a bottle of water from the fridge. "What are we having?"

"Beef stew in bread bowls." Mama smiled proudly.

"Yum. So where is Carrie if she isn't in here elbow-deep in flour?"

"Resting. I made her lie down. She looked exhausted." Doreen turned her attention back to the dough.

"I'll let you get back to dinner." Will headed upstairs, knocked on Carrie's bedroom door, and opened it when she called out to come in. He found her leaning against the carved walnut headboard of her bed, pretty pillows spilling out from behind her as she read a book. He closed the door behind him. "Hey."

"Hey. How was your day?"

"Apparently, harder than yours."

She chuckled as he sat next to her. "Mama insisted that I take some time off. Who am I to argue with that?"

"Who, indeed?" Leaning in, he hesitated, but when she met him halfway, he kissed her firmly on the lips. "Are you okay?"

"I'm great." She put a bookmark between the pages of her novel before closing it.

"You seemed upset this morning. I was a little worried."

Carrie sighed heavily. "Mama ruined my mood, that's all."

"What happened?"

"Just her delusions," she said dismissively. "Tell me about your day. Was Donnie better?"

"Marginally."

"I feel like it's my fault he's acting like a jerk."

He ran his hand over her thigh. "It isn't. He's always a jerk. Can we not talk about Donnie right now?"

A smirk curved her lips. "What would you rather talk about?"

"Your mother-in-law is completely enthralled by her dinner preparations."

"And?"

He moved his hand higher. "I think we need to go for a run."

"A run?"

"I want to be alone with you."

"I like the sound of that." Carrie smiled. "Meet you downstairs in ten?"

"It's a date."

Going into his room, he found a pair of running shorts and a T-shirt, hurriedly dressed, and then splashed cologne on his cheeks.

By the time Carrie came into the kitchen, looking like she'd put in as much effort to get ready for their run, Will was sitting at the island, drinking a bottle of water and talking to Doreen about dinner.

"Are you ready?"

"Are you off to exercise again?" Mama asked.

"It's my fault," Will said. "I hate running alone."

"I have to work off dinner before I eat it," Carrie said. "I'll be back in time to help you finish up."

"I'm not worried about that. I'm worried about you wearing yourself out. You should be resting."

Carrie dismissed her concerns with a smile. "We won't be long."

Will walked with her out of the house, feeling a bit guilty

for causing Doreen concern. "Should we tell her we're sneaking off to be alone so she won't worry about you?"

"Somehow I don't think that would be any easier for her."

Picking up his pace to a trot, Will resisted the urge to reach out and grab her until they were far enough down the trail to be out of view. Pulling her against him, he kissed her on the lips. "You have no idea how disappointing it was to wake up without you."

"Oh, I think I might."

"I was worried that your bad mood this morning was regret."

Stepping out of his arms, she entwined her fingers with his and started down the path again. "Mama had one of her Mike delusions. It knocked the wind out of my sails."

"You had wind in your sails?"

She blushed and smiled widely. "I had a lot of wind in my sails."

"Me too."

"Good."

"Last night was amazing."

"It was." She hugged him around his waist as they turned off the path a few minutes later. Stepping inside the cabin, Carrie looked at the little bed and couldn't help the fluttering low in her belly. They'd made love on that bed, and neither seemed capable of pretending that they weren't here to do the same thing again.

"Once they're done shooting here"—Will closed the door behind him—"I think we're going to have to invest in a twin-size bed for our hideaway."

"That cot is a bit cozy, isn't it?"

"Just a bit."

"Not necessarily a bad thing, is it?"

Putting his hands on her hips, he used them to steer her directly to the bed and stretched out on his side so they both could fit on the small mattress. Will ran his fingertips down her arm, smiling at the way goosebumps rose on her flesh. "Not completely."

"I kind of like it," she whispered, her lips brushing against his.

"You want to keep it?"

"Maybe."

"Whatever you want."

"Whatever?" she mumbled against his lips.

"Whatever."

Carrie kissed him thoroughly before pulling back enough for her to look into his eyes as she ran her fingers over his cheek. "I may hold you to that."

Within moments, the passion between them flared and she was lying on top of him, her legs straddling his hips as he pushed her shirt over her head. When their clothes had been discarded, Will tucked her beneath him, promising with his eyes all the things he didn't dare put into words.

———

CARRIE HAD to admit that she didn't mind having guests after Donnie's troop went to stay at another inn. In fact, she was actually enjoying the company as she, Mama, Will, and Grant played their second game of Scrabble on a Friday evening.

Will grinned as he set out all of his letters and let out a triumphant whoop.

"That is not a word," Carrie insisted when Will started counting up his total.

"Actually, it is." Grant frowned.

"How do you even say that?" Doreen asked.

"Omnidirectional," Will read. "It's like, equal all around."

"Like, equal all around," Carrie repeated and then frowned as she found his word in the dictionary. "Omnidirectional: sending or receiving in all directions."

"Oh, booger," Mama said, making everyone laugh.

"That puts me in the lead," Will taunted.

"Don't get too comfortable, Michael," Mama told him playfully. "There is no way you are winning this game."

Carrie's heart dropped to her stomach when Mama called Will Michael, but she'd hoped she'd misheard. She hadn't. She could tell by the way Will's mouth was hanging half-open. Looking at Grant, Carrie found he had the same horrified look.

The mood around the table shifted with that one word. Carrie's eyes glazed over with unshed tears, and Grant shifted uncomfortably. Mama was the only one who hadn't noticed how her words had affected everyone else.

Despite the altered mood, they finished the game. Once all the tiles had been played, Will confirmed that he'd won. Mama started to clean up, but Carrie looked at Will.

"Let the guys clean up," Carrie said. "We need to start dinner, Mama."

Mama chuckled as she stood. "Winner should have to clean up anyway."

"We've got this," Will said.

Carrie led Mama to the kitchen, but her mind was a million miles away. As Mama looked at the menu on the wall, determining what they'd planned for dinner, Carrie silently hoped that something would click in Mama's head and she'd remember Mike was gone. She'd hoped Mama would realize Will wasn't Mike. That Will was someone else—someone

Carrie was coming to care for—and then things could somehow be normal.

She'd hoped a lot of things. It hadn't done a damn bit of good.

As they'd played the game, Doreen called Will by the wrong name several times. The guilt twisted in Carrie's gut each time. By the time they finished making the baked chicken dish for dinner, Carrie was ready to get Mama off to bed. She'd sat through dinner faking smiles and doing her best to pay attention, but the only thing she'd heard was when Mama once again referred to Will as Mike.

Carrie was emotionally drained by the time she finally did manage to get Doreen into bed. She was tempted to go straight to bed herself, but she and Will needed to talk about this change in Doreen's perceived reality.

"Hey," Will said when she walked into the kitchen. She noticed the wine on the counter and went straight for a glass, taking a long drink. "Carrie," Will warned as she gulped. "Stop. Slow down or you'll get sick."

She set the glass down and shook her head at him. "I don't know what to do. I don't. I don't know how to make her see that you are not Mike."

"Take it easy." He rounded the island and put his hands on her shoulders. "It's been a long day. We're exhausted. Let's not worry about this until tomorrow."

She shook her head. "Do you really think it will be any better tomorrow?"

"It might be. Maybe whatever clicked in her mind today will be reset when she wakes up."

"Right." She sighed.

"Come here." He pulled her into his arms.

She cursed quietly as she buried her face into his chest. "I hate this so much."

"There is nothing we can do to fix it," Will said. "Let's focus on making the most of what we have, okay?"

Leaning back, she furrowed her brow. "Oh, God. You've been reading up on the support groups again."

"Just making sure I know what to say."

Laughing lightly, she held his gaze. "You don't have to say anything. This is exactly what I need."

"You want to sit outside for a while?"

She shook her head. "Not tonight. I'm so drained."

"Okay." He put his arm around her shoulder. "Let me tuck you in."

The relief she felt at his understanding was almost enough to make her crumble. For the first time in a very long time, she felt like she had someone she could lean on. Yes, she could depend on Natalie to help with Mama and running the inn on occasion. And she could count on her dad if there was a busted pipe or a tree that needed cutting down, but this was different. Counting on Will was different. The bond they'd forged was intimate, and not because of the sex.

More than anyone else, she'd come to count on him and his emotional support. Part of her felt that wasn't fair to him, but she was really good at ignoring that part. She was really good at ignoring anything that made her second-guess the time they were spending together. She needed him more than she was willing to admit, even to herself.

"Will you stay with me for a while?" she asked as they started up the stairs.

"As long as you like."

"Until I fall asleep."

Putting his hands on her hips, he guided her into her

bedroom before easing the door shut and following her to the bed.

Guilt again tugged at her as she looked at the picture resting on her nightstand. Mike had his arm around her, pulling her close as they smiled at the camera. She reached out and laid the photo facedown as Will curled behind her.

"Do you think we'd get along?" Will asked.

She chuckled. "Probably. He was quite the prankster. I think you guys would have given each other a run for your money. He was a handful."

"There was a lot of laughter in your marriage."

"Yes," she said as she stretched out beside him. "There was. This house used to be filled with laughter. It's sad really, how quiet things are now." Rolling over, she rested her head on his arm and slipped her hand under his shirt so she could run her fingers over his skin. "I feel like I'm betraying her somehow," Carrie confessed on a whisper.

"What do you mean?

"She thinks that you're Mike. Letting her believe that somehow feels like I'm cheating her of something."

"Of what?"

"I don't know. Reality, I guess." She closed her eyes tightly. "I know that I lie to her all the time, but this seems different."

"Maybe because now you're not only telling her a lie, you're living it."

"So are you." Carrie leaned up so she could look into his eyes. "I'm sorry. This must be incredibly unsettling for you."

"It is, but I get it." He ran his hand over her hair. "She has Alzheimer's, Carrie. She's not being malicious."

"I know, but... I should have corrected her. I was too shocked, but I should have snapped out of it and corrected her."

He shook his head. "No. Not unless you think that's what's best for her. I can take it. You have to do what's right for *her*."

Stroking his face, she whispered, "Thank you." Lowering her head, she said, "Maybe you're right. Maybe tomorrow will be better."

CHAPTER 17

When Carrie awoke the next morning, alone in her bed, she held on to the hope that Doreen would be back to recognizing Will.

With an apron over her clothes, she pulled out a bowl and got to working on blueberry pancakes before the kitchen was invaded. She'd just finished the first batch when Mama came down, dressed and ready for the day.

"It's chilly this morning," Doreen said. "First snow will be falling before too long."

Will came in behind her. "I hope not."

Turning, Doreen smiled at him and there was a dramatic pause as Carrie waited for her response.

"Is your daddy up yet?" she asked him.

Carrie's mood spiraled downward. "Mama," she said sadly, "can you slice some fruit?"

"Of course, dear. What would you like?"

"Whatever." Carrie looked at Will, wanting nothing more than to lean into him and let him make her feel better.

She resisted, even though she suspected Doreen wouldn't have thought twice about it.

It was after lunch before Carrie had a chance to be alone with Will. He was in the den, reading his script, when she came down from helping Doreen get settled in for her afternoon rest. He looked up and smiled when he found her leaning against the doorframe watching him.

"She asleep?" he asked.

"Yeah."

"How are you?"

"Exhausted."

"You should sleep too, then."

She shook her head and crossed the room. "No amount of sleep could make me feel better."

She sat next to him, and he pulled her with him as he leaned back on the couch. He wrapped her in his arms and held her tight. His hand rhythmically stroked her back, gently, softly, slowly. She closed her eyes as she snuggled against him. Finally, for the first time all day, she was able to relax.

When Carrie opened her eyes again, it took several moments for her to realize she was in the den, curled up against a warm body that was snoring softly. She slowly eased back, verifying that it was Will rumbling beneath her. After wiping her face to make sure she wasn't drooling, Carrie shook him gently. "Hey."

"Hey."

"I think we dozed off."

"Apparently." He grunted as he sat up and then looked at his watch. "Shit. It's almost four o'clock."

"We slept for two hours? I'd better check on Mama."

"Hey," he said before she could get off the couch. "I finally got to wake up with you."

"So you did." Carrie smiled as she pushed herself up. Climbing the stairs, she brushed her hands over her hair and her face. Taking a breath, she pushed the door to Doreen's room open and her smile fell. "Mama?" Walking to the bathroom, she found it as empty as the bed. "Oh no," she whispered. She trotted downstairs, calling out for Doreen.

Will met her at the foot of the steps. "What's wrong?"

"She's not upstairs."

"She's probably in the kitchen working on dinner," he assured her.

But the kitchen was empty as well.

Carrie went to the back door. "It's still locked. She didn't go out this way."

"Is it possible that you didn't see her?"

She looked at him in disbelief and then pushed past him and headed for the front door. "Shit," she hissed when she found the lock released. Yanking the door open, she stepped outside, hoping to find her mother-in-law on the porch. The space was empty. "Damn it. It's getting cold, Will."

"We'll find her. She couldn't have gone far."

"We don't even know when she left."

"We'll find her," he repeated.

They turned at the sound of gravel crunching as a vehicle headed up the driveway.

"There's Nat. I'll send her out to look in the stores. Mama has a short list of places she likes to go." Carrie didn't wait for Natalie to get close to the house. She started running toward the truck, meeting it as it neared the house.

"Lose something?" Natalie asked when Carrie reached the driver's side window.

Sitting in the passenger seat, Doreen smiled brightly as she waved at Carrie, completely oblivious to the fuss she'd caused.

"Mama. Where did you go?"

"I needed some fresh air, honey."

"She was almost to the highway," Natalie said.

"You and Mike looked so cozy. I didn't want to wake you."

"Will," Carrie whispered when her friend looked at her with confusion.

Natalie nodded. "Gotcha."

"You scared us," Carrie said to Doreen. "Please don't walk off like that. We didn't know where you were."

"I'm a full-grown woman, Carolyn. I can take a walk if I want to."

"I know. Please let us know from now on. *Please*."

"If you're done with the lecture," Doreen said, not even trying to hide her frustration, "I'd like to get started on dinner."

"That would be great," Carrie said flatly. "Go on ahead. I'll see you at the house."

Natalie reached out the window and squeezed Carrie's hand before easing off the brake and driving the rest of the way to the house.

"You okay?" Will asked when Carrie finally reached the porch.

"I think I need to start bolting the doors so she can't get out without me."

"Do you want me to call someone?"

She nodded, trying not to let the misery show on her face. "Yeah. I guess it's time."

———

WILL'S entry into the kitchen was greeted with a curse from Carrie. He couldn't help but smile. "That doesn't sound good."

She frowned as she looked at her reddened fingertips. "Potholders can only do so much."

"You okay?"

She grinned when he kissed her fingers after examining them. "I'm better now." Her smile faded when she looked into his eyes. "Something wrong?"

Will hesitated, not wanting to say what he had to say. "Donnie let us know that we wrap at the end of the week."

"Oh," she said after a few seconds. She held his gaze for a long time before pulling her hand away and turning to the dish she'd pulled from the oven. "Well, it has been almost three months. That's how long Donnie expected it to take when he reserved the rooms."

"Right." Will watched her busy herself with dinner.

"So you'll be leaving by the end of the week, then."

"Donnie put in the call to start making flight plans."

Carrie stuck a meat thermometer into a chicken breast. "I'm sure you'll all be excited to get back to California before the cold weather sets in."

Will creased his brow. "I don't give a damn about the weather."

"Well," she said lightly, "you would if you'd spent another few weeks here. It'll be snowing before long."

He gently grabbed her arm and turned her to face him. The touch of anger that he felt at her seemingly dismissive tone faded as he saw the sadness in her eyes. It was a look he was becoming increasingly familiar with, yet it never failed to rip at his heart.

"It's not like we didn't know this was coming," she whispered.

"I know."

"You can come visit. I won't even charge you for a room." She tried to laugh at her joke, but it sounded miserable.

"I'll take you up on that." He wrapped his arms around her. "I'm sorry."

She shook her head. "You have nothing to apologize for, Will."

"I feel like I do."

Pulling back, she looked at the thermometer. "Dinner's ready. Would you please let everyone know?"

Will wanted to press the issue, but she turned her attention to dinner and he took the hint. He gathered what was left of the inn's guests, and they sat around the table. While everyone else was excitedly chatting about how close they were to wrapping the shoot, the knot in Will's stomach grew so tight, he could barely eat his dinner. He was thankful when his co-stars left the table and started settling into their evening routines.

Carrie offered Will a weak smile as she cleared the table. However, once she disappeared into the kitchen, she didn't reemerge for some time. Finally, he went to find her, but the kitchen was empty. Peering outside, he verified that she wasn't sitting by the fire, so he made his way upstairs.

He finally found her backing out of Doreen's room. Looking over her shoulder at him, she put her finger to her lips. As soon as she latched the door, he took her hand.

"Come with me," he whispered.

She hesitated in following him to his room, but he tugged her with him.

Once inside, he shut the door behind them and then spoke in his normal voice. "What do you think I'm going to do? Ravage you?" he asked, pulling her against him.

She smiled and wrapped her arms around his waist. "You usually do."

"I've yet to hear a single complaint."

"And I doubt you will." Carrie kissed him. "Unless Mama is in the room next door."

"I want to talk to you." He pulled her with him to the sitting area.

Dropping onto a chaise, he watched her sit across from him in an oversize navy blue-and white-striped chair. He took her hands and leaned close so she would have no choice but to hear what he was saying. "I don't want you to worry about us."

She gave him one of her fake smiles. "Why would I worry?"

"Because you wouldn't be you if you weren't worrying about something."

"There is that." She dropped any attempt to hide her concern and her smile faded into a frown. "I thought we'd have more time."

Will tucked her hair behind her ear. "We're going to be fine. I'll call you all the time. E-mail, text, video chat. Whatever it takes to keep us going."

Carrie inhaled slowly. "You're going to get back to California, back to your life, and I'm going to stay here. That will change things, no matter how much we say it won't."

He squeezed her hands and looked into her eyes. "I'm willing to try. Are you?"

She nodded slightly. "I am. I told you that already."

"It's not like we'll never see each other again. I can fly back anytime."

"I know," she whispered.

"We can make this work."

Lifting her gaze to his again, she smiled, this time with

more confidence. "Of course we can." Leaning forward, she kissed him gently and cupped his face. "And we will. We'll make it work."

Will frowned as he watched the line between her brows deepen. "What are you thinking?"

"What to tell Doreen. I guess I'll tell her you're going on a trip."

His heart sank. He hadn't even considered what his sudden disappearance might do to Doreen. "Will she be okay?"

"Yeah. She'll forget all about you by the end of the day." She smiled, but he didn't believe her failed attempt at being light. "She'll be fine. I can handle it."

Clutching her hands, he held her gaze. "I need you to promise me something, Carrie."

"Don't go there, Will," she warned as her smile faded.

"You don't even know what I was going to say."

"You want me to promise to put her in a home if she gets too hard to handle."

He shook his head. "I was going to make you promise that if she gets worse because I've left that you'll let me know so I can try to make it better."

"Oh." Squeezing his hands, she let out a deep breath. "And how would you do that?"

"I don't know. Call her or something."

"That's nice," Carrie said softly. "I'm sure she'll be fine, but I'll let you know."

"And if she gets to be too much..." He watched her glare at him but held on to her hands when she started to stand. "Listen to me, Carrie. Carolyn," he said more firmly when she refused to look at him. "Tell me. I'll help you any way that I can."

The burst of irritation that had filled her face faded. "I have to tell you something," she whispered.

"What?"

"My name is not Carolyn." She smiled when his brow creased. "The name on my birth certificate, the name my parents gave me, is Carrie. Just Carrie. Mama started calling me Carolyn about a year ago. I have no idea why."

"But Natalie calls you that sometimes."

"As a joke."

A stunned laugh left him. "I've called you Carolyn so many times, and you never corrected me."

She grinned mischievously. "I know."

"Why?"

"I kind of like it when you call me that," she said with a shrug. "Like it's a term of endearment or something. I figured it was time for you to know."

"I guess it is. I'm a bit disappointed, though. I felt like we shared something special."

"I'm sorry."

"No, don't be," he insisted. "It's not your fault that your mother-in-law renamed you. What else don't I know about you?"

"So many things," she teased.

"I'll bet." Kissing her again, he let it linger, loving the feel of her mouth on his. "Can I still call you Carolyn?" he asked, making her laugh.

CHAPTER 18

"What is this?" Carrie asked as she entered the small cabin the next evening.

Will smiled. "Well, it is my final week here, at least for a while, and I wanted to do something special."

She turned and looked at him, disappointed at the reminder. Time had passed quickly, and he'd told her the cast would be working long hours wrapping up the film. "How did you do this without my knowing?"

He smiled, clearly proud of himself for sneaking dozens of roses, a bottle of champagne, and some fruit out to the cabin without her realizing it. "I have my ways."

"Very sneaky."

"I have to be where you are concerned." He pulled her to him. "Has anyone ever told you that you are a bit of a control freak?"

She grinned. "A lot of people, actually. It's not necessarily a bad thing, I'll have you know."

"No, it's not. Not at all. I've quite enjoyed getting a little spontaneity out of you when I can."

"Have you?"

He moaned his confirmation as he leaned down to kiss her. The kiss lingered, threatened to ignite, but he pulled away. "I have a plan for this evening."

"So do I." She smirked.

"Don't worry, that is in my plan, but first..." He moved away from her to light several candles and then pulled his phone from his pocket. He scrolled through his music for several seconds before selecting a playlist and setting it on the counter. An old Frank Sinatra song filled the room.

"You've thought of everything."

"I tried." He held her close while they slightly swayed to the music. "I should have done this for you a long time ago."

Lifting her head from where it had been resting on his shoulder, she searched his eyes. "Being alone with you is enough for me, Will. This is nice—wonderful—but I don't need this."

"But you deserve this. You deserve to be pampered and romanced."

"You've done everything right," she assured him with a kiss.

"I hope so. I really hope so. I don't ever want you to doubt that I want to be with you."

She kissed him again. "I won't."

"The time that we've shared has meant so much to me."

"I know," she whispered against his lips. "It's meant the world to me too."

"I feel like you've helped me reconnect with something inside of me, something that was missing."

Fear started to settle around her heart. For someone who was so adamant that their relationship wasn't ending, he was certainly laying the reassurances on thick. "Are you going to talk all night?"

He grinned. "I was trying to make the most of our time together."

"The way I see it," she said as she stepped back and pulled her shirt over her head, "you can talk to me on the phone any time you want, but this could be the last chance you'll have for who knows how long to lay me down on that little bed. You're wasting an awful lot of time telling me things I already know."

Will tightened his arms around her waist, and he lifted her several inches off the floor as he kissed her hard and continued his march to the cot. He leaned down, his mouth staying locked with hers as he eased her down.

———

THE SOUND of laughter drifted up to Will's room as he peered through the sheer curtains. Carrie and Mama had been walking through their little garden, pulling vegetables and talking. He couldn't make out what they were saying, but every now and then their giggles filled his ears and made him smile. His smile froze, fading a touch, when a strange warmth settled over him. If he didn't know better, he'd think the feeling was contentment. Maybe even happiness.

Sitting on the arm of the chair next to the window, he continued watching but with less focus on Carrie and Doreen and more on whatever was shifting inside him. Some time passed before he realized what he was feeling—nostalgia. A strange and unexplained sense of calm that only came from feeling at home. Watching Carrie and Doreen together brought the same sense of normalcy from his childhood. Something Will hadn't missed in years.

His mom and grandma used to garden when he was younger. They'd bring in baskets of carrots, tomatoes, and cucumbers that would be cut up for snacks or to be used in salads at dinnertime. His family would talk over each other during the meal as multiple conversations happened at once. Sometimes Will or his brother would reach across the table for something, only to have their father lightly swat their hands and remind them to ask for things to be passed to them.

"There's no need to climb on the table," he'd explain every time.

Will's smile faded with the memory. How had he gone from having Sunday dinners around crammed tables to feeling like staying on a movie set was more important than being with his ill father? How had he gone from a childhood where family was everything to feeling like paying his mother's bills was pulling his share of caring for her as she aged? How had his stage persona—that empty version of himself he shared with the world—become *real*?

Sliding off the arm and sinking into the chair, Will let his eyes swim out of focus. He couldn't imagine Carrie ever saying that paying Mama's bills was enough. He couldn't imagine her ever putting her job above Mama's health. As a matter of fact, she hadn't. The moment Donnie pushed to have Doreen removed from the home, Carrie had pushed back. She'd given back money she couldn't afford in order to protect Doreen—a woman who wasn't even her blood relative.

Leaning forward, resting his elbows on his knees, Will silently chastised himself for turning into everything he loathed. Juliet triggered him because she was shallow, self-centered, and would do anything to advance her career. Will had to admit he wasn't much different than her. This year had changed him, the guilt had worn down his ego, but he couldn't recall the last time he'd called his mom to check in.

He was distracted with the movie, with the networking, with the fan interaction. When he wasn't, he couldn't get his mind off Carrie. Everything came back to him, to what he wanted to focus on. And there was no part of feeling guilty that he wanted to focus on. Sure, he'd paid his father's medical bills, but when it came down to what really mattered, Will had failed his family.

He'd failed his parents and his brother.

Slouching in the chair, Will pulled his phone from his pocket and stared at it for a long time before scrolling through his contacts and finding his mother's phone number. Swallowing hard, trying to breathe through the shame that was threatening to choke him, he tapped the screen to connect the call.

CHAPTER 19

Rain was quickly moving in when Carrie walked onto the porch Saturday morning. The weather seemed fitting for the day. She was glum, despite the last few weeks having been especially nice. Ever since Donnie and Juliet had left, leaving her with only the more pleasant of the cast, Carrie had enjoyed having guests at the inn.

Now, standing out in the chill of the early autumn morning, she accepted hugs from her guests as suitcases were carried to rented cars. Natalie had taken Doreen to get her hair done at Carrie's request. They had both grown so accustomed to having these people in their house, Carrie wasn't sure how Mama would handle sending them off, especially since she had come to think that Will was her son.

"Try to walk down the stairs from here on out," Grant suggested, giving Carrie a tight hug.

She laughed. "I'll do my best."

"I need a date to the premiere," he teased. "You'd look great on the red carpet."

"Oh, you surely can find someone who has had more plastic surgery than I have."

"That's right, let me down easy." Grant looked over when Will stepped out on the porch, suitcase in hand.

If any of the actors had caught on to the affair that was happening under their noses, they'd kept it to themselves. Carrie doubted that any of them had not figured it out. No one could take as many runs and random disappearances as she and Will had over the last few weeks without incurring suspicion.

"I'll see you around," Grant said, forcing Carrie to tear her gaze from Will.

"The next time you find yourself trapped in Iowa," she said as he started toward one of the waiting cars.

Looking at Will, she swallowed, despite how dry her mouth had suddenly gone. He gave her a sad smile as he stepped to her.

"Call me. Let me know you got home safely."

"I will." Taking her hand, he squeezed it tightly. "I'll come visit soon."

"That'd be nice." She smiled.

Putting his back to the waiting cars, attempting to block them from view, he lifted her hand to his mouth and kissed it. "If you need anything," he whispered.

Carrie nodded. "I'll call."

He cupped her face for a moment before sliding his arms around her and pulling her against him. He held her tightly, giving her a moment to memorize his scent and the feel of his arms before finally easing his hold on her.

His eyes locked on hers as she leaned away from him. "I'm going to miss you like crazy, Carolyn."

She smiled. "Me too, William." Holding his hands in hers,

she looked down at them, watching his thumb brush over a charm dangling from her bracelet. "You'd better go," she finally said, lifting her gaze to his face. "You don't want to miss your flight."

"Are you going to be okay?"

"Hey, I was okay when you got here, wasn't I?" she asked as lightly as she could.

"Barely. Promise me that you'll take care of yourself."

She lifted her hand, holding up three fingers. "Scout's honor." When he curled his hand around hers, pulling it to his heart, she sighed. "I'll see you soon."

He nodded and held her gaze for a few more heartbeats before bending down and grabbing his suitcase. "Soon," he agreed, turning away and walking down the stairs.

Carrie stepped to the banister, leaning against the solid structure as she watched him leave. She smiled and waved when Grant rolled his window down and yelled another farewell her way and then told Will to hurry his ass up.

The driver took Will's bag and stuffed it in the back as Will opened the door to the SUV and turned around one last time. He hesitated before waving and disappearing behind the tinted windows.

One by one, the vehicles pulled away. Her heart ached as the last one, the one carrying Will, started to move forward. Despite their promises to keep in touch, she feared that as soon as he left, the spell would be broken and their relationship would be forgotten. She tried to trust him, tried to believe what he'd told her, but the reality of their lives and the distance between them was too much for her to ignore.

She watched Will's vehicle disappear around the bend before heaving a sigh and looking up at the overcast sky, cursing the cooling weather and the rain that was sure to come before the day was over. Back inside, she closed the door and looked around the foyer as Will had done the day he'd arrived. She already hated how quiet and lonely the house felt.

Stopping at the den, she thought of the impromptu get-togethers that had so frequently happened there. In the dining room, she began gathering the place settings. There was no need to have the table set. She and Doreen usually ate in the kitchen.

Upstairs, she stripped the beds one by one, starting on the third floor and working her way down to the second. When she came to Will's room, Carrie stared at the bed for several minutes before sinking onto the plush mattress and pulling his pillow from under the comforter. Holding it to her chest, Carrie dipped her face down and inhaled deeply, recognizing his scent. The ache in her heart grew. He'd only been there a few months, but having someone to share her life with—even if they did so in the shadows—had been so wonderful. He'd eased more of the burden weighing her down than she figured he'd realized. Probably more than she'd realized.

The night before, after making love, he had curled her body against his and told her again that they were going to make it. She believed his determination, his desire, but she couldn't quite allow herself to believe that it would happen. Time would take its toll; distance would seem to grow. Eventually, someone was going to have to give up one home for the other, and she couldn't really see herself living in California any more than she could see him in Iowa.

Their lives were different. Incompatible. And she couldn't hide from that forever.

The sound of floorboards creaking pulled her from her thoughts, and Carrie realized that tears had filled her eyes. Blinking rapidly, trying to hide them, she went to work on removing the pillow from the case, as if she'd been doing that all along.

"You guys got back pretty quick," she said, hoping her voice sounded lighter than she felt. "How'd it go?"

When she didn't get a response, she turned and her forced smile fell. She had expected to find Natalie standing in the door, but instead Will was there, watching her with an uncertain look. Her heart lifted, but that logical part of her refused to let her excitement grow.

"What are you doing here?"

He stood in the door staring at her. "I couldn't leave."

"You couldn't?"

"Well, I could." The corner of his mouth tilted in that way it did when he was uncertain. "But I didn't want to."

Damn it. Her heart lifted, begged her to let the happiness in. "You didn't?"

"No. I didn't." His half smile faded when she continued to stare at him. "This reaction of yours, is this a good thing?"

"What?"

"I kind of had this whole running into each other's arms reunion playing in my head, and you're just sitting there."

Finally, she let the smile she'd been fighting light her face. "You surprised me."

"Clearly."

She set the pillow aside as she stood. "You came back."

"I did."

Trotting across the room, she threw her arms around his neck, laughing as he pulled her against him. "You came back!" She kissed him several times before hugging him again.

"That's more like it." Will squeezed her tightly. "That's much more like it."

"How long are you staying?"

Will eased her down and shrugged. "As long as you'll let me, I guess."

Her smile widened, but it only lasted a moment before concern caused her to frown. "But what are you going to do here, Will? Watch me take care of Mama?"

"Sure. Why not?"

"Because you're going to be bored out of your mind. That's why."

"Hey," he whispered. He took her face in his hands as his mouth met hers. He kissed her sweetly. "First things first. I'm here. I didn't want to leave. That's all that matters right now."

When her smile returned, he leaned down and kissed her again. As it lingered, she felt that familiar need filling her. Pulling away, she sucked at her bottom lip, still wet with his kiss. "Hold that thought."

She dug into her pocket, fishing for her phone. After pushing a few buttons, she smiled at him and held her hand out until he captured it and took it to his lips for a kiss. "Hey," she said when Natalie answered. "How long till you're done?" She bit her lip when Will turned her hand and kissed her wrist. "Well, I need you to take your time. I need at least an hour. Something came up," she said, causing Will to laugh quietly. "Thank you."

She tossed her phone aside and gave him a seductive look. "You came back."

"You keep saying that."

"I still can't believe it."

"Well," he said, yanking her against him, "let me try to convince you."

Carrie exhaled slowly. She rolled her head back when he dipped his head to capture her neck with kisses. His hands slid under the hem of her T-shirt and began pushing the material up. The process was painfully slow and seemed to take forever until he finally lifted her shirt over her head and tossed it aside.

His arms went around her waist, and he pulled her against him as his mouth crashed into hers. He kissed her deeply, his fingertips digging into her sides as hers dug into his shoulders, trying desperately to not melt into a puddle at his feet.

She felt like this was the real beginning of something. Not a fling, not a passing moment in her life, but something real. She'd been holding back, not wanting to believe this could last, but at that moment, she wanted it to. Wanted to believe in what he was offering her. She felt her heart give in a bit, and warmth rushed through her—not a physical heat, but something so much deeper.

Breaking the kiss, she put her hand to his cheek and brushed her thumbs over his lips.

He came back.

The air rushed from her body. Even though she had given Will the right to be with her, she hadn't given him the right to touch her so deeply, to make her feel things she'd never wanted to feel with anyone other than Mike. But here she stood, nearly naked, her heart racing as Will stared into her eyes, and her heart started to ache with something else. She wasn't feeling lust and loneliness any longer. This was something more. Maybe love, maybe something close, but it was strong and undeniable, and it hit her so hard that she rocked back slightly.

Carrie leaned into him, kissed him tenderly, afraid he'd see what she was feeling if she kept looking into his eyes.

Using her hips, he steered her toward the bed as she went to work on the fly of his jeans. She had managed to release it before she bumped into the bed. Will cupped her head in his hand as he eased her back. Once she was lying down, his hand drifted over her shoulder and between her breasts, traveling lightly over her skin until he'd found the waist of her jeans. Carrie swallowed hard and let her eyes close as he went to work on removing her pants. Her only movement was to lift her hips so he could ease the denim down, leaving her clad in lacy black boy shorts and a red satin bra.

"You are so beautiful," he whispered.

Opening her eyes, she smiled when she saw his intense desire had faded to something softer, something that seemed more like what she'd been feeling moments before.

Sliding his hand beneath her, he slipped the hook of her bra, slid the straps off her shoulders, and watched as her breasts became visible. Leaning down, he slowly kissed each one, using the warmth of his mouth and the gentle pressure of his tongue to awaken them, suckling the nipples until they stood out, begging for more.

Closing her eyes again, Carrie licked her lips. The heat of his breath moved over her breasts and her stomach as he placed soft kisses along her flesh. She moaned, feeling his heat between her legs. Thrashing at the feel of his nose brushing over her, she bit her lip and willed her body to take his sweet torture.

When he exhaled against her center, Carrie's back arched up and her hands balled into fists as his moist breath taunted her. Gently putting his nose against her, he slowly moved his head back and forth, eliciting a sound from deep in her throat.

In response, he pressed his mouth against the lace of her panties and moved methodically, slowly bringing all of her to life. She was on the verge of begging for more when he moved away from her and began placing moist kisses over her thigh as he sat back.

Lifting her leg over his shoulder, Will gently massaged the muscle of her thigh as he turned his head and opened his mouth over the back of her knee. As his kisses moved lower down her leg and she felt his breath on her ankle, she reminded herself to breathe.

Opening her eyes, she looked at him, watching him watch her as he pressed his mouth into the arch of her foot for a moment before slowly lowering her leg and starting on the other one, this time working from her toes up.

By the time he made it to her other knee, Carrie could have sworn that a simple touch would have sent her soaring into the heights of a climax she had never known before. God, the things this man was doing to her was putting her every nerve on edge, begging to be the next to receive his gentle touches and soft kisses.

Hissing when he finally made it back to the top of her thigh, Carrie threw her head to one side, grinding her teeth together in a desperate attempt to keep her composure. When he gently pulled at her panties, she helped by lifting her hips slightly. Looking down at him, she watched as again his eyes filled with the burning intensity that had shaken her.

This time, Carrie forced herself to keep her eyes on his when he looked at her, and she felt certain he was seeing into her soul. Swallowing hard as he tossed her panties aside and slowly moved back up her body, she watched him lower himself to her, not closing her eyes until she felt him against her and heard him inhale her scent deeply.

She was jolted when he finally made contact with her soft flesh. The moment his tongue touched her, Carrie moaned from deep within, and when he tasted her deep inside, she gasped as her muscles clenched against her will.

Again, Will moved his head, pushing his mouth harder

against her. A moment later, she was groaning wildly, her back arched, her legs wrapped around his shoulders, holding him to her as her body released all that he had slowly built up within her.

As soon as she started to relax, Will stood up and jerked his pants off. She closed her eyes and took several breaths as she listened to the familiar sound of a condom being torn open. A moment later, he slithered up her body and looked down at her. His hands brushed her hair from her face, and he smiled as he slipped into her.

Rolling her hips to meet his, she grinned at the look in his eyes. He looked like he could stay in this moment forever. It didn't take long for her to realize he was getting close to coming; she could hear it in his moans. It amazed her that she knew his signals.

Touching his face, she held his gaze as they moved together, and she felt something akin to love grow inside of her. She embraced it as he leaned down and kissed her again.

Digging her fingers in his hair, she held him there, his mouth locked with hers as her body began another climb to ecstasy. He pulled back enough to put his forehead to hers and whisper her name as he thrust his hips forward, burying himself so deeply it made her gasp. He slowly pulled back and thrust again. The next time was all it took for every muscle in her body to tense and cling to him.

That was all he needed to finish himself, and she clung to him as he groaned with the power of his release.

CHAPTER 20

Will moved carefully as he put a playing card on the very top of an intricately designed stack. When the queen was balanced, and he was certain the card wouldn't fall, he leaned back and took another from the table.

"What are you doing?" Carrie whispered from the doorway.

He hesitated in turning his head, as if the air current would make the cards go tumbling down. "Architecture," he answered in the same hushed tone.

"It's beautiful."

He looked at the cards, carefully balanced on top of each other. "Thanks."

He followed the same procedure as before, moving slowly, steadying the card, and then pulled back.

"Are you okay?"

He was okay. He was fine. But he was restless. He'd spent more time the last few weeks pacing, wandering, wondering, and fidgeting than he could remember. He and Carrie had fallen into a routine that he knew was normal for most people —other than the fact that he was now answering to his girl-friend's dead husband's name where Doreen was concerned. He was quite certain that wasn't the norm. "Um. I'm bored out of my mind."

"You don't say."

He considered his work of art before taking a deep breath and blowing, destroying his card castle. When her arms slid around his shoulders from behind, he couldn't help but smile. "I don't know what to do with myself."

"I can tell."

"Suggestions?"

She kissed his cheek and whispered, "Nothing appropriate for the middle of the morning."

Will smiled, but his lips fell quickly. "Three weeks without working, and I'm going insane. This is pathetic."

"It's not. You're used to being active."

He started gathering the cards. "I was looking forward to relaxing."

"Which you have done."

"In abundance."

She chuckled and gently nipped his earlobe. "What would you like to do?"

"I have no idea."

Carrie pulled her arms from around him and sat in the chair next to him. Worry seemed to fill her eyes. "Ready to go home yet?"

"That's not what I'm saying."

She smiled, but the effort didn't look sincere. "Just checking."

Will took her hand. "I'm not used to not working."

"Well, you were considering a change in direction."

"I still am." He picked up a few cards and let them fall again. "I wish I knew what direction that was."

"Now is as good a time as any to figure it out. You said before that if you weren't acting, you'd write."

Will looked at her with raised brows. "And?"

"And...there's an office right down the hall. Get in there and write something."

"Write something? Just like that?"

She shrugged. "Why not?"

"What am I going to write?"

"Don't ask me." She put her fingertips to his cheeks and kissed him softly. "But whatever it is, at least I won't have to keep watching you mope around."

When she left, Will gathered the mess of cards on the table and contemplated her words. After piling up the cards, he walked into her office and sat in front of the monitor. He stared at the screen for several long moments before moving the mouse to bring the computer to life. Then he stared even longer before opening the program. The white screen stared back at him, the cursor blinking, waiting for him to make some kind of decision.

"Okay," he sighed, putting his fingertips to the keyboard. "Write something."

———

CARRIE DEBATED KNOCKING on the office door. The last thing she wanted to do was disturb Will, but she hadn't seen him for two days. She knew he'd eaten because she'd found his dishes in the sink, but she hadn't actually seen him.

She tapped on the door, pushed it open, and poked her head inside. "Good God, you look like hell."

Will smiled at her. "Thanks."

"Lunch is ready."

He shook his head and sighed. "I'm on a roll."

"So it's going well?"

"I don't know about that, but I'm writing."

"Can I see?"

"Not yet." He closed the document as she neared the desk. "Maybe when I'm done."

"What are you writing?"

"Um, I don't know. I'm writing whatever. When I think it's good enough, I'll let you see."

"Fair enough. Would you like me to bring you something?"

"I'll come out for lunch soon. Promise."

Leaning over the desk, she waited for him to kiss her, but once he did, she frowned deeply. "You need to shave."

"I need to bathe."

"I was being nice," she commented, leaving him to his writing. She went back to the kitchen and smiled at Doreen. "Mama, would you like to help me make some marinade for the chicken? Something garlicky to go with pasta?"

Doreen hesitated before meeting Carrie's gaze. "Have you seen the cat?"

They didn't have a cat. They'd never had a cat. "In the den," she lied.

"She's always disappearing."

"She's sleeping, Mama. How about we start dinner?"

"What is Mike doing in there?"

"Paperwork."

"Your father never had to do so much paperwork."

Carrie went to the pantry to find the olive oil. "Things are different now, Mama." Coming into the kitchen carrying several ingredients, she set them on the counter.

"Have you seen the cat?"

Carrie sighed. God, how she hated days like these.

Putting Mama to bed several hours later was such a relief, Carrie almost felt guilty. Her guilt eased, however, when she walked into the kitchen to find a haggard-looking Will filling two wineglasses.

"Ah, just like the good ol' days," she said.

He smiled. "I'm sorry. I don't mean to neglect you."

She kissed his cheek. "I get it."

"You do?"

She nodded as she accepted a glass. "Back when I had a life beyond this inn, I used to get caught up in the kitchen. Imagining new recipes or improving old ones. I don't have much time for that these days, but I do remember that creating something can be addicting."

"Yes, it can."

"I worked crazy long hours sometimes. Drove Mike nuts."

Putting his arm around her shoulders, he guided her to the back door and out to the patio where a fire was already roaring. "How was Mama today?"

Carrie sank down and so did her mood. "Honestly?" Swirling her wine in her glass, she frowned. "She seems to be fading more and more quickly. Every day seems to take a larger piece of her mind."

He was quiet for a moment. "I'll put this project on hold—"

"No. You won't. There isn't anything you can do, Will."

"I can be here for you."

Reaching out, she took his hand and squeezed it. "You are. And that means the world to me."

CHAPTER 21

Over a month passed before Will let Carrie see his script. Though he knew the work still needed polishing, he couldn't wait to hear feedback from someone. So, with a bottle of wine and his nerves on edge, he dragged her to the den and sat her down. An occasional laugh would leave her, sometimes her brow would crease, but she refused to explain until she finished her second read through.

He'd stopped asking her why she was reacting the way she was when she'd threatened to make him leave her alone. So, he sat watching her face, trying to get an idea of what she was thinking. Not knowing was torture, but he couldn't make himself stop. At one point, she'd sent him to check on Mama, who was sound asleep. And then she'd sent him for wine. But other than that, he'd sat watching, waiting, silently begging for feedback.

As he sat, he realized how much he had been neglecting her lately. She insisted he wasn't—that being there was enough —but she looked exhausted. The light that usually shone in her eyes seemed to have dimmed. Mama's mental state continued to deteriorate, and with it, Carrie's ability to have a positive outlook.

She hadn't said as much, but in the little bit of time she and Will spent talking about the situation, Will had sensed she was beginning to accept the reality that Doreen's Alzheimer's was progressing quickly.

Putting his hand on Carrie's knee, he squeezed gently.

She smirked but didn't take her focus off the page. "Stop pestering me."

"I'm not."

Lifting her gaze, she cocked a brow.

"I was thinking how amazing you are."

She laughed quietly and lowered his script. "Bribing the judge?"

"No," he said sincerely. "Recognizing that I've been a bit self-absorbed the last few weeks. Longer if I were honest. Now that I'm talking to my mom more often, I really don't want to get back into the cycle of ignoring the people who are important to me. I'm sorry I haven't been more present. I know you need help with Mama."

Gently touching his cheek, she drew a deep breath as the sadness in her eyes deepened. "I appreciate your support, but taking care of Doreen is on me, Will. I'm just... I have to start facing some truths that I've done my best to ignore for a really long time."

"Such as?"

"The Alzheimer's isn't the only thing going on here. Her diabetes is getting worse. She gets tired so easily these days. I think Natalie is right. I think she's been right all along. No matter how hard I try..." A sheen of tears coated her eyes. "No matter how hard I try, I do not have the money or the capability to keep her here much longer."

"Money isn't an issue," he said softly.

"Will—"

"You listen to me," he said with a tone that let her know he wasn't debating this. "Money is *not* an issue when it comes to keeping Mama in this house."

"I'm not taking charity from you."

Brushing her hair behind her ear, he gave her a smile. "Helping Mama live out her days in her home is not charity. It's me looking after someone I care about. If we need to hire another nurse, we'll hire another nurse. Whatever we need to do, we'll do it. Money isn't an issue."

"She's only sixty-four. She could live another twenty years."

"Yes, she could."

"You're going to pay for a nurse for twenty years? That isn't—"

He put his fingers to her lips to stop her argument. "When someone does something nice for you, Carolyn, you say thank you."

"Thank you." Dropping the papers, she leaned into him and hugged him tightly.

He kissed the top of her head. "You're welcome. Now..." Picking up the papers, he exhaled heavily. "Finish reading this, please. You're killing me."

———

CARRIE BLINKED SLOWLY as her eyes tried to focus on the numbers on the clock. Nearly three in the morning. Seconds passed before she jolted. Something had stirred her from her sleep, and that usually spelled trouble. Grabbing the monitor that she kept beside her bed, she squinted until she could confirm that Mama was tucked between the sheets, sleeping soundly.

Glancing over her shoulder, the dim moonlight revealed the other side to be empty. Will had gotten out of bed at some point. That must have been what caused her to awaken. Sliding her feet into her slippers, Carrie headed to the bathroom to check on him, but he wasn't there. Moving, silent as a ghost, she searched until she found him pacing in the den with his phone pressed to his ear.

When he turned, the smile on his face was as brilliant as she'd ever seen it. His eyes met hers, and the excitement there was obvious. He waved for her to come in and grabbed her hand as he listened to whatever he was being told.

"Thanks," he finally said. "Thank you so much. I'll call you back in the morning." He barely ended the call before dropping his phone onto the sofa and pulling Carrie into a big hug. "That was my agent."

Carrie's heart sank. That was all he had to say. Between the excitement on his face and the relief his voice held, she already understood what was happening.

Will leaned back and put his hands on her face as he laughed lightly. "He loves my script. It's still rough. There's still work to be done. But he loves it." Will shook his head. "He wants me back in LA right away so we can start working toward the next steps."

Yeah. That's what she'd feared.

"I don't want you to worry." The smile on his lips fell as he grew serious. "I'll only be gone for a few days. Maybe a few weeks at most. But I'll be back as soon as I can. And if you need me for anything," he said, "call. I'll be there."

For a moment, just a heartbeat, she believed him. However, he pulled back and grabbed his phone. When he looked at her again, the raw happiness had returned. "I gotta book a flight and pack a bag."

He held her hand as he led them upstairs. While he rambled about his project and all the people he wanted to work with, she sat on the edge of the bed smiling and nodding at the appropriate times, but she wasn't hearing him. She was silently reminding herself that she had known all along this day would come. She'd known his desire to go back to California would win out eventually.

The hours flew by until Carrie sat across from Will, sipping coffee as Mama chatted lightly over breakfast. Will had told Mama about his trip and, as he'd done to Carrie, promised he wouldn't be gone long. The more times he said that, the less Carrie believed him.

He was leaving. Going back to his life, back to the life that he loved. Something told her that once he stepped foot back in his world, this one would quickly fade from his mind. As she'd done all night, Carrie smiled at the appropriate times but couldn't force herself to engage in the conversation or genuinely share in his excitement.

Within hours, Natalie had shown up to stay with Mama, and Carrie was on her way to take Will to Des Moines International Airport to catch a flight to LA. They were silent most of the way, but as they exited the highway, Will looked at her.

"Do you think Mama understood?" he asked.

"I'll talk to her about it when I get back. She'll be fine."

"Do you understand?"

For the first time since he'd gotten off the phone with his agent, he sounded uncertain.

Carrie glanced at him and saw concern in his eyes. She did understand. This was his life. This was his dream. He had to chase it. He had to try. Asking him not to, asking him to stay with her, would be unfair.

However, the fear in her stomach was like a hot rock. He'd told her about how he'd missed spending time with his ill father because of his career. How his career had driven a wedge between him and his brother. She wasn't family. She was... She didn't know what she was, but she wasn't ready to ask either. Offering him a smile, she said, "Of course I do. And I'm happy for you, Will."

Putting his hand on her thigh, he squeezed it gently. "I'll call you tonight and let you know what I find out."

She stared straight ahead, clutching the steering wheel. "If you decide to do this, how long will it take to finish?"

"I don't know. I'll find out as much as I can before we talk, okay?"

"Okay."

A heavy silence felt like a wall between them until he asked, "What are you guys going to do while I'm gone?"

"Oh, the usual," she answered as lightly as she could. "Keg parties and orgies with the neighbors."

He chuckled. "Save that for when I get back. There is nothing I'd like to see more than Mama drinking from a beer bong."

Carrie laughed as she turned into the airport. "I'm sure there are pictures somewhere. I hear she was pretty wild in her younger days."

"I bet."

Her amusement faded as she followed the lane for passenger drop-off. Within moments, she was pulling up to the curb in front of sliding glass doors and watching people dragging suitcases.

"It's only for a few days," he said.

"You'll be back before you know it," she agreed. Releasing her seat belt, she pulled the lever to pop the trunk and climbed out of the car. Meeting him at the back of the car, she stood back as he grabbed his suitcase.

He set the bags down and slammed the trunk shut before looking at her. Closing the distance between them, Carrie slid her arms around Will's waist and leaned into him as he squeezed her tightly.

He pressed his lips gently to hers. "I'll call you tonight."

"I'll be waiting."

He picked up his bag and stepped onto the curb. Putting his fingers to his lips, he blew her a kiss. She offered him a smile and then turned and walked away.

CHAPTER 22

As Carrie feared, a few days of Will being in LA turned into a week, a week turned into two, and that turned into a month. His calling every night turned into every other, and that turned into every few days.

She didn't want to let her fear and doubt take over, but it was becoming more and more clear every day—she was losing him to his old life. When they did talk, the excitement in his voice was unmistakable. He was loving everything about what he was doing. He talked about things she didn't understand and people she didn't know. He did his best to keep her up-to-date and include her in what was happening, but she was too far out of the loop. She tried to care, tried to catch up, but the reality was, she had no idea how to talk to him about his project. She didn't speak that language or understand that culture. She didn't fit in that world.

When he asked about her day, all she could report was Doreen's deteriorating health. She didn't have a project or a passion to share. All she had were updates on Mama, and none of them were good. The difference between Carrie's and Will's lives was shining brightly now—as she had suspected it would the moment they'd parted ways.

No one was to blame. Will was in his world, and Carrie was in hers. And those two worlds were on opposite sides of the universe. Losing him saddened her, but the outcome had been inevitable. She'd always known this, just as she'd known that it was inevitable that she'd someday lose Doreen to her illness.

"You look a million miles away," Mama said, pulling Carrie from her thoughts as she aimlessly stirred the cup of hot tea she'd poured.

Carrie didn't know why she'd filled a mug. She hadn't wanted the drink, but she'd needed something to occupy her while she hovered around the kitchen while Mama searched high and low for something she couldn't name or describe. They'd been making a grocery list when Doreen had gotten distracted. That had been almost an hour prior.

Blinking back to the present, she tilted her head curiously at the strainer in Mama's hand but didn't comment on it. "Oh, just thinking."

"About what?"

She cleared her throat and lied. "Thanksgiving dinner. It's not that far away, you know. We should add that to our shopping list."

Doreen's eyes lit with happiness as she put the strainer down. "Oh, let's have the works. Turkey, stuffing, cranberry sauce, potatoes, pies. I want it all."

"Who's going to eat all that stuff, Mama? It's just the two of us." As soon as the words left her, Carrie's smile fell. She looked at the older woman with horror. She waited, but Mama didn't seem to realize that Carrie hadn't included Mike.

"And homemade rolls," Mama continued. "We haven't had homemade rolls in so long."

"Rolls would be great."

"Will Natalie be here this year?"

"Probably for dessert. She hates her mother's pumpkin pie."

"I don't blame her," Mama said. "I tasted it once at a bake sale. The crust was terrible."

Carrie laughed when Doreen pulled her lips tight and shook her head. Carrie marveled that the woman could remember how bad a pie tasted, when this morning she'd looked at the nurse who'd been assisting her for months as if the woman was a stranger.

When her cell phone rang, Carrie couldn't help the way her heart lifted a little at the sound of Will's ringtone. "Add whatever you want to our shopping list, Mama. I'll be right back."

She waited until she was stepping out of the kitchen before answering. "Hey," she said warmly.

"Whatcha doing?" Will asked.

"Mama and I were planning Thanksgiving dinner. Should we expect you?"

"When is that?"

"Two weeks."

He sighed heavily. "Ah, babe, I don't know."

She had been expecting that, but his rejection still cut at her heart. "Well, what are you going to do?"

"I usually crash somebody's party. That's how we do it out here."

She could hear the smile in his voice. She didn't smile in return. "How's the project going?"

"Great. It's going so great." As always when he talked of his work, his excitement was evident, but she couldn't bring herself to share in his happiness this time. "We're still working on getting some investors. It's coming together."

She sat on the sofa in the den. "When do you start filming?"

"We're a long way from that, I'm afraid."

She closed her eyes tightly. "Any idea when we'll see you?"

"I don't know. I know I promised to be home right away"—his tone was full of regret—"but I really didn't expect this ball to get rolling so fast. There's so much going on between this and promoting Donnie's shit. I feel like my head is spinning."

"I don't mean to add to it," she said quietly.

"You're not. I miss you. Maybe you and Mama can come out here. I'll have dinner catered," he offered. "You won't have to lift a finger."

Carrie dismissed the idea with a laugh. "That sounds nice, but I don't think busy airports and traffic would be advisable for her."

"How is she?"

"She's moving a little more slowly these days. She seems to have lost the connection she had made that helped her recognize Jenny. She keeps treating her more like an inn guest than a helper. She wants to keep serving her drinks and telling her about the history of the inn."

"I'm sorry."

"Well... It was bound to happen."

"And you?"

"I'm okay," she lied. And it was a lie. She hadn't been okay for some time. She was sad that they were drifting apart and devastated that she couldn't do anything more to help Doreen. The threads of her life were fraying faster than she could mend them. Without Will there, she felt helpless. And alone.

"I am going to be home soon." His voice was the same one he used when he was holding her tight, reassuring her on those particularly difficult days. The tone wasn't nearly as soothing when it was on the other end of a telephone.

"Yeah. That'll be nice."

"Maybe I could pop in for Thanksgiving and head out the next day."

She closed her eyes tightly. Oh, how she wanted to see him, but not as a fly-through. "I don't know, Will. I don't want to confuse Mama. I don't think it would be good for her if you are just coming and going. She probably wouldn't understand that."

"Yeah. I don't want to confuse her," he agreed.

Carrie listened to the silence for a moment before clearing her throat. "I need to go. We were getting ready to head to the store."

"Hey," he called before she could hang up. "I miss you like crazy."

"I miss you too. We'll talk soon." She hesitated a moment before ending the call.

Talking soon didn't have the same meaning it had when he'd first left. Talking soon now seemed to be whenever he could squeeze her in. She tried not to feel bitter about that, but anger and resentment tugged at her mind when she thought about the situation too much.

Exhaling her frustration, she walked back into the kitchen. "What do you say we splurge and have lunch while we're in town?" Carrie's stomach dropped when she realized the kitchen was empty. The purse that she'd left on the counter was gone. "Oh, God," she muttered. Not only had she put the checkbook in the bag, but she'd dropped her car keys in there as well.

She ran through the house and onto the front porch in time to see the leaves in the driveway starting to settle. Carrie immediately called Natalie. When Mama pulled these kinds of stunts, she always let Natalie convince her to come home. Sinking her teeth into her lip so she didn't cry, she waited for Natalie to answer and explained that, yet again, Mama had taken the car and disappeared.

Natalie had the list of Mama's go-to places memorized—the grocery store, the salon, and her favorite restaurant were the most likely stops. If Natalie didn't find her at one of those, she'd go to a few of Mama's friends' homes. After that, the panic could officially set in.

Walking back into the empty house, Carrie looked around and suddenly felt overwhelmed. Not only by Mama but by Will. Mostly Will, if she were honest with herself. He'd left, and she had a growing sense that he wouldn't be coming back. Sinking onto the stairs, Carrie sat, phone in hand, and waited until the front door opened almost an hour later.

"This is getting to be a habit," Natalie pointed out after she escorted Mama into the house. "What happened?"

"We were making a grocery list, and I got a phone call. I was distracted. Thank you for bringing her home."

"What about your car?"

"I'll call my dad. He'll pick it up. What was she doing when you found her?"

"Shopping. I convinced her that you needed her to come home right away. By the time we got here, she thought we'd been out to get our hair done."

Carrie closed her eyes and rubbed the crease in her brow that was threatening to become permanent.

Natalie sighed as she squeezed Carrie's shoulder. "Honey, where is your head these days?"

"I don't know. I'm tired."

"No word from Will, huh?"

"That was the distraction." Carrie frowned. "He called."

"When is he coming back?"

"I don't know. Let's get in the kitchen before she runs away again."

Natalie held firm to Carrie's shoulder. "Are you okay?"

Carrie's spirits sank even lower. "Can we not do this right now? I'd like to make sure Mama doesn't escape. Twice in one day might do me in."

She sensed Natalie's gaze on her as she fixed them all tea and Doreen rambled on about how Mike needed to come in from the fields. An occasional glance toward her friend confirmed the concern on Natalie's face. Carrie wanted to slam one of the teacups down and scream.

Yes, Mama was doing worse. Yes, she was becoming more difficult to handle. Yes, Carrie was overwhelmed and on the verge of breaking down.

But she didn't. She ignored Natalie's concern and Mama's incessant talking and eased into a chair at the table. She smiled sadly as Mama started telling one of her stories. It was one that both Carrie and Natalie had heard a thousand times, but neither stopped her.

When their cups were empty, they helped Mama upstairs, tucked her into bed, and silently walked back downstairs.

Natalie gathered her purse from the table by the front door and gave her friend a hug. "I'm here if you need me" was all she said before leaving.

Carrie pulled her keys from her pocket and bolted the door that would keep Mama a prisoner inside her own home. Walking into the kitchen, she double-checked to make sure the back door was bolted as well. Once she was convinced

Doreen couldn't escape again, Carrie sat down at the table and sighed loudly.

———

WILL LOOKED AT HIS WATCH. Damn it. He wasn't sure how this always seemed to happen, but the hours seemed to slip away before he noticed. Given the time difference between California and Iowa, he knew Carrie would be in bed. He didn't want to wake her, or worse, wake Mama and give Carrie more problems than she already had. Leaning back in his desk chair, he ran his hands over his eyes.

He'd thought being in front of the camera was exhausting. Taking on production was damn near killing him. That was no excuse. He knew it was no excuse. He needed to be more aware, more considerate. Carrie had sounded so completely worn down the last time they'd spoken.

Looking at his phone, he noticed the date and realized that had been days ago.

He hadn't called her in days.

But to be fair, she hadn't called him either.

Pushing himself up, he took his phone with him to the kitchen and filled a wineglass. His wide-open contemporary home seemed so cold now. So empty. Hollow. That was the word that had first come to mind when he'd returned. His home seemed hollow. Standing in front of the floor-to-ceiling windows, he looked out at the view. The vision of the lights twinkling below had been the reason he'd bought this house. He could look down on the world from his living room. Somehow that had seemed so damned important back then.

Now, the lights were a distraction from the view he wanted to see. Bright stars twinkling above wide-open fields. A fire burning in front of him, keeping him warm. A soft hand to hold.

"Screw it," he breathed as he pulled his phone from his pocket.

It was well after Carrie's bedtime, but Will didn't care. He needed to hear her voice. He needed the reassurance that she was waiting for him and to reassure her that he really was working to get back to her as quickly as he could. Before he could find her name in his contacts, the phone rang. He frowned, debating if he should ignore the call from his agent in lieu of calling Carrie.

He didn't. He answered with the intent of brushing his agent off as quickly as possible. However, within minutes, he was sitting at his desk, scrolling through his script to resolve a question.

CHAPTER 23

Thanksgiving had brought a dark cloud with it. The holiday hadn't had the warmth and cozy feeling of family. Will was in California, and Mama had sat with a blank stare. The entire day had been a juggling act of emotions. Carrie had sent her dad away as soon as the meal had finished. She hadn't wanted to deal with him insisting over and over that Carrie was no longer able to care for Doreen.

He'd told her long ago that it was time to put Mama in a home, and Carrie wasn't up for an argument. Instead, she'd sent him home, put Mama to bed early, and then sat with a glass of wine, silently cursing Will for abandoning her.

She'd considered calling him but hadn't wanted to disrupt his plans. Actually, truth be told, she hadn't wanted to hear how happy he was without her. She hadn't wanted to hear one more damn word about his project and how all his dreams were coming true while her life was crumbling around her. Instead, she'd cried herself to sleep and woken up with dread.

As ten a.m. approached, Carrie once again looked at the

monitor. Mama still hadn't woken. She hadn't stirred. Not once.

The silence in the house had taken on an eerie effect. The air was heavy with the dread that had felt suffocating since Carrie rolled out of bed. Every breath she took seemed more difficult than the last. The coffee in the mug that was cradled between her hands had long since turned cold while she stared out the window at the overcast sky. The wind blew the fallen leaves around the backyard, and every now and then she thought she saw a few flakes of snow dancing through the air.

Sighing heavily, she walked to the sink and dumped her coffee, looking down at what remained of the Thanksgiving dishes in the sink. She'd been too tired the night before to empty the dishwasher and reload it, so she'd left them in the sink. Seeing the dried cranberry sauce stuck to a dish, she wished she hadn't been so lazy.

Then again, she hadn't really been lazy. She'd been exhausted emotionally, physically, and mentally. Something told her this day wasn't going to be any better than the one before. Something told her this day was going to be worse. Much worse.

Never in all the years that she had known Doreen Gable had the woman slept past eight a.m.

When Carrie looked at the clock again, it was a few minutes after ten, and she knew she couldn't linger in the kitchen any longer. She walked to the bottom of the stairs and looked up at the landing. She stood there for several moments before putting her hand on the railing and pulling herself up the stairs.

Standing outside Mama's bedroom door, she closed her eyes and took a deep breath, bracing herself for what she knew to be true before knocking on the wood. "Mama?"

The woman didn't answer.

Swallowing hard, Carrie pushed the door open, and tears sprang to her eyes at the sight of the woman still curled up under the blankets.

"Hey," she called out cheerfully as she marched to the window and pulled the curtains back. "Come on, sleepyhead, time to rise and shine."

Turning, she looked at the bed. Mama hadn't stirred. Carrie went to the closet and started sorting through clothes. "You need to dress warmly today. It's starting to snow."

Carrie grabbed a heavy cardigan from the closet and turned, hoping to see Doreen glaring at her—irritated at being woken up. She still hadn't moved. Carrie's heart grew even heavier. Slowly walking to the bed, Carrie stared at the lump under the blankets, and tears fell down her cheeks.

"Don't do this to me, Mama," she whispered. "Please don't do this." She put her hand on Doreen's shoulder and gently nudged her with no response. Closing her eyes, Carrie exhaled loudly, resigned to the truth.

Moving to the window, Carrie fiddled with the sweater in her hands for a long time as she stared out at the trees. "Mike died, Mama. Almost four years ago. He walked into a convenience store and some kid came in behind him with a gun. The doctor told me he didn't feel a thing, that he was dead the moment the bullet hit him."

The snow was falling more steadily and would start accumulating soon, leaving a layer that would hide the world until it melted away. Knowing how the Iowa winters went, Carrie suspected that wouldn't be until spring. Mama would hate having people trek through the snow to bury her. She'd hate that they'd be cold. She'd hate the inconvenience snow could bring to a funeral.

"Christmas is coming," Carrie whispered. "Maybe this is the year we'll keep it small. I know." She smiled. "We say that every year, and every year we drag everything out and go all out, but maybe this year we really should keep it small. It's just the two of us, after all." She choked on the words.

Snatching a tissue from the box on the nightstand, Carrie wiped her eyes and nose and took a deep, calming breath. She didn't have time to stand there and cry. There was so much to be done. So much to plan for. So much to think about. Even though she should have, she had avoided planning Mama's funeral. She hadn't had the heart. She'd regret that now, she knew, but some things she didn't have the strength to face until she had to.

She'd done that with Will. She'd done that with Mama's illness. Why wouldn't she continue that trend now? Carrie sniffed when Natalie called out her name. She hadn't been expecting company, but she was glad someone had shown up or she likely would have stood staring out the window all day.

Avoiding the inevitable.

"Care?" Natalie asked from behind her.

Carrie swallowed and slowly turned.

Natalie's brow was creased, but the moment realization hit her, her eyes widened and her mouth fell open. "Oh no."

"Can you call someone?" Carrie asked in a voice that sounded emotionless to her ears. "I don't think I can."

Natalie moved to the bed, looking down at the bundle under the covers. "Oh no, Carrie. What happened?"

"She just didn't wake up. Can you call?"

"Come with me."

"I should stay. She wouldn't want to be alone."

"Carrie," she whispered.

"Please," Carrie begged on a whisper. "Please, make the call."

Swallowing, Natalie nodded. "Okay. Okay. I'll be right back."

As soon as Natalie left the room, Carrie put her face in her hands and sobbed.

———

WILL PULLED his phone from his pocket when Carrie's ringtone sang out to him. The old theme song from *Rocky* grew louder as he pulled the phone from his pocket. He thought the inspiring song suited her even though she'd laughed at his choice, but he'd explained that she was stronger than she realized and tougher than anyone would expect.

Even so, he was concerned after her second attempt to reach him in such a short time.

"Will," Marvin, his new assistant, said. "Are you coming?"

Will silenced his phone, making a mental note to call Carrie the moment he had a chance. Following Marvin into the meeting, he smiled and shook hands as he was introduced and then sat in a plush leather seat, preparing to have smoke blown up his ass.

He only half listened. While he was excited about the project, the semantics they were discussing were things Will didn't care much about. Marvin was the one he had hired to deal with the minor details. Will wanted to get into the work of making his movie a reality. He didn't want to deal with all the numbers and the ass-kissing. But he'd made the mistake of insisting that he be involved on every level. He wanted to have a say in everything so his movie was his vision and not someone else's.

He'd officially turned into one of *those* writers, and this was his first project.

He'd felt so good at the start of this. He'd felt accomplished and in control. Those feelings hadn't lasted long. Now he felt like he was drowning in details and meetings and brownnosing.

This was something he'd wanted for so long. And he was living it. Yet he was miserable. The hustling from meeting to meeting. The networking and meet and greets were squeezed in between interviews about the movie he'd made with Juliet Ramirez—the project that he'd hated every moment of making.

The project that had only been tolerable because of a beautiful innkeeper and her delusional mother-in-law. Damn it. He had promised Carrie this wouldn't happen. He'd promised he'd be home within days...then weeks. Now it was closing in on two months since he'd left her standing at the airport. He barely found time to call her.

He wouldn't blame her if the reason she had been calling was to break up with him. To tell him to not bother calling her or making lame promises anymore. He deserved to be kicked to the proverbial curb for his neglect. He should send her flowers. And candies. And something for Mama. Mama deserved an apology from him too.

He didn't realize he was nervously tapping his fingers until Marvin subtly nudged his arm.

"We were talking about casting," he said to Will, pulling him back to the meeting.

Will laughed softly, pushing thoughts of Carrie and Doreen from his mind so he could focus on the task at hand.

———

CARRIE FROWNED as she closed her phone. She'd called Will twice. The first time she'd left a message asking him to call her back. This time she'd simply hung up when his voice mail answered. Natalie and Jenny had called almost everyone else: friends, extended family who they rarely heard from, and members of the church and other groups Mama used to attend.

Carrie's dad had come over and called the funeral home that had taken care of Mike. Carrie was grateful for the three of them stepping in and taking over, but it left her with time to think, and she was beginning to realize that wasn't a good thing. Sticking her phone in her pocket, she looked around the kitchen. Before long, it was going to be overflowing with cakes, casseroles, and every kind of salad imaginable. People would be filing into the house to pay their respects to the woman who had passed away.

Carrie wanted to cook, she wanted to bake, to create something to focus on, but she knew it was pointless. Whatever she made would never be touched. Instead, she reached under the sink and pulled out a bottle of cleaner and sprayed the counter. Taking a towel, she started scrubbing. She moved the toaster to the side, carelessly brushing the crumbs to the floor and spraying the countertop again. She moved the blender, then the mixer, then the coffeemaker.

When the counter was clean, she started on the refrigerator. Opening the door, she looked at the food inside. The fridge was stuffed with the uneaten Thanksgiving feast. She'd have to get rid of it all to make room for the food that was coming. Standing there, looking inside at all the containers, Carrie felt overwhelmed.

Reaching in, she pulled out a bowl and looked at what was left of the cottage cheese Mama had had with her lunch the day before. Carrie tilted the bowl from side to side, watching the contents shift for a moment before turning and throwing it with an angry grunt. The dish shattered against the wall, sending shards of glass and curds to the floor.

Turning back to the refrigerator, Carrie pulled out an uneaten pumpkin pie, and angry tears spilled down her cheeks. The pan slammed into the wall, denting the deep-red paint and splattering it with the orange insides of the pie. That was followed by a casserole dish full of homemade mashed potatoes.

Natalie ran into the kitchen. "What the hell are you doing?"

Carrie threw one last dish. She thought it must have been gravy by the way it splattered. She choked out a sob as clumps of food slid down the wall. "Cleaning out the fridge."

Natalie looked at the mess of broken glass mixed with splattered food and frowned. "You could have asked for help."

CHAPTER 24

N atalie walked into the kitchen as Carrie tossed her phone down. "Still no answer, huh?"

"No. Nothing."

"Do you have any other way to reach him?"

"No."

"What about Grant? I could give him a call."

Carrie tilted her head and narrowed her eyes. "Why... Why do you have Grant's number?"

Natalie widened her eyes. "Oh. Um. You know...when you were in the hospital and everyone was so worried..."

Carrie debated pressing her on the weak answer, but she didn't have the energy. Closing her eyes, she rubbed them and realized how irritated they had become. "I wish I could sleep."

Natalie walked to the counter and snatched up a bottle of pills. "The doctor called in a prescription for you. Your dad picked it up." She opened the bottle. "Take one, for God's sake."

Carrie swallowed a pill, and then Natalie pulled her to her feet and walked with her upstairs. At her door, Carrie paused, looking down the hallway at the room where Mama had died sometime the night before. "The house is too quiet."

"Enjoy it while you can. It'll be a madhouse tomorrow."

Carrie lay down, and Natalie tucked a blanket around her. "If Will calls—"

"I'll wake you," Natalie promised.

Carrie slept through the night, waking up the next morning amazed at how many hours had passed. Heaving a sigh, she looked out the window. The day was overcast and gloomy. She wondered if she could get away with taking another of those pills and sleeping through the day as well.

Though it was appealing, she knew if she gave in to the urge now, she might again, and weeks could pass before she managed to crawl from the bed.

One moment, one step, one day at a time, that's what Mama had told her when Mike died. That was the only way to get through, and in this moment, she needed to get her butt out of bed. Pushing the covers back, she forced herself to get up and face the day. She was certain Will would have called her by now. She was eager to find out his plans for coming back.

That was the last thought she had before drifting off. When she woke, the sun was shining, and Carrie felt like she'd been in a coma for weeks. She felt hungover from the pill she'd taken. That was exactly why she didn't take pills. She slept too deeply and wouldn't hear if Mama called out to her.

She sat up and froze when she realized where her mind had gone. Mama hadn't called out to her. Mama was gone.

Closing her eyes, Carrie let out a shaky breath and refused to let her tears form. There would be plenty of time for that. Right now, she needed to hydrate and get some food in her stomach to ward off the effects of the pill she'd taken. In the kitchen, she found Natalie already up, reheating a breakfast casserole that someone had brought the day before. "You're up early."

"Well, I didn't sleep nearly as well as you did."

"I didn't think it was possible to sleep as well as I did. Even so, I don't like feeling so out of it this morning." She waited, but Natalie didn't tell her what she wanted to hear. "Did Will call?"

Natalie's face said it all. "No, honey, he didn't." She frowned as Carrie sank onto a stool. "He will. You left him a message, right?"

"Yeah."

"So he'll call."

She reached for a coffee mug and tried to smile. She failed. "I could use him right now."

"Maybe you should call him again."

Carrie looked at the clock. "He'll still be sleeping."

"I think this is a call worth waking up for." Reaching into her pocket, she handed Carrie her phone.

Taking her mug with her, Carrie sat on the sofa in the den. She sighed in frustration when the call went directly to his voice mail. "It's me again," she said after the tone. "I need you to call me. As soon as you can. It's important." She hung up and dropped her phone on the coffee table. "Where the hell are you?"

———

WILL WASN'T sure how he'd ended up in New York. His days were a bit of a blur. He couldn't remember the last time his life had been so hectic. This was a good kind of hectic, though. This wasn't the hectic of trying to find work, trying to reassure producers he was still a player in the movie business. This was the kind of hectic he needed his life to be.

He was moving beyond the mundane meetings and getting into the good stuff. Other than this trip to New York. This trip was all about the movie he'd filmed with Juliet Ramirez. They had several interviews and dinners lined up. He'd enjoyed promoting his work a lot more when it was work he had cared about. But he had to get through this.

Get through a few parties, a few questions, a few false smiles, and he could get back to focusing on what was important—his project and finding time to answer his damn backlog of phone calls. At the top of that list was the woman who had called yet again this morning.

Her voice let him know something was wrong. He was certain he knew what it was.

Carrie was furious with him. He hadn't returned her calls. Hadn't sent those flowers he'd intended to send. Only now, he was beginning to think he was going to have to buy out a florist to get back in her good graces. And he'd do it too. He'd make things right with her, but he couldn't do it half-assed.

He'd find time. He'd make time.

Just as soon as he had a moment to breathe.

CHAPTER 25

Sensing someone in the door to the den, Carrie slowly opened her eyes. Natalie gave her a reassuring smile. Carrie knew she looked like hell. The black dress she'd worn to Mama's funeral did nothing but highlight how pale she was and how dark the circles under her eyes had become.

She had considered caking her face with makeup, but that would only make her look worse. Streaked foundation and mascara had never been on trend.

"He's still not answering." Carrie dropped her phone on the couch and exhaled heavily. "I don't know why I keep calling."

Natalie had done an amazing job at not bad-mouthing Will until one of Mama's friends mentioned a picture she'd seen on the front page of a tabloid. There were photos of Will with one very lovely Juliet Ramirez on his arm at several different events over the last few days. Quite a bit of buzz was brewing about whether or not the two were dating, and the friend had wanted to know if Carrie had suspected anything while the stars were staying at the inn.

Carrie had smiled stiffly, shaken her head, and gone straight to the office with Natalie on her heels. They had found the photos online, and Carrie had broken down in tears.

Several hours later, with an empty house, Carrie leaned back on the sofa and the photos ran through her mind again, only stopping when Natalie stood over her looking concerned.

"I made you some tea," Natalie offered. "That's what Mama would do, right?"

Carrie's heart grew heavy as she nodded. "Thanks."

Setting the cup on the coffee table, Natalie frowned deeply. "Have you thought about what you're going to do?"

"About the estate or about Will?"

"Both, I guess."

"Well, I can't afford the estate, so I guess I will sell the house and...if Will hasn't dumped me without bothering to let me know, which I suspect he has, I'm pretty sure him going to parties with Juliet Ramirez while I buried Mama was a deal breaker."

"I'm sorry, babe." Natalie moved to the sofa and put her arm around her friend.

Carrie shook her head. "Don't be. It's not like we ever could have worked out anyway. He'd only been here a few weeks and wanted to go back to his real life. It's better that he left now instead of, you know, five years of marriage and three kids from now."

"There is no such thing as fairy-tale endings anyway."

"No, there's not. Thanks for my tea," Carrie said, changing the subject.

"I'm here for you through this."

"I know. And I am so thankful for that."

Natalie gripped Carrie's hand. "You'll always have me."

"Maybe I should marry you."

"Maybe." Natalie smiled. "Our children would be way better-looking than his."

"I don't know if I'd go that far. He's pretty cute."

"Hey," Natalie protested, making Carrie genuinely smile for the first time in days.

Her smile faded quickly though. "I kept telling myself not to count on him, that we were too different, but I didn't expect things to end like this. I expected him to at least tell me he was over me. I don't know how to process this disappearing act of his."

"Try not to dwell on it. You have so much else to deal with right now. And he's not worth the heartache that you'll find if you go looking for answers."

"It was piss-poor timing on his part."

"I know. But you have to deal with what you can handle, and you can't handle everything."

"So I should just get over it? Is that what you're saying?"

"No, but you need to recognize that some guy who would drop off the face of the earth without so much as a word when you've told him that you need him is not worth the effort. Let it go and deal with the things that can be dealt with."

"Like selling Mama's house," she said in a strained voice.

"If you want to keep it—"

"I can't. I could never afford the upkeep and taxes."

"Don't make that decision right now."

"I made it a long time ago, Nat. I was able to keep her here. That's what was important," Carrie said as tears filled her eyes. "I can't afford it. I wish I could. I'd stay here forever, but I can't. The time has come. I have to let go."

"I'm sorry."

Carrie shrugged. "It's okay. I'll be okay."

Natalie dug in her pocket and produced the prescription.

Carrie almost resisted, but she was exhausted, and even if she knew she'd feel like hell the next day, she held out her hand.

"Take this now and by the time you finish your tea, you'll be ready to crash," Natalie said.

Carrie chuckled. "I'm ready to crash now."

"I know," Natalie said as Carrie took the pill. "I can see it. I'm worried about you."

Squeezing Natalie's hand, Carrie wished she could reassure her. Instead, she redirected the conversation. Natalie's job was a safe topic. Mama and Will had nothing to do with Natalie's job. Within half an hour, Carrie was feeling tired enough to make her way upstairs.

She looked at her phone one more time after changing and brushing her teeth but opted not to try Will again. She wasn't going to continue setting herself up for that disappointment. Falling into bed, she stared at the ceiling, watching shadows play until she drifted off.

Sometime later, Carrie rolled over, cursing whoever dared to call in the middle of the night. Finally, when she woke up enough to recognize the ringtone, her heart seized in her chest. She weighed answering until it stopped ringing, sending Will's call to her voice mail. She tried to swallow, but her throat was tight and her chest was heavy with anxiety.

She was still holding her phone, her hands trembling, when he called again. She hesitated but finally answered. "What?" she demanded, her voice shaking from a mixture of nervousness and fury.

He exhaled heavily on the other end of the line. "I know I'm an ass. I am so sorry that I haven't called. I have been so busy. I tried to—"

"She died," Carrie blurted out.

"What?" he asked, breathless, as if the air had been robbed from his lungs.

"Mama. She died."

"Oh my God, Carrie. Oh, baby, I'm so sorry." He sounded every bit as sincere as he had all the times when he'd promised her that nothing would change between them. "What happened?"

"She died in her sleep. Sometime during the night, I don't know when. She looked peaceful." Carrie ignored the tears that started burning her eyes. She was used to how tears sprung up every time she spoke of Doreen's death. "I think she's finally where she wants to be. I like to think her mind is finally whole again and she's with her family. As she should be. She was buried in the plot next to Mike."

"I'm sorry. I should have been there."

"Yes," she stated bluntly, "you should have been."

"I didn't know."

"Well. You didn't return my calls, Will. If you'd returned *one* call." Carrie closed her eyes and silently chastised herself. She'd gone over and over in her mind a thousand times what she would say if she ever talked to him again. Every time she practiced it, she'd managed to stay calm and cool. However, the reality of hearing his voice twisted her anger into something that was out of her control.

"I know. I know. I could tell that you needed to talk to me. I could tell something was wrong, but I—"

"Had to take Juliet Ramirez to a few parties?"

He sighed again. "It wasn't like that. I can't ignore her when I see her, Carrie. We'll have to work together to promote the movie when it releases."

Carrie nodded. "And I had to bury my mother." She closed her eyes against the silence, hating that she wanted to reach out to him, to smooth over the words she knew had stung him, but she remained silent as well.

"I'm almost done here." He used that damned soft tone of his—the one that felt like his words were caressing her soul. "I'll be home soon."

"No," she said with a hard tone that she didn't recognize. "Do not come here."

"Carrie."

"You promised. You promised to be here, Will. You promised to help me through this, and when I needed you the most, you were off doing who the hell knows what with that woman who treated Mama like trash."

"It wasn't like that."

"What was it like, Will? Was it like when your father was sick?" The silence on the line was thick and heavy. Her arrow had struck the mark. She'd cut him deep. Good. He deserved it. "You let me count on you," she said with a cool tone. "You let me depend on you, and then you left me. I needed you, and you weren't here."

"I know," he whispered.

"No. You don't know. You don't have a clue, you selfish bastard. You should have just left me alone. You had no right to come in here and make me care about you, make me *need* you, and then walk away. You have no idea how cruel that was."

"Carrie—"

"I don't want you here. I don't even want to think about you."

"I know I messed up—"

The laugh that left her was so bitter, it was almost frightening. "You can't even begin to imagine."

"You know what you mean to me, Carrie. What Mama meant to me."

"Don't." She closed her eyes against his words. "I have to pack up this house, sell what I can't keep, sell the house. I have to sell my home, Will. I have to leave this place where my only sense of family has ever been. I do not have the time or the energy to deal with you and your oversized ego."

"Carrie," he pleaded, "I'm sorry. I'm so sorry."

"Don't call me again." Ending the call, she dropped the phone on her nightstand and snatched several tissues out of the box, covering her face as a sob escaped her.

———

WILL DIDN'T SLEEP after Carrie hung up on him. He didn't even try. He spent all those hours replaying her words, the months he spent at the inn, and the long year before that. His brother had said similar words when Will had shown up for their father's funeral. His brother had called him a selfish bastard too.

Coming to see his brother was right had taken months, and processing the guilt had taken longer. Hell, he was still processing it. Hearing those words from Carrie, the woman who had always been so understanding and forgiving, had been a harsh slap of reality Will had needed but would give anything to have not heard.

The anger in her voice, the pain and the suffering, had been so obvious. Even in her voice mails, he had heard something was wrong. Why hadn't he called her back? Why had he allowed himself to put her on the back burner of his career?

Because that was how he was, he realized somewhere around

three a.m. He was a selfish bastard who always put his career ahead of the people he cared about. He was a self-centered Hollywood elite who stepped on people to stay in the spotlight. That was another bitter pill his brother had forced him to swallow.

He was everything he hated about the movie industry and the superficial people who fought to survive there. Staying prominent had been more important than his ailing father, and it had been more important than Carrie.

The realization made his stomach turn and bile burn up his throat.

By two in the morning, Will had beaten himself up to the point of becoming numb to his own self-loathing. By four a.m., he was trying to sort out what the hell he could do to make things right. And by six a.m., he was at the airport climbing onto a plane headed not to Des Moines, but to Chicago. The closest airport to the little town where he'd grown up, the town where his family still resided.

Several hours later, Will parked his rental car in his brother's driveway and looked at the small ranch where Brad and his wife had lived since their first year of marriage. That was over twenty-five years. For twenty-five years, Brad and Anne had stayed in one place, raised two kids, and had supported and loved each other through all the ups and downs life brought.

Will's life had been parties, traveling, and awards shows. Fake friends, faker lovers, and business associates who disappeared once they got what they'd needed from him. Even his nieces, whom he loved dearly, tended to only reach out when they wanted VIP concert tickets or money their parents hadn't been willing to lend them. Brad and Anne? Will hadn't spoken to them since...Christmas of the year before. Almost a year. And that had been out of holiday obligation.

Part of Will wanted to back out of the driveway and leave

before he had to deal with this confrontation. The other part of him knew if he didn't face this now, he never would. He and his family would continue to grow apart.

Taking one big, deep breath for courage, Will climbed from the car and headed for his brother's front door...and hopefully toward mending the first of many bridges he'd burned.

CHAPTER 26

The humming of the road beneath his tires hypnotized Will as he drove. Though his eyes were seeing the path before him, his mind was on the litany of mistakes he'd made.

He'd called Carrie on Christmas morning, hoping the spirit of the season would grant him a little clemency. She hadn't answered. After moping his way through New Year's Eve, he'd finally confessed to his mom and brother that he hadn't only hurt them with his inability to put his career aside when needed. He'd hurt Carrie—someone who had come to mean the world to him.

They had listened, his mom had even been a bit sympathetic, but in the end, his brother told him what Will had known all along: he would never fix the damage he'd done to his relationship with a phone call. His mom had agreed. If Will wanted to make things right with Carrie, he had to face her. No matter how hard that might be.

He couldn't remember the last time he'd felt so much fear gripping his heart. Facing his family again after so long had been difficult, but he'd known, at the end of the day, they were his family. They would find a way to forgive him. They'd accept him back into their fold and find a way to move forward.

He didn't have that guarantee with Carrie. She had no reason to forgive him. They had no unbreakable ties. Will couldn't remember a time in his life when he needed forgiveness as much as he did now. He also couldn't remember a time when he deserved forgiveness less.

When the GPS told him to prepare to turn, Will's heart dropped to the pit of his stomach. As he reached his destination, the guilt in his gut started to consume him. He felt like he was being swallowed by it until he couldn't feel anything but the shame of his actions. After parking his car, he grabbed a piece of paper from the passenger seat and memorized the notes he'd jotted down. Swallowing hard, Will climbed out of the car with the dozen roses he'd bought on his way into town.

He slowly walked across the light dusting of snow that covered the ground until he stopped and looked at the stone at his feet.

Doreen Elaine Gable.

Tears burned Will's eyes, and his guilt tightened into a lump in his throat. "I'm sorry," he managed to say. Looking around the cemetery, he gathered his thoughts before continuing, "I'm not sure if you can hear me or not, Mama, but if you can, please forgive me. And if you have any sway," he said with a slight smile, "maybe you can convince Carrie to give me another chance."

He put the flowers on her headstone and ran his fingers over the engraving that identified the woman buried there. "If she forgives me, I promise I'll be better. I swear to you, I'll take care of her. I won't let her down again."

———

CHRISTMAS AND NEW Year's Day passed with as little bother as Carrie could manage. Her spirits hadn't lifted since Doreen had died. If anything, she guessed they'd sunk lower than ever. Settling the estate had happened more quickly than she'd expected. Then she'd had to get the house on the market. As soon as the time had come, a cloud had settled over her soul. Memories lived in every room. This home was all she had left of the family she'd loved so much, and she was finding it more and more difficult to think about leaving her home.

It was too late, though. She'd accepted an offer and signed the papers.

She'd considered keeping the property more than once. She and Natalie had discussed remodeling a portion of the house to have the tearoom that Carrie had dreamed of so many times before, but ultimately Carrie knew she could never manage to make the money she'd need to keep the house.

The only reason she'd been able to afford to stay this long was because of the unexpected guests she'd housed for three months. Hollywood's elite.

Will.

She shook the thought of him from her mind before missing him could take hold of her heart. She still thought of him—it was impossible not to when his face was on the television and every gossip rag at the grocery store checkout. Rumor had it, he had backed out of a project and his friends were concerned for his future in Hollywood. At first, she'd been concerned too, but she refused to read more than headlines, which she convinced herself she wasn't really reading— simply glancing at.

Damn it. He'd consumed her thoughts again.

Moving to the window, she looked out over the property and focused on her life. Her real life. The life that she couldn't simply walk away from.

For the first time since the foundation had been laid, this house had left the Gable family. Carrie knew Mama would hate it, but what choice did she have? The house and everything in it, as negotiated, now belonged to someone else. Someone else would be living here, cooking in this kitchen, laughing in the den, drinking wine around the fire pit.

She looked around the kitchen until her gaze fell on the island, where she'd spent so much time with Doreen. "I'm sorry, Mama," she said sadly. "I can't do this alone."

"Maybe you don't have to."

Startled, Carrie looked to the door, and her sorrow instantly hardened into anger as she met Will's timid gaze. "What are you doing here?"

He let his breath out slowly and shrugged. "I was hoping we could talk."

Carrie roughly wiped her eyes, hating that he'd caught her crying. "I don't have anything to say to you."

"I screwed up, Carrie."

She scoffed and turned away from him.

"I know," he said, "I did what I promised I wouldn't do. I let the distance take me away from you. I'm sorry."

Turning back to him, she shook her head. "I don't need your apology. I don't. I need some peace and quiet in my life. I need to process everything that is happening. I don't need you distracting me."

"I'm not trying to distract you."

"That's what you do," she said with a hard edge to her tone. "Don't you see? That's all you were. That's all we were. A distraction. Something to take our minds off what was happening around us."

"We were more than that."

"If we had been more than that, you wouldn't have left me. You wouldn't have left me here, alone, needing you. You would have been here, Will. If I meant half as much to you as you swore that I did, you would have been here. I needed you."

"I know. I know you did. I am so sorry."

"*Stop* apologizing."

"I'm sorry." He laughed a little, and then he looked at his hands. "There is no excuse for how I've behaved. I let that life pull me in. I forgot how all-consuming it can be. How everything else fades into the background. I fell back into my old life without thinking about how I was hurting you. After you called, when you told me about Mama, I went home...to Indiana. I stayed with my family and made things right with them because I knew I couldn't...I wouldn't have the right to ask for your forgiveness until I'd earned theirs. I did that. It was hard and humbling, but I did it. I want you to know that I do care about you, more than you know, and I will regret, for the rest of my life, that I lost you."

Carrie narrowed her eyes at him. "You didn't lose me, Will. You threw me away."

He flinched, like her words were a slap across his face. "I made decisions that I wish I could take back."

"Decisions? I saw the pictures of you with that...anorexic witch. That woman who acted like Mama and I were something to be scraped off her designer shoes. You know how she treated us. Yet there you were, smiling pretty with her hanging off your arm."

"My job—" he started.

"Screw you *and* your job, Will! I don't even remember how

many times I called you. To tell you Mama was gone. To ask you to come to me. To beg you to help me. I needed you *here*. I needed you with me, like you promised you would be, and you were out living it up while my life shattered around me."

"I know."

Resting her palms against the cool tiles of the island, she glared at him. "You always say that you know, but you don't know. You don't have a clue what I've been going through. She's gone. Everything is gone. Mama. The house. My life as I knew it. It's gone."

"Mama's gone. But the house... The house is still yours."

She shook her head. "I signed the papers this morning."

Will looked down for a moment before meeting her gaze again. "I don't deserve your forgiveness, Carrie. I know that. I ruined what chance we had, but I did... I *do* care about you. More than you can possibly understand. I will probably never know what our life could have been like, but I couldn't live with myself if I didn't at least try to take care of you. I promised so many times that I would. No matter what happens, I need to know that you are where you belong, in this house, with no threat of it ever being taken away from you."

She creased her brow. "What are you talking about?"

He reached into his back pocket and pulled out a stack of folded papers. "This is the deed. This house will never leave your name again."

She stared at him, disbelieving. "You bought the house?"

"I made sure that you didn't do something that you would regret for the rest of your life. Trust me," he said with a wry smile, "you don't want to go down that road."

She gawked at him as he slid the papers onto the island between them. "How dare you."

He looked taken aback. "You didn't want to sell it."

"Don't pretend to know what I want."

Stepping closer, he held her gaze. "I know you didn't want to sell your home, Carrie. You told me. You told me that you wanted to stay here, you wanted to open a restaurant. You wanted Doreen here to help you run it."

His reminder stabbed at her heart, and hot tears stung her eyes. Rage ignited inside her. "Are you seriously trying to buy your way out of this?"

He stared for a few moments before shaking his head. "No. I promised I'd take care of you. I failed. You're angry at me for not being here, but someday you'll be happy I did this."

She shook her head and scoffed at how absolutely obtuse this man was. "All you've done is prolonged the inevitable, Will. I *cannot* afford this house. If I could, I never would have sold it to begin with."

"The money from the sale will last a long time."

"You think I'm going to take your money?" she asked quietly.

"You have to," he said calmly. "We've signed the papers."

"I'll cancel the agreement."

He shrugged. "You can't. We've closed on the deal."

Frustration filled her gut and made her stomach churn. "I won't stay here. I won't live in your house."

"*Your* house."

"The hell it is," she said angrily. "I will not allow you to buy your way out of your guilt."

"It's not just guilt," Will said just as hotly. "I don't expect you to forgive me, but you can't give up something that is this important to you because of your anger toward me, Carolyn."

The name drove an arrow of pain through her heart. "Don't call me that! Don't you *dare* call me that!"

"I ruined things between us," he continued, ignoring her outburst, "but that doesn't mean I don't care. That doesn't mean I'm not going to help you when I can. You know as well as I do that you'll regret selling the house."

"That's not your concern, Will. Not anymore."

He sighed and shook his head. "The night we spoke, when you told me Mama died... I didn't sleep. I kept replaying every mistake I've ever made over and over. I knew I had to fix my relationship with my brother. I'd known that a long time, but I was too scared to try. I deserved whatever he said to me because he was right. *You* were right. I always end up putting my career first. I don't mean to. It just happens. I don't even realize what I'm doing until it's too late. I went home the next day. I went to my brother, and we had a long talk. Several, actually. It took some time, but I didn't leave until I'd fixed things."

"And now you're here?" she asked.

"I don't know if I can make things right between us. I messed up, Carrie. I own that, but I think you need to recognize I wasn't alone in screwing this up. You weren't exactly tripping over yourself to call me before Mama died."

She narrowed her eyes. "What?"

"Before Mama died, how many times had you called me to check in, to say hello?"

"You were busy," she reminded him.

"Yeah, I was. But the phone goes both ways."

She crossed her arms and tilted her head. "You are a world-class son of a bitch."

"I've been told that a time or two. But you can't lay all the blame on me. I should have reached out to you when you called. I agree. I messed up. So did you, Carrie. Because before Mama died, I was the only one making an effort to stay connected. Other than a few messages on social media, I was the only one reaching out."

She lowered her face, embarrassed by the truth he was stating. She hadn't called him as often as she should have. She'd made a lot of excuses why she hadn't, but the reality was, she didn't have any more of an excuse than he had.

He threw his hands up as if he was giving up trying. "The house is yours. Do with it what you want. If you really can't accept that I did this, sell it. But I think you'll regret that. Almost as much as I regret...throwing you away."

Carrie stood, watching him leave, furious that he'd have the nerve to walk away when she was still fighting with him. But then his words sank in and she eased the clench of her jaw.

He had damn near crushed her when he'd disappeared.

But the reality was, she was damn near crushed already. She'd been broken when he'd found her. He'd been broken too. Wasn't that what had bonded them? Their mutual need for someone to listen, someone to be there. He'd done that for her in abundance. But how much had she given in return? Really? She'd tried to support him, but the reality was, so much of their relationship had been him comforting her, and she hadn't even noticed until he'd stopped.

Closing her eyes, she exhaled some of her frustration. The anger and grief that had been consuming her turned into something else. Shame.

As much as she wanted to blame him and be angry at him, she was as guilty of neglecting him as she'd insisted he was her. Sure, she'd called when she'd needed him, but she'd also spent a fair share of her time fuming that he hadn't called her. She had been so convinced that he was going to leave her once he got back to California that she'd all but left him first. And then she'd pointed her finger at him, as if he were the only one to blame. They were both to blame. They were equally guilty of not trying hard enough. Whether it was fear or selfishness or just plain stupidity, they'd both had a hand in their own downfall.

He was right, they'd both made mistakes.

Rushing out of the kitchen, she caught up with him in the foyer. "Hey," she called, her voice thick with the emotions raging in her chest. "You do not get to come in here and dump all of this on me and then walk out on me again."

He looked down for what seemed an eternity before looking at her with sorrowful eyes.

"You broke my heart," she whispered harshly. "You left me. You promised me you would help me and then you left me."

"I know."

"I needed you."

He nodded. "I know. I'm so sorry."

"What am I supposed to do now?" she asked.

After another long silence, he shrugged. "Do you think... Can you forgive me?"

She swallowed hard. "I don't know. I'm so hurt."

"I love you," he said softly.

His words took her breath away.

"I love you, but I realize that I ruined what we had. I put us second, and I failed you. I'm sorry for that," he said. "I'm trying to be better. I think you and Mama made me better, you helped me see what was important, but I tripped up. I lost the ground I'd gained. I'm as confused and lost now as I was when I first came here. I know you must be feeling that way too. Maybe it is too late for us to try to fix each other again, but I won't ever forget how you helped me realize that I needed to change. I'll never forget what we meant to each other. I do need to know that you're happy. You won't be happy if you leave this house, Carrie."

Carrie shook her head. "Do I look happy to you? I've lost everything, Will," she said just above a whisper. "I feel completely broken and alone. I lost the only mother I've ever known. And you. I've lost you. You made me feel alive again and then walked away. It's all gone. Everything we had—even if it wasn't real—is gone."

"It was real," he said quietly. Closing the distance between them, he brushed his fingers over her cheek, and just like the first time, she felt his touch all the way to her soul. "Carrie, it *is* real. I took it for granted. I took you for granted. You have no idea how many times I wanted to come to you and tell you how sorry I was, but I didn't want to make things worse for you. I didn't want to hurt you any more than I already had. I got pulled back into that life, Carrie. I got pulled in and I couldn't see anything but what was right in front of me. I jumped in, and I got lost. Like I always do. But in here"—he put his hand to his heart—"I never let you go. I got lost, but I didn't let you go."

"You did." She exhaled slowly. "But I got lost in my life too. Mama..." Her voice choked off as emotion hit her like a sledgehammer to the chest. "She's gone, Will."

"I know," he whispered.

His face sagged when she choked out a sob. Reaching out, he pulled her to him and she let him. As soon as he wrapped her in his arms, in that safe place that she'd missed so much, she crumbled.

"I'm so sorry," he whispered as he stroked her hair.

He held her tightly as she finally let go of some of the anger that had been buried deep inside of her. She hadn't even realized how deeply the pain ran until that moment. Something about Will had always made it okay for her to feel—to *really* feel. Now that she was, she couldn't seem to control the sobs racking her body.

"I'm sorry," she whispered when she finally managed to pull herself together.

He put his hands on her wet cheeks and shook his head. "No. No. I'm sorry. You shouldn't have had to go through that alone. I would give anything to go back, just so I could be here." Pulling her against him, he wrapped her up again and kissed her head. "You're everything to me, do you know that? You are everything. I know I don't deserve it, but I'm begging for your forgiveness. For one more chance."

Leaning back, she sniffed and wiped her cheeks. "And your movie?"

"I sold the rights. It's out of my hands. There is nothing there for me now."

Her breath lodged in her throat. "Oh, Will. You wanted that so much."

"I thought so. But then I realized everything I want is here."

Shaking her head, Carrie stepped back. "What happens when you go back?"

He shook his head. "I'm not going back."

"Oh, Will. The movie premiere, the interviews, all those things that took you from me this time—they aren't going to go away. That's your life."

"I don't want it, Carrie. I don't. That life has cost me too much."

"But that's who you are. You can try to change that, but we both saw what happened last time. That life is in your bones. You can't walk away from your life any more than I can walk away from mine."

He put his fingertips to her chin and turned her face to his. "I let you down. I hurt you. Knowing that is like a knife in my heart, Carrie. I'll never forget what that did to us. I'll never let it happen again. I'm done with that. I'm not going back."

She shook her head slightly. "Listen, I...I took an awful lot of frustration out on you because you weren't here. Maybe... maybe some of that was jealousy. You were off fulfilling your dreams, and I was here watching Doreen die a little each day. I think I resented that a little. That wasn't fair to you."

"Nothing about what you were going through was fair, Carrie. Don't kick yourself for this."

"Why not? I've certainly been kicking you an awful lot. I've been unfair to you, Will. I'm sorry. You can't walk away from your life for me. It wasn't fair for me to expect that from you. Los Angeles is your home. It's where you work. It's part of you."

"Carrie—"

"We can compromise. Don't you think?" she asked. "We can make this work. We just have to try. With Mama gone, there's no reason why we can't split our time. Right? Maybe that isn't ideal, but we can try. If you want."

He smiled as he put his hands to her face. "I do. I want that more than anything."

"Me too." She looked around the foyer. "Thank you. For saving my home."

"You're welcome."

She shrugged. "You know, if I'm going to open a restaurant in here, I'm going to need to remodel. I don't want people traipsing through our living space. I'm going to need to put a wall up, expand the den. I'm going to need a bigger kitchen. That's going to keep me pretty busy. But then again, I guess you'll be busy doing your movie premiere stuff. So...we'll have a lot of things to juggle."

He grasped her hands and brought them to his lips to kiss them before looking in her eyes. "We can do it. I know we can do it."

She smiled. "Yeah. We can do it."

He held her gaze intently. "I do love you."

"I love you, Will."

He pulled her to him, wrapping his arms around her and kissing her so passionately, she had to pull away to catch her breath. It reminded her of the first time he'd kissed her. The sensation rolled through her, consuming her. Smiling, she ran her hands over his hair.

"I missed you like crazy," she whispered.

"I missed you." He kissed her gently one more time. "The first time I start acting like a self-centered movie star, you have my permission to hit me over the head with a frying pan."

Carrie chuckled. "I'm going to need that in writing." Her smile faded a bit. "Promise me one thing."

"Anything."

"You won't forget me again."

He kissed her lightly. "That never happened, Carolyn. And it never will. You are unforgettable."

THE WOMEN OF HEARTS SERIES:

Hidden Hearts

Burning Hearts

Stolen Hearts

Secret Hearts

OTHER TITLES:

California Can Wait

Seducing Kate

The Rebound

Unforgettable You

ABOUT THE AUTHOR

As a teen, Marci Bolden skipped over young adult books and jumped right into reading romance novels. She never left.

Marci lives in the Midwest with her husband, kiddos, and numerous rescue pets. If she had an ounce of willpower, Marci would embrace healthy living, but until cupcakes and wine are no longer available at the local market, she will appease her guilt by reading self-help books and promising to join a gym "soon."

Visit her here:
www.marcibolden.com

 facebook.com/MarciBoldenAuthor
 twitter.com/BoldenMarci
 instagram.com/marciboldenauthor

CPSIA information can be obtained
at www.ICGtesting.com
Printed in the USA
BVHW042131040822
643864BV00004B/38